FOREVER IN LOVELY BAY

POLLY BABBINGTON

AUTHOR

AuthorPollyBabbington.com

Want more from Polly's world?

For sneak peeks into new settings, early chapters, downloadable Pretty Beach and Darling Island freebies and bits and bobs from Polly's writing days sign up for Babbington Letters.

© Copyright 2025 Polly Babbington

All rights reserved.

This book is a work of fiction. Names, characters, businesses, places, events, and incidents are either the products of the author's imagination or used in a fictitious manner. Any resemblance to actual persons, living or dead, or actual events is purely coincidental.

1

Fleur Champion stood at her kitchen window stirring a pot of tea and gazing out at blue-grey waves tumbling onto Lovely Bay's shoreline in the distance. It was a cosy sort of morning, the air damp from an early drizzle, but with brightness to the sky promising that if things went well the clouds would burn off and sunshine would arrive. You could but live in hope. She stood for ages, waiting for the tea she'd just made to brew, staring out the window doing nothing at all but thinking and thinking and then just for good measure having a little bit more of a think, too. Mornings with nothing too pressing to do were the mornings our Fleur cherished. Not much going on, peaceful, grounded, and the faint hum of Lovely life stirring outside her little seaside cottage. Just how she liked it and wanted it to remain, forever, of course.

She heard Patrick clomping down the stairs and smiled as he entered the kitchen in tartan pyjama bottoms and no top. That was a good way to start a morning; her cherished morning just got a little bit better. Blinking a few times, she couldn't quite believe what was in front of her eyes or that Patrick, mmm, mmm, was actually part of her life. Nudging around the kitchen table, he looked out the back door as Fleur took bacon, eggs, and sausages out of the fridge and pottered around getting a pan from the cupboard. 'Morning.'

'How did you sleep?'

'Well. Apart from that downpour and thunder in the middle of the night...'

'It scared the life out of me.'

'Me too.'

'I didn't think you'd woken up.'

'I did.'

'It was so loud.'

Fleur held up the box of eggs. 'I thought I'd do a fry up and then we'd go for a walk. Fancy that?'

Patrick chuckled. 'I've had worse Saturday morning offers. Sounds right up my street.'

Fleur laughed to herself. Out of the two of them she knew whose Saturday morning was better. 'I know you love a good fry-up and it gives me an excuse to pretend I'm only having it because you are. Plus, it has to be better than the fruit and yoghurt I've been eating all week.'

Patrick shook his head and frowned. 'Is there really anybody who doesn't like a full English? Asking for a friend.'

'There can't be, surely?' Fleur unwrapped a packet of bacon from the deli and dropped it into the pan. As it sizzled away to itself, she sliced bread into triangles for fried bread and watched Patrick as he stood on the terrace outside the back door with a mug of tea in his hand. He'd now been around for a while, and to be frank, she was surprised by that. She'd half-thought somewhere in the depths of her mind, that he might have done what her ex-husband had done; gone off her by now, traded her in for a better model, called it a day, but so far, so good. He still gave her goosebumps every time she looked at him, which was a very good bonus when he was standing half naked just outside your kitchen. When she let herself revel in the fact that he'd given her a ring to document whatever it was that they had she'd felt like a teenager in the first flush of love. Holding her hand up to the window, she turned it this way and that so that the diamonds sparkled in the light. As she watched the glimmers, the little swoony jump thing in her heart that always happened when she thought about Patrick made itself known.

The world had turned in mysterious ways for our Fleur. She'd gone from being serially on her own, through a slow-moving but persistent line of not very fabulous relationships to being a significant other to someone she loved very much. Sometimes she actually thought that none of it was true – not Patrick, nor the cottage, nor Lovely. That she would wake up alone still in the house on the green, rummaging around in humdrum, not really sure what was going to happen in her life and not all that happy, either.

If that had been the case and all of this was indeed a dream, her dad would still be alive, her mum wouldn't be living van life, her sister would not be Down Under, and she would still be floating around in the monotony of life. There would be no other words for it but mildly miserable with a side of bored thrown in for good measure. Not that she'd thought she was miserable when she'd been in the house on the green before moving to Lovely. Not at all, actually. Then, she'd thought she was okay. Now, she really *was* okay. The hunk of a man directly in front of her standing shirtless in her garden looking down at his phone told her that well enough. Gulp.

As Fleur cracked eggs into the pan, she glanced at Patrick and smiled. His head was bent slightly, light catching on bed hair and he was frowning a touch and leaning forward with a bit of a furrow on his face. She'd learned the look well and she would have laid money on it that he had a problem at work. Watching him type away furiously with his thumbs, it hit her how utterly unexpectedly glorious it was to have him in her life. Solid, dependable, quietly funny, Patrick who now seemed as much a part of her world as the cottage itself. Shifting the eggs around the pan with a wooden slice, she mused the situation as if in a little delicious private daydream for one.

In a way, it felt quite alien to be part of something, a unit, to be someone else's significant other, if that indeed was what it was. For so long, she'd told herself she was perfectly fine on her own. *More than fine. Absolutely marvellous. Not in need of anything at all.* She'd convinced herself she didn't need anyone to help with the messiness of life or indeed the *anything* of life. She'd raised Lucy, handled her divorce, and rebuilt her world bit by bit without a lot of fuss and froth and a whole lot of gritting of teeth. And yet, here was a man who had managed to slip into her life, as if he'd always been meant to sit around, drinking tea and reading his phone while she fried bacon on a Saturday morning. Niceeeee.

As Saturday morning companions went, he wasn't too shabby, better than the last one, anyway. It was strange how love had crept up on her when she most definitely had not, like not, not, *not*, been looking for it in any shape or form. She'd been so busy surviving, trying to keep things together and getting on with the gigantic move to Lovely Bay that the idea of being with anyone let alone someone like Patrick hadn't even been in her peripheral. In actual fact, it had seemed like some far-off fantasy that she would be part of a relationship unit ever again. Stranger things and pigs flying, though, because here she was doing just that. Flying up there with the pigs was oh-so nice and how very, very pretty those pigs were up there. With fab, sculpted abs on.

The man poking his head around the back door told her that he was not a fantasy and very real. *And breathe.* 'Need a hand with anything?'

Fleur shook her head, smiled, and joked. 'No, I'm fine. You sit there and look pretty.'

Patrick laughed and went back to his phone. She glanced

over at him again as she waited for the bread to brown. Sometimes she wondered why he was with her and that he was the one getting the short end of the stick. Punching? Wasn't that what they called it? There was nothing particularly dazzling about her existence or her, for that matter. The razzle-dazzle of Fleur from days gone by was long gone. Just plain old Champo bobbing along in life – single mum, notebook maker, and occasional overthinker. What was it, exactly, that had drawn him and her together? Why and how did they click? Whatever it was, from her side of the fence, it worked. There would be no boat rocking going on.

'Do I have something on my face, or are you just admiring me?' Patrick winked.

Fleur startled, realising she was twirling and whirling and lost in her own thoughts. She fired back as quick as a flash. 'You wish.' If only he knew how much she'd been admiring him. By the truck load.

'What's going on in your head? You look as if you are deep in thought.'

'Nothing. Just thinking about breakfast and I don't know, stuff.'

'Stuff, right. The breakfast smells amazing. How is it that frying bacon smells so good? I think I could live on it. Add fried bread and life couldn't get any better. It's a good job I've done a lot of work this week or it would be going straight to my arteries.'

Fleur flipped the bread over in the pan, letting it soak up the last of the bacon grease before plating everything up. Two heaped plates of fried bread, bacon, eggs, and sausages. She carried them over to the table, tried not to think about the calories and put one down in front of him. 'There you go. One full English for your arteries and cholesterol levels.'

Patrick rubbed his hands together. 'You spoil me.'

'Someone's got to.' Fleur chuckled and thought about how

nice it was just to have *companionship*. She hadn't realised how much of a gaping hole not having someone to share the everyday with had been until it had been filled by the man sitting opposite her. She turned her hand and let the diamond forever ring catch the light and then sat lost in her thoughts as she tucked into her breakfast.

'You're doing that staring thing again.'

Fleur shook her head. 'Just happy, I suppose. After those few manic months with Lucy and Mum and this, that, and the other. It's nice to just sit down and breathe, right?'

Patrick tilted his head. 'Yeah. It's nice to be happy...'

'It really is.'

Fleur nodded as she popped another forkful of bacon into her mouth. The funny thing was that she was forever happy, not just day-to-day happy, or regular happy, or yeah happy, but tightly happy, stay-with-me happy. One thing she knew for sure; she wanted it to remain.

Let's hope that what was in our Champo's future would keep it that way. That the cards dealt in the next part of Fleur's story would be good ones. Our Champo wasn't sure if she should hold her breath.

2

Fleur sat in a lobby adjacent to a reception desk at the doctor's surgery on the outskirts of Lovely Bay and looked up at the posters on the wall. One told her not to forget to screen her breasts by way of a picture depicting two pink hundreds and thousands covered doughnuts. It did not make her laugh or want to check her breasts. Another spoke about dementia choices depicting a woman in the most revolting beige cardigan she'd ever seen. A third advertised free community transport with a picture of a little pink minibus. An Ed Sheeran song jangled on the radio and a gigantic plant in the corner looked as if someone was giving it lots of love. As she looked through into the middle of the waiting room, past an Art Deco glass door and beautiful timber floorboards, she thought to herself that even the doctor's surgery in Lovely was nice. It was a far cry from the surgery she'd belonged to where she'd lived before. In that place, she'd always felt slightly grubby when she'd sat down. It had never been clean and whenever she'd been there, she'd felt as if she'd leave with something a lot worse than anything she'd gone in with. Sitting on the chair wondering how long she would have to wait, she earwigged on a conversation between the receptionist and a woman in overly bright, wide-leg floral trousers and a white shirt. The woman's long dark straggly hair reached below her bottom and made Fleur feel a bit queasy. Just as she was sitting there, wondering what a palaver washing such long hair would be a message came in from Lucy.

Lucy: *Hi Mum, how are you?*
Fleur: *Just at the doctor.*
Lucy: *Oh yes, for the check-up?*
Fleur: *Yep. You good?*
Lucy: *I'm fine. I'm in London and waiting to get a train back. I just heard from Dad.*
Fleur: *Is he OK?*
Lucy: *They've got an exchange date to move.*
Fleur: *Great.*

Fleur didn't think the news was great, but pretended otherwise. Lucy didn't need to know her views on her ex-husband Ben and his moving escapades. She'd learnt a long time ago to keep her views on Ben in a tightly closed box.

Fleur: *Excellent, that's good.*
Lucy: *Just in time for the baby.*
Fleur: *How fortunate. I hope their move goes well.*
Lucy: *Once the baby has arrived, they'll be able to settle in, and I'll be much closer which is good. I can't believe I am going to have a brother or sister!*
Fleur: *Exciting!*
Lucy: *I should be home in a few hours if the trains are on time. See you later.*
Fleur: *See you then xxx*

As Fleur waited for her appointment, she watched the comings and goings of the reception area, including a doctor in a black dress with highlighted hair who looked way too young to know what she was doing as far as Fleur was concerned. How had it come to be that doctors were younger than her? The world didn't hang around, that was for sure. She idly sat thinking about all sorts and read through yet another poster telling her not to talk on her mobile phone in the waiting area. Glancing down at her phone again, she reread Lucy's texts. There was no doubt that Lucy was happy about Ben's baby which Fleur saw as a good thing. They'd had a long conversation about when the baby arrived and Lucy was very happy about having a sibling albeit one who would be many years younger than her. Fleur had to wonder, though, what it would be like in reality. When the baby arrived would Lucy be happy or would she have her nose pushed far out of joint? Fleur hoped it wasn't going to be the latter because she knew very well who would be the one dealing with the fallout. If it did, our Champo would be the one picking up the pieces.

Despite the fact that Fleur could not stand Ben's partner Sarah, thought that she was more than irritating and acted as if she knew everything, overall, Sarah *had* been nice to Lucy. Fleur would give her that. She was well aware that Ben's new partner could have had a totally different approach to Lucy and it may have gone a very different way. Sarah had included Lucy in the pregnancy from the word go and had even taken her along to a couple of midwifery appointments. Lucy was well into how the birth was going to go and positive about everything. What was there for our Fleur to complain about? Nothing, apart from the fact that the whole situation made her feel ever-so-slightly uncomfortable. Plus, she knew for sure that she didn't want the birth and the baby's arrival playing out on what felt like her doorstep but that ship had sailed and was on its way to port. She would have to buckle up and take it on the chin.

With a funny gagging feeling in her throat as Fleur watched the woman with the long hair grab it and tuck the bottom into the waistband of her trousers, she mused the Ben and Sarah situation. She was going to keep her distance, sit back, watch, and see what happened as real life took hold once the baby was born. She'd tried her darndest to be happy for them and hoped that everything would go well. However, she had a feeling in the back of her mind that when things hit the fan, Sarah's perfect Instagram posts and lack of reality would not end well.

It would be interesting to observe whether what Sarah had learned in her psychology degree, would all go down the pan once push came to shove. Fleur could but wait and see. One thing she *did* know: she was not up for being any part of the fallout. All she hoped was that Lucy didn't get caught in the crossfire. Time would surely tell.

3

A few weeks later, Fleur was sitting in the deli with a cup of coffee in front of her, scrolling on her phone, wondering if it was possible to get one-day shipping on Amazon Prime for a bookbinding tool that she really didn't need but wanted to try. As she stared at the listing, she looked at the one-click button and felt very tempted to give it a go, then reminded herself that she already had hundreds of bookbinding tools. The temptation to do the one-day shipping and have the tool arrive that afternoon was so good she could almost taste it. As she pondered, and nibbled on a piece of chocolate-covered peanut brittle and took a sip of her tea, she reasoned that adding a few more things to her basket would mean she'd kill a few birds with one stone, so in theory it was a good deal. Just as she was finishing off the order realising she had completely failed at resisting she looked up to see Patrick walk in. He smiled, waved, and then stopped to chat with Alice for a bit before ordering a coffee and coming over to sit down.

'How are you?' he asked, putting his cup down on the table and pulling out a chair.

'Yeah, good. How was the job? How did it go? Did everything work out okay in the end?'

'Yeah, *really* good. The team is there and ready to go and there weren't any problems which is a miracle but I won't hold my breath. I love it when it goes smoothly...'

Fleur nodded. 'That's great. You can relax now.'

'Yeah, I'm fine.' Patrick took a sip of his coffee. 'How's Lucy? Any news about the baby or anything?'

'No, no, nothing.'

'Oh, okay, excellent. No news is good news...'

'Ben sent me a message to ask if I could contribute to paying for that dance festival she's doing in Manchester.'

'You're kidding me, aren't you?' Patrick looked up sharply.

'I know.'

Patrick sighed. 'I thought he was the one who encouraged her to do it. He's pathetic.'

'That's a bit steep.'

'I'm just imitating him.' Patrick didn't sound happy.

Fleur was well aware that Ben was not Patrick's favourite person. She tried to steer the conversation away, but he moved it right back to Ben.

'He seems to think that because he's moved house and is having a baby you have a bottomless pit of money to pay for things now. Grr, he really gets my goat. Making you pay for the festival when he was the one who kept on about it.'

Fleur wrapped her hands around her coffee and watched the steam curl upwards. 'You're not going to let this go, are you?'

Patrick scoffed, leaning back in his chair. 'I'm just trying to give you the other side of it. Would you, if it were me? If the situation was reversed?'

Fleur considered for a second. 'Probably not.'

'And he's closer now which makes it more irritating.' Patrick took another sip of coffee. 'It just annoys me. It was bad enough before but now he's moved what twenty minutes from Lovely it's worse. Of all the places he could've gone.'

Fleur raised an eyebrow. 'It's a free country.'

'Oh, don't give me that.' Patrick shook his head. 'Anyway…'

Fleur didn't argue. She might not have been as vocal about it, but she had thought it was odd when Ben had announced he was relocating so close but had tried to let it go. 'Whatever.'

Patrick shook his head and tutted. 'I bumped into them. They were in Lovely last weekend.'

Fleur stilled. 'What? You didn't mention that.'

'Didn't want to make a thing of it.'

'And yet here we are.'

Patrick gave her a look. 'They were meeting Lucy.'

Fleur softened. 'That's right.'

'I need to rein myself in. I just hate the way he acts like he's Father of the Year. I don't know, maybe it's just me picking up those vibes and being unreasonable. You should've seen Lucy; she was all over the place.'

Fleur's chest tightened. 'What do you mean?'

'I mean, she looked like she didn't know whether to be happy or what about the baby and stuff. She was trying so hard to be excited, but you could see it all over her face how she wasn't sure deep down. Ben just lapped it up. That's what annoys me the most.'

Fleur swallowed, looking down at her coffee. 'Did she say anything to you after?'

Patrick hesitated. 'Nope.'

Fleur sighed. 'I'm surprised you thought she looked like that. She's been fine about the baby with me. I just hope that when the baby comes it's a positive outcome for Lucy.'

'So do I.' Patrick's jaw tightened. 'And now that Ben and Sarah are living so close, it's going to be right in her face whether she likes it or not.'

Fleur sighed and looked out the window. She couldn't be doing with any further issues with Lucy. She'd had a gutful of them and, to be frank, she was a bit sick to the back teeth of it. 'I'm crossing my fingers that it will all work out well.'

You could but live in hope.

4

Fleur was in the throes of going down to the market to her stall. Patrick and Lucy had left not long after breakfast to set everything up and she was at home getting a few last bits together and making something for dinner for when they got home. Removing the lid from the slow cooker, she plugged it in, took a jug of homemade stock out of the freezer, eased it from the sides of its container and dropped it in. Unwrapping paper from fresh fish from the kiosk on the harbour, she added it to the pot and then popped out into the garden snipping loads of fresh herbs from the little herb garden she'd planted near the back door. After throwing those in too, she dumped in fresh garlic, sprinkled on dried herbs for good measure, and poured in a generous amount of white wine, hoping her thrown-together amalgamation would make a lovely stew for later that evening. She was sure that she, Lucy, and Patrick would be exhausted after a long day working at the market and knew that her future self would be pouring her a glass of wine and putting her feet up when she got in. Racing around, opening cupboards and jars, and popping things in the pot, she thought about the day ahead and all she had to do.

After wiping down the sides and scooping dishes into the dishwasher, she went up to do the beds. As she pulled up the covers on her bed, tightened the duvet, and plumped the pillows she thought about Lucy and how she was now compared to just before she'd given up ballet school. Now, Lucy was like a different person; the change in her was striking. The counsellor who'd been suggested to Fleur by Birdie seemed to share a similar opinion. Pondering how Lucy's sessions with the counsellor had turned out, as far as Fleur was concerned, the whole experience had been brilliant from start to finish and Fleur rarely said that about anything. Lucy had shown radical improvement from the very beginning; it was amazing to see how simply talking to somebody could help but in Lucy's case it had done and worked like a dream.

Fleur mulled the Lucy situation over and over as she finished making her bed, tidied up her bedroom, moved to the mirror, and started brushing her hair. After twisting it up into a clip, she blobbed a few huge dollops of BB cream onto her face, rubbed it in, and dusted on some blusher. Looking in the mirror, she smiled. Lucy wasn't the only one who was looking better. Fleur did too and it felt good to appear somewhat human again. She nodded as she smiled at her reflection, popped some perfume behind her ears, and decided she was ready for the day.

The market was already bustling by the time Fleur arrived. She parked her car near the harbour and began unloading a couple of last-minute notebooks and journals, locked her car and made her way towards the stall. Just as she'd turned down by the harbour wall, she saw Birdie carrying a tray of coffees coming the other way. Birdie stopped and smiled. 'You're looking well.'

'Morning, Birdie. Thanks. Is one of those for me?' Fleur joked.

'Ha, help yourself.' Birdie nodded to the left side of the tray. 'That one is how you like yours.'

'Lifesaver. Thank you.' Fleur took one of the coffees and sipped. 'Fab.'

Birdie smiled. 'All part of the service. I've just been chatting to Patrick. How's our Lucy doing? She looked great as far as I could see.'

'Really well. The counsellor was fantastic, but I'm still taking each day as it comes. So far, so good, though. No more fainting and she's put on weight. Yeah, all around she's fine.'

'Good. That's all you can do.'

'Thank you again for recommending the counsellor.'

'Not at all. If you need anything, you know where I am.'

'You're a good person to know. The word-of-mouth recommendation worked in this case.'

'The best way.'

'Yep. Anyway, how are you?'

'Oh, you know, getting on with it. Right, I'd better trundle on. It's so busy today already. The sunshine helps...'

'Yes, I'll go and relieve the troops.' Fleur held her coffee up. 'Thanks for this. I owe you one.'

Fleur strolled through the market and smiled here and there at a few people she knew. She'd come to love market days and her little notebook stall. There was something soothing about the rhythm of the market; the chatter, the sea air, the cry of gulls over the harbour, happy Lovelies strolling here and there, the lighthouse in the distance. For Fleur, it was a reminder of how far she'd come since moving to Lovely Bay and how it had turned out to be one of the best decisions she'd ever made in her life. Not that she'd thought it at the time, but now here she was in the swing of it and dare she think it, but living the dream.

Once at the stall, she put her stuff down, kissed Patrick and Lucy, and sat down. 'How are you getting on?'

'Not bad at all.' Patrick swooped his arm in the direction of the trestle table. 'Looking good.'

Lucy smiled and wiggled her phone to indicate the payment app. 'We've sold loads already. The nice weather does wonders.'

'And because your mum's notebooks are brilliant. People can't resist them.' Patrick laughed.

Fleur rolled her eyes. 'Flatterer.'

As Fleur sat on the stool at the back of the stall and watched Lucy speak to customers and observed Patrick chatting to Colin from the riverboat, she smiled. Here she was with a new partner, Lucy seemingly thriving, sitting at her own market stall observing the general public fall in love with things she'd made with her own two hands. What a turn up for the books. People watching, sipping her coffee and letting the market and Lovelies drift by, Fleur felt a little pop of contentment in her core. Long may it last. More importantly, it had better blooming well stay.

After having a quick shower and getting rid of the day at the market which felt as if it was clinging to her skin, Fleur went downstairs in a soft, beige tracksuit and stepped into the kitchen, smiling at the sight of the lovely Shaker doors and the warmth of the little kitchen at the back of the cottage. Opening the window a touch to let in some fresh air, she caught a glimpse of the sea down at the end of the lane and really did think as she had done when she'd been at the market, that she was exactly where she was meant to be; living her best life in a little market town in a cottage by the sea.

Taking a mixing bowl out of the fridge with bread dough she'd made the evening before, she scraped the bowl clean, kneaded the dough into a rounded shape, covered it in poppy seeds, and placed it into a Le Creuset that had been heating in the oven. Just as the bread was finishing baking and Fleur was getting everything ready for dinner, she heard Patrick's car pull up. She almost did a double take when she opened the door to go out and help. She hadn't noticed quite how different Lucy was, but as she looked out onto the driveway it hit her like a tonne of bricks. With a gigantic storage tub in her arms, and even after a long day at the market, Lucy looked radiant and full of life. It was a far cry from earlier in the year when she'd been so frail that Fleur had wondered if there was something seriously wrong with her. Now, Lucy glowed; her hair looked as if it could reflect light, her cheeks were filled out and she beamed as she walked in through the back door. Fleur felt the last of the worries she'd had about Lucy float off down the lane. Oh, how nice that relief felt, indeed.

Lucy chuckled and smiled as she walked towards the front door. 'It smells amazing. We could smell it halfway down Lovely Pott Lane. We're starving.'

Fleur made a funny face. 'Oh, just a fish stew I threw together this morning before I left. French-style thing.'

Patrick popped the lid on the boot. 'You just threw it together?'

'Yep, just before I left this morning. Homemade bread, too.'

'It smells absolutely fabulous,' Lucy gushed.

'You're just saying that because you've been on your feet all day and you could eat anything.'

Lucy raised her eyebrows. 'Ooh, I love that bread. We haven't had that for ages.'

Fleur smiled to herself. What had happened to her daughter who had barely been able to put any food in her mouth? Hopefully, all of them had seen the back of *that* Lucy. This Lucy was so much nicer to have around.

Half an hour or so later, after Lucy and Patrick had showered, the three of them were in the kitchen. Fleur placed a steaming pot in the centre of the kitchen table, freshly baked bread mingled with garlic and herb smells and all felt good in the world. As they tucked in, Fleur watched across the table and felt ridiculously happy at how well Lucy looked. Brighter, happier, and just, well, different. It wasn't just that she was eating better, or that the gauntness in her cheeks had disappeared. Nope, it was that there was a lightness about her as if some unseen weight had lifted. It felt very good that the weight was nowhere to be seen.

Patrick dunked a piece of bread straight into the stew. 'Throwing it together seems to have worked out perfectly. This is so good.'

Lucy hummed in agreement as she scooped up a spoonful. 'This is exactly what I needed. The market was nuts today...'

Fleur watched as Lucy tore into the bread, eating with the kind of appetite she hadn't seen in her for months, if ever. 'Have to say, Luce, you're looking well, better than well, actually. There's a glow about you. What have you done differently?'

Lucy glanced up and shrugged. 'Nothing. I just feel amazing. I love my job and I don't know, I just don't feel *stressed* anymore.'

Patrick smiled. 'Good.'

'Apparently, working at a market all day with fresh air, good food, and no pressure makes you happy,' Lucy joked. 'Who knew?'

Fleur leant on her elbow, chin resting in her hand. 'Well, whatever it is, it's working. Honestly, Luce, a few months ago, you looked like the wind could knock you over. Now, you're glowing.'

Lucy laughed. 'I'll take the compliment.'

Patrick bantered. 'Miracles do happen.'

Fleur narrowed her eyes a bit as Patrick and Lucy chatted about the market and discussed a problem they'd had with the payment app after Fleur had gone home. Lucy was radiant, her energy entirely different from the fragile, exhausted young adult she'd been not so long before. Fleur didn't know what had shifted, but whatever it was, she hoped it stayed.

She swirled her wine and sipped. 'So, what's actually brought on this sudden transformation with you, Luce? Have you finally joined a secret wellness retreat without telling us? If so, I need some of it. Ha.'

'No, nothing really. I think I've just started taking care of myself properly. Sleeping more. Eating better. Turns out, when you stop stressing about everything, your body actually thanks you for it. I feel really good lately. Better than I have in a long time. I'm just pleased not to be at ballet school. It was all-consuming and now I'm not there, I realise that I was way out of my depth.'

Patrick eye-rolled. 'I should try eating better and less stress.'

'Might take a few years off your worry lines.' Lucy joked.

'I do not have worry lines.'

'You do.'

'I absolutely don't.'

'Mum?'

Fleur held up her hands. 'I'm staying out of this.'

Patrick rolled his eyes and Fleur laughed. Inside she felt a huge sigh of relief that Lucy really *was* on the mend. She was okay, or actually better than okay, and it had been a long time coming.

Lucy laughed, shaking her head. 'I promise, I don't have a guru or anything.'

Patrick swirled his wine in his glass. 'You're not secretly seeing someone you haven't told us about yet, are you?'

'Excuse me?'

'A secret boyfriend, Luce. Is that it? You've got that look. That soft look. The one people get when they're all happy and content.'

Lucy rolled her eyes, but there was the slightest hesitation before she answered. 'No, I am not seeing anyone.'

Fleur turned her head to the side. 'You hesitated.'

'I did not.'

'You did,' Patrick pointed his spoon at her. 'You definitely hesitated. Gotcha.'

'There isn't anyone. You two are imagining things.'

'If you say so.' Fleur wasn't entirely convinced, however, she didn't care; as long as Lucy was happy, *she* was happy.

'I still think there's more to this story.' Patrick winked.

Lucy sighed. 'I think I've just stopped worrying about everything. For so long, I was running myself into the ground—stressing about what I looked like, worried about ballet, stressing about people, overthinking everything and I think my body just gave up on all that. So, I've been taking it slow. Just letting myself be for once.'

'Well, whatever you're doing, it's working. You do know that, don't you?'

'Yeah, hope so.'

Fleur nodded. 'Alright, well, as long as you're not keeping some massive secret from us...'

Lucy laughed, shaking her head. 'There is no *massive* secret.'

Patrick smirked. 'Which implies there's a small one.'

Lucy rolled her eyes and joked. 'Shut up and drink your wine.'

Fleur laughed, wondering if Lucy *was* keeping something to herself, but decided she would let it be, because, whatever it was or whoever it was, Lucy was happy and that was all that mattered. Hopefully.

5

The following week, Fleur thought about the life hack of putting her phone on airplane mode when she wanted to stop herself from scrolling social media. Flicking the toggle on meant resisting the temptation to scroll through Sarah, Ben's partner's, social media. It was very hard, though, not to give in. Contemplating switching it back she forced herself not to, telling herself that if Sarah thought that Fleur was scrolling through her social media, she'd love it. Fleur really didn't want to give her that pleasure, even unknowingly. However, she'd just come off the phone with Lucy, who was staying at Sarah and Ben's, and Lucy had told her that she'd just been taking a video of Sarah doing a pregnancy dance with her fully formed bump front and centre.

Lucy's conversation was full of fun and laughter and she'd thought both the dance and posting it on TikTok were hilarious. Fleur, not so much. She was very tempted to have a look but forced herself not to. Telling herself she did not need, want, or essentially *have* the time to waste an hour doom-scrolling people dancing in their kitchens, she moved away from her phone, opened her laptop, and started to answer work emails. About twenty minutes later, the temptation of Sarah dancing with her baby bump was just way, way, *way* too much. Pathetically, she gave in and succumbed to her ex-husband's new partner's social media dances which held their own special kind of addiction.

It had to be said that Fleur was definitely more than befuddled and a lot shocked when she saw the video. She couldn't quite believe her eyes. Part of her wondered if it was a deepfake image because who in their right mind would jiggle and gyrate in their knickers and bra and gigantic oversized pink fluffy slippers at nine-plus months pregnant and publish it to the world? However, she very much knew it was real because her own daughter was the one who had taken it. Pressing pause for a second, she let what she'd seen sink into her brain—her ex-husband's new partner, pregnant with their baby gyrating to a soundtrack where a rapper informed Fleur, and anybody else who watched, that she had been pregnant for way too long.

Fleur watched in astonishment, or was it horror, as Sarah started to rap the words herself and cradled her hands over her gigantic, bare baby bump. Groaning into the cup of peppermint tea she was drinking, she watched agog as there was a slight pause in the video. Sarah feigned for a moment whether her waters had broken, and then the music started again and she continued to gyrate to the rap. Fleur continued to let her chin drop to the floor. Shaking her head, she took another sip of peppermint tea, not really sure what to think. At least Sarah was positive about the whole thing. There was that.

She didn't know whether to laugh, cry, or what to do but reflecting on the video, she wondered if it was good for Lucy to be involved but decided it wasn't any of her business. She had to talk to someone about it, though, and picking up her phone, she dialled Cassy.

'Cass, how are you?'

'Yeah, good, thanks.'

'Where are you? Sounds like you're somewhere busy.'

Cassy sighed. 'I'm in Sainsbury's, just grabbing some bits to make a meatloaf. I've literally been eaten out of house and home by the boys. I don't know where they put it, I really don't. Same old, same old.'

'Well, three boys would do that to you.' Fleur laughed. 'What can I do for you? Did you want to chat about the training on Tuesday?'

'Well, no, actually, I'm just phoning you to tell you to go on TikTok and have a look at Sarah's video. I don't mean to be mean, but—'

Cassy interrupted. 'Ha, I know that voice. You *do* mean to be mean so you are being mean...'

'Caught red-handed.'

'Were you going to say you didn't want us to slag her off but?' Cassy laughed.

'It's unbelievable! You *have* to have a look. I can't believe Sarah is gyrating with her baby bump on show when she's about to drop. Lucy just phoned me and told me she'd taken a video. I mean, what can she possibly want to get out of broadcasting herself rapping? I must be too old. I don't get it.'

'Wait a minute, I'll have a look. Hold on.' A few seconds later, Cassy was back. 'Wow. She really does love herself, doesn't she? It's quite unbelievable that Ben is with someone who does all this. Literally, the post before is one of her psychology babble books pointing out the dangers of digital life!'

'I know. Maybe it's just the thing these days, that you put yourself all over social media when you're pregnant.'

'No, I don't think so. I didn't do that, did I?'

'I know, but it wasn't quite around then, was it?'

'We're not that old! It was. No, come on, most people don't

do that sort of gyrating dance thing when they are about to give birth. What even is that music? Did someone make that up, especially for that dance? Pregnant for too long, man? I mean, really?'

'Who knows?' Fleur questioned. 'Honestly, I don't even know what to say, which is why I phoned you to get your take on it.' Fleur shook her head as she stared at her phone screen. 'She's overdue. She could pop at any moment, and she's cavorting around like she's about to launch a world tour.'

'It's actually impressive. I mean, she's got balance, I'll give her that. If I'd tried anything like that at nine months pregnant, I'd have needed a forklift to get back up. I couldn't even put my own shoes on.'

Fleur snorted. 'Right? I could barely roll over in bed, let alone do a dance routine and thrust my nether regions about.'

'Maybe she's trying to shake the baby out?' Cassy suggested. 'Like a human snow globe?'

Fleur burst out laughing. 'It's possible. I mean, at this point, I wouldn't be surprised if she's got an entire social media strategy planned out.'

'That'd be a great series,' Cassy mused. 'Day One: Aggressive Squats. Day Two: Belly-bouncing to Club Remixes. Day Three: Interpretive Dance to Whale Noises.'

'You can't make it up.'

Cassy sighed. 'I mean, fair play to her. She looks fantastic. I was an absolute mess when I was that far gone. The only thing I was dancing with was a box of biscuits and the heartburn that came after.'

'Same,' Fleur agreed. 'My idea of exercise was waddling from the fridge to the sofa.'

'Exactly. I couldn't even sit comfortably, let alone attempt what she's doing. This is why I have trust issues with influencers. They make pregnancy look like a fun little adventure when in reality, you're sweating, swollen, and trying not to cry because you dropped your last piece of toast on the floor.'

'The truth right there and yet, there she is, doing a full-on music video like she's starring in Pregnant: The Musical.'

'Honestly, though, what is Ben thinking? Like, does he see her setting up the tripod and just, what, carry on with his day? Or is he the one filming it?'

'This time it was Luce.'

'Right.'

'I hadn't thought about that. Please don't tell me he's usually the cameraman. I can't deal with that level of cringe.'

'Imagine him giving her feedback,' Cassy snorted. 'Like, "Babe, let's do another take, but this time, really feel the lyrics."'

'Stop, I'm actually dying. If he ever starts doing couples dances with her, I will officially combust.' Fleur chuckled.

'Next thing you know, they'll be in matching pyjamas doing a reveal to a drum roll.'

Fleur groaned. 'I hate that I can picture it.'

'Look, all jokes aside, good luck to her.'

Fleur nodded. 'I suppose and at least Lucy thinks it's funny. I was a bit worried she'd feel weird about the baby and all that goes with it, but she seems fine.'

'Yeah, I guess it's better than her sitting around feeling left out. Maybe this baby will come out dancing at this rate.'

Fleur smirked. 'If it does, I hope someone gets it on camera.'

'Sarah will have a tripod set up in the delivery room. "Hey guys, welcome back to my labour vlog—don't forget to like and subscribe!"'

'Stop.'

Cassy chuckled. 'Right, I better get this meatloaf stuff bought or the boys will start eating the furniture. Keep me updated. This could be the most entertaining thing to happen all week.'

'Will do.' Fleur rolled her eyes as Cassy hung up and

chuckled to herself. She put her phone down and stared out into the garden for a moment. Sarah's social media antics aside, the whole new baby situation had the potential to be a tricky one to navigate but so far so good. Champo nodded; she'd just watch from the sidelines and see how it all panned out. Her popcorn was ready and waiting.

6

Fleur woke up to her phone vibrating aggressively on the bedside table. Groggy, she reached for it, barely cracked open one eye, desperately wanted to go back to sleep, and squinted at the screen. Three missed calls and eight unread messages. She frowned and sat bolt upright. It wasn't even seven. Who in their right mind was calling her so early?

Another buzz. This time, a voice note from Cassy. That was never a good sign. Cassy only sent voice notes if something major had happened—either an emergency with one of the boys of which there had been a few or on one memorable occasion, a limited-time sale on Le Creuset. Yawning, Fleur hit play.

'Oh my goodness!' Cassy's voice blasted through the speaker. 'When you wake up, check your messages. I've been up since the crack of dawn and am losing my actual mind. Haha! You're not going to believe this but Sarah posted from the hospital car park. It's happening. I repeat, it is *happening* and doesn't everybody know about it? The whole of England knows. The King has issued a press statement. I thought her socials were about her psychology business. Anyway.'

Fleur blinked. Before she could fully process it, a message came through from Lucy.

Lucy: *Mum. Don't freak out. But Sarah's in labour.*

Fleur groaned, rubbing her face, and whispered to herself. 'Oh, for god's sake. I don't care.'

Patrick stirred. 'What's going on?'

'Sorry, didn't mean to wake you. Sarah's in labour.' Fleur held her phone up in front of her face and scrolled through the messages.

Patrick made a noise that was half yawn, half grunt. 'Right. Okay. And?'

Fleur side-eyed. 'And apparently, everyone I've ever met thinks I need to be alerted about it immediately.'

Patrick flopped onto his back, staring at the ceiling. 'Right. So, she's having a baby. That is what happens at the end of a pregnancy. Not exactly breaking news. Really?'

Fleur rolled her eyes. 'Yes, but apparently, there's drama.'

Patrick sighed clearly gearing up for whatever nonsense was about to unfold. 'Go on, then. Hit me with it. She's the only one to ever have such a bad birth, rah, rah, rah. Then it will be the most magical baby ever, then how much she loves breastfeeding.'

Fleur chuckled and scrolled to Lucy's next message and read aloud. 'Sarah's waters broke at home, but instead of going straight to the hospital, she filmed a labour vlog first. She made Dad record her getting ready for the hospital twice because she didn't like the first take. Then she tried to do a transition where she went from breathing through a contraction to doing her hair.'

Patrick squinted. 'You're joking?'

'Weird, right?'

Patrick let out a low whistle. 'That woman is unhinged.'

Fleur continued to scroll. 'Luce, filmed some, too.'

Patrick sat up. 'Oh, brilliant. So now she's on unpaid camera duty as well as big sister duty.'

Fleur groaned. 'I knew I should've had a word with her about this. But I thought she was sensible and wouldn't get sucked in. Clearly, I was wrong.'

Patrick grabbed his phone from the bedside table. 'Well, let's see if they've gone fully unhinged yet.'

Fleur narrowed her eyes. 'What are you doing? I didn't think you *did* social media?'

'Checking Instagram and her other socials, obviously.'

'Patrick—'

Patrick was already scrolling and within seconds, he sniggered. 'Yep. There it is. She live-streamed from the hospital car park. This woman is actually unreal.'

Fleur grabbed the phone from him, and sure enough, there was Sarah, sitting in the passenger seat of their car, mid-contraction, one hand dramatically clutching her bump, the other perfectly framing herself for the camera.

Sarah panted into the screen. 'So, we're officially on our way to have this baby! Can you believe it? Oh my god, I'm so excited but also in so much pain, like, owww!'

Fleur winced. 'I can't watch this.'

Patrick hooted. 'Hang on, I want to see what Ben's doing. Cannot stand the man and this is gold. Good luck to him the next time he walks into the pub.'

Ben appeared on Patrick's screen and looked absolutely dead behind the eyes, gripping the steering wheel like a man questioning all his life choices.

'Ben, say hi to everyone!' Sarah trilled.

Fleur shook her head as Ben gave the camera the weakest, most defeated wave in history.

Patrick's eyes rolled. 'Oh, mate. He looks ruined already. I have to say this is funny.'

Fleur sighed. 'I don't know whether to laugh or be horrified.'

'Laugh. Definitely laugh.'

Fleur shook her head. 'I swear to goodness, if she has a ring light set up in the delivery room, I will lose my mind.'

Patrick grinned. 'You know she will.'

Another message came through from Lucy.

Lucy: *Mum. She's STILL filming. She just asked a midwife if they'd mind recording the birth from a good angle.*

Fleur dropped the phone onto the bed. 'Nope. I'm out. I refuse to engage with this level of insanity. She's off her rocker.'

'Not all there.'

Fleur dragged herself out of bed. 'I need tea and then I need to debrief this with Cass.'

Padding downstairs, as she pulled her dressing gown on, phone in hand, Patrick followed behind her. By the time Fleur had a mug of tea in front of her, Cassy had sent another voice note. 'Have you seen the latest update? Sarah's just posted a poll on Instagram asking people to guess how dilated she is. I have left my own body.'

'I refuse to believe that is real.' Fleur said to Patrick.

Patrick, still scrolling, let out a bark of laughter. 'Nope. It's real.'

Fleur clutched her forehead in faux drama. 'This cannot be, someone who is in my daughter's life and meant to be a role model.'

'Well, technically, it's Ben's life. He looks like he wants to throw himself out of the window, so small victories?'

'I almost feel bad for him. But then I remember who he is, and I don't.'

Patrick raised his mug in a toast. 'To karma. And to whatever poor midwife has to put up with them today. She will need a lot of patience.'

Fleur shook her head. 'You just know there's going to be a full-on birth announcement with a professionally edited photo and some ridiculous caption.'

'What do we reckon?'

'"So blessed to have documented every single moment of my labour journey for you all" with some aesthetic picture of her holding the baby while Ben looks like he's aged ten years in the background. I hope Luce has the sense to keep out of it.'

Patrick grinned. 'I give it four hours.'

Fleur exhaled, resigned. 'Three.'

They clinked their mugs together in agreement and Fleur shook her head and hoped it wouldn't all go to pot. She had a horrible feeling she was going to be proved wrong.

7

Fleur had just finished clearing up the sitting room. Patrick had gone upstairs for a shower because he was getting up super early the next day to drive to Norfolk, and she'd spent a very pleasurable hour on a notebook perusing binge with the aid of a nice gin and tonic with a slice of lime and sprig of lavender. As you do. Feeling quite smug about how well her latest notebook had turned out and how it was wholly just for her and her only, she looked at her phone as it rang with a video call on WhatsApp. She glanced at the screen: *Lucy*. Fleur and Lucy had been texting on and off all day about the new arrival but Fleur had not yet had a proper call from her.

Patrick, with wet hair and pyjama bottoms, walked in rubbing the back of his hair with a towel. Fleur turned her phone around and he raised an eyebrow. 'I reckon she's calling to debrief you on the greatest birth ever documented. Brace yourself.'

Fleur knew the birth and the baby would be the main focus of Lucy's call. She smiled but there was an odd little tightness in her chest as she pressed to accept the call. 'Hey. How's everything over there? I bet you're tired...'

Lucy let out a small, exhausted laugh. 'Mum. I am dead, like I now know what it feels like to die. I don't think I've ever been so tired in my entire life. Ballet school is nothing on this and I thought that was bad.'

Fleur leaned back against the sofa and joked. 'Why, exactly? Did you give birth, too?'

'Might as well have. Mum, it was chaos. You have no idea.'

Patrick shot Fleur a knowing look and mouthed, *Oh, I think we do.*

The pair of them had watched Sarah's socials too many times to not know what was going on or how the birth had gone. Fleur stifled a laugh. 'Go on, then. What happened?'

Lucy groaned. 'Well, for starters, Dad panicked, obviously. He literally left the hospital bags in the car and then lost the car keys, so I had to go back down to the car park and get them while Sarah was live-streaming her contractions. She was pretending to be fine but really, she swore a lot at Dad. When I say swore, I mean the worst word. You must have seen the contractions, did you?'

Fleur pinched the bridge of her nose. 'How was Sarah?'

'Oh, she was loving it in between. Like, full-on thriving. Between contractions, she was giving commentary, like some kind of reality show contestant. "I can do this; I was made for this."'

Patrick openly shook his head and whispered. 'Thriving? Don't make me laugh. Wait until she's been up all night.'

'How did the midwives take it?' Fleur was mindful not to turn the conversation into a full-on rant about Sarah but couldn't really help herself. She already had a fair idea of what the midwives would have been saying.

Lucy rattled on. 'At one point, one of them had to say, "Sarah, love, you have to put the phone down."'

'You're joking.'

'I swear on my life. Dad looked traumatised through the

whole thing.' Lucy sighed dramatically. 'Anyway, fast forward to the actual birth, and she was all sweaty hair and stuff and she was swearing like really, really badly and like every other word. Honestly, I was shocked and she did this really deep sort of voice, like, I don't know, an animal or something...'

Fleur tried to piece that information with the picture-perfect version she'd seen on Instagram. 'How did she end up looking as she did in that photo you sent me?'

'It's the lashes,' Patrick said solemnly as if he had a clue.

Lucy giggled. 'Anyway, the baby is here now but yeah, Sarah swore so much. It was long. Honestly, I don't even know what day it is anymore.'

'So, you two are at home now?'

'Yeah, and Dad is shattered. It was, well, a lot.'

Patrick caught Fleur's eye and pulled a face. Fleur took a deep breath. 'Right. You need to be careful. We don't want any collapsing from you or anything.'

Lucy sighed. 'Mum. Can we not start with that? I am fine. That hasn't happened for ages since I stopped ballet. I wanted to be there. It was actually nice and I really, really love him, Mum. He's so tiny and perfect, his little toes, oh my goodness, and I don't know, I just feel like I want to be here for him, you know? Like I *need* to be. Bonding is what Sarah called it. She did a module on female and sibling bonding at uni...'

Fleur closed her eyes briefly. She had expected Lucy to be happy about the baby's arrival but she hadn't expected the intensity of it all. Here her daughter was very emotionally involved with something that at the end of the day wasn't much to do with her at all. Sometimes she didn't know what to say for the best. 'He is your little brother, after all.'

'I know, but it's more than that. I feel like... I don't know, like I *want* to be involved. Like, be properly there for him. You know?'

Fleur felt deeply conflicted. On one hand, she was glad Lucy felt the connection. It was good, healthy, and just all-around nice. On the other hand, it was early days and Sarah's post-partum fantasy would soon wear off, that she knew for free. She swallowed her thoughts and tried to sound happy. 'That's really lovely, Luce. I'm glad you feel that way.'

'Yeah.' Lucy hesitated slightly and narrowed her eyes. 'So, would you want to come to the hospital and meet him?'

Fleur froze. God no. Full-on, flat-out, hard no. Just in case there was any doubt: no. She'd known the moment was coming, of course she had, and she'd given it a fair bit of mulling over, but as the words came out of Lucy's mouth, she felt completely unprepared. There was no way on earth she was going to the hospital. She felt a little bit like some kind of evil, ugly, old witch in a fairy tale but didn't care. 'Hmm.'

'I mean, no pressure, obviously. But, you know, it might be nice. I know it's weird and complicated and everything, but at the end of the day, he *is* my brother. And I think you'd like him.'

Fleur gripped the edge of the coffee table and swallowed. It was all too awkward and had been since Sarah had been on the scene.

'Mum?' Lucy prompted.

Fleur cleared her throat. 'Yeah, I umm, I just... We'll give them some time. It's all very new.'

Patrick raised his eyebrows at Fleur from the other side of the sofa and whispered. 'Just say no, if you don't want to go.'

'Mum, honestly, you don't have to. I get it. But I think it might be less weird than you think it will be.'

Would it, though? Fleur wasn't so sure. Nope, it would not. Not only could she not be faffed, she didn't want to have to suffer Sarah in all her baby glory acting as if she was the only woman on the planet to have ever given birth. She imagined walking into the hospital or Sarah and Ben's house, Sarah looking smug as heck, Ben looking awkward, Lucy sitting there, completely in love with the baby, and Sarah probably filming the whole thing and harping on about how good it was to be a merged family. Fleur was a flat *no* but there was no way she was going to present it like that. She'd just make an excuse until all the baby arrival glow had worn off. 'Ahh, umm, I'll see.'

Fleur grimaced. She wouldn't see and wouldn't be going. End of. She loved Lucy and put her at the fore of almost everything. This, however, was going too far. She'd watch from the sidelines and keep her distance and see how everything turned out. It was none of her business, she wasn't interested in bonding and at the end of the day just simply didn't want to know. Lucy was going to have to suck it up and take that on board.

Fleur had just sat down with her late evening cup of cocoa, feeling quite pleased with herself for ignoring her phone for a whole hour, when Patrick wandered in, cocoa in one hand, phone in the other, grinning like a man who had found something truly ridiculous.

'It's happened,' he said, plonking himself down opposite her.

Fleur frowned. 'What's happened?'

Patrick held up his phone. 'The official birth announcement has dropped.'

'Already?'

Patrick scrolled with one hand as he took a sip of coffee. 'And, surprise, surprise, it's not just any old baby announcement —it's a Sarah special. Give me strength.'

Fleur sighed and reached for her phone and sure as eggs is eggs, there it was. A full-on, professionally edited post, so polished it could have been featured in a high-end baby magazine. Sarah was in the hospital bed, looking like she'd just stepped out of a spa treatment, full make-up, perfectly curled hair, and skin so glowy it had definitely been filtered to high heaven. The baby, swaddled in the softest white blanket, lay in her arms like a perfectly arranged prop. Ben was in the background, sitting in the hospital chair, staring at the camera with the hollow-eyed look of a man who had aged twenty years overnight.

Fleur zoomed in on his face. 'He looks done in.'

Patrick chuckled. 'I am enjoying this way too much. That is the face of a man questioning every life decision that led him to this moment.'

Fleur scrolled to the caption.

Welcome to the world, our precious little poppet. Our hearts are bursting! The most magical, empowering, raw experience of my life. So grateful for my amazing partner who has been my absolute rock through this journey. I couldn't have done it without you. #Blessed #NewMum #BirthWarrior #PostpartumGlow #LoveMyTribe #FourthTrimesterMagic

Fleur made a faux gagging sound. "'Fourth Trimester Magic?'" She repeated and swiped to the next photo a black-and-white shot of Sarah looking down at the baby, eyes dramatically misty while Ben rested his head exhaustively in his hands beside her.

Patrick leaned over. 'Yeah, that's not normal. No one looks like that in labour. Lucy probably took that. Have you heard from her?'

'Not for a bit.'

Fleur scrolled further. There were more pictures. A soft-focus close-up of their hands intertwined. A posed shot of Sarah breastfeeding with perfectly arranged hospital sheets and artful lighting.

Patrick shook his head. 'There's more staging in this than a wedding. You do have to wonder...'

'How did she even have time to do all this?'

'She probably hired someone, a Birth Content Specialist or I don't know...'

Fleur groaned and clicked on the comments section, which was even worse than she had anticipated.

Omgggg! Sarah you look INCREDIBLE, how is this even possible?!
Ben is such a supportive King, you can see the love in his eyes.

Fleur blinked. 'The love in his eyes? You have got to be kidding me.' She knew Ben well and had never seen him looking as bad.

Patrick smirked. 'Maybe they mean the love of sleep. You know, the love he used to have before it was cruelly ripped from him forever.'

Fleur scrolled further down the comments.

Thank you for sharing this journey with us, it's so special to be a part of it.

'A part of it? Why do these people think they're part of her birth? It's so fake.'

Patrick snorted. 'Because *she* made them part of it. There's probably some poor sod out there who's been refreshing her page all day, convinced they had a personal role in this labour.'

'This is unhinged. Give it a week, she'll be doing New Mum Skincare Routines and reviewing postpartum recovery tea.' Fleur buried her face in her hands for a second. 'This cannot be my ex-husband and my daughter is part of it. Why me? Why?'

'Oh, but it is and it's only just beginning.'

Fleur's phone buzzed with an image from Lucy: a picture of Sarah, lying in her hospital bed, baby nestled against her, makeup still fully intact, looking unnaturally serene, and Lucy bobbed down beside her looking at the baby. Fleur shook her head. 'Nope. Nope. Can't do it. If I see any more of this, I'll throw my phone out the window.'

Patrick grinned. 'I mean, at least she's committed. Some people just post a picture and move on.'

Fleur exhaled, rubbing her temples. 'It's the comments that get me. The people who actually think she looks like that after giving birth. Shall we place bets on how soon the postpartum fitness journey begins?'

'A week, maybe less.'

Fleur typed out a suitably nice message to Lucy, pressed send and with that, shut off her phone, picked up her cocoa, and decided a much stronger drink would be required in the next few post-baby weeks. She would remain resolute, calm, nice and pleasant on the outside while on the inside she would try not to get too rattled at all. Another thing she had to navigate as Lucy's mother. Sometimes she felt as if it was all really a bit too much.

8

The best part of Fleur's day normally arrived at around 7:30 pm, when the cottage was quiet, she'd eaten, and had wrapped up her workday. She liked to call it her notebook time. In the sitting room, with the gingham curtains open, she arranged her personal notebook on the coffee table along with her laptop, a tablet, a half-read paperback, and her phone. All she needed was a nice glass of wine, and all would be right with the universe. Life in her little cottage tucked away from the world as she knew it, really was quite good. Turning over one of her notebooks covered in a beautiful strawberry and paisley fabric, she smiled as she remembered finding the fabric in a little haberdashery shop down near Portsmouth. She'd strolled into it one day on her lunch hour when she'd been giving a training course in a small business centre. On spotting the fabric, she had immediately fallen in love. She'd bought a yard of it and now here it was covering one of her books. It was one of the reasons she loved bookbinding; each book came with its own special memory of where and how it had started off. Nodding at the little pastel pink page marker annotations poking out the side and the pink and grey elastic pen holder she'd made, she felt quite pleased at another one of her creations and a job well done.

Pulling the elastic band off and over the front, she flicked to one of the tabs and started to consult random notes that had tumbled out of her mind a few weeks previously. After that, she turned to the side again and flipped to the section on places she liked the look of; little restaurants she'd passed, places she'd seen on her socials that she wanted to visit, exhibitions, and museums and pretty much anything that took her fancy. Flipping through she remembered things here and there and decided that she needed to get out there and start visiting some of the places in her books. There was a whole section on a museum she wanted to go to in Surrey, an art gallery doing an Art Nouveau collection in London, and a house down near Dover that detailed things that had gone on under the White Cliffs in the war.

Getting to the section on travelling and far-flung climes she was surprised at how many notes she'd made. For someone who'd only been out of the country a few times, there was a whole list of countries she wanted to visit. Unfortunately, the places on her list were more or less dreams; ones she'd never quite had the time, inclination or money to fulfil. Forever dreams that really were never going to happen. Turning over the pages, she read through notes she'd made about visiting Hawaii, somewhere she'd always wanted to go, and smiled as she remembered that her dad had always said he'd fancied going to Hawaii too. This was why our Champo liked her notebooks; they took her back to other times, let her remember her thoughts and helped her mind zoom back to days gone by.

Tucking her feet up under her, she sat back on the sofa, sipped her wine, and got lost in notes, lists and words. Continuing to read notes she'd made the year before about Hawaii, the more she read and pondered, the more she felt like throwing caution to the wind and booking a holiday. As she perused the length of the flight, the cost, and a few hotels she had found, she nodded as the notion became less and less like a pipe dream, and more and more attractive by the minute.

Reading her notes about Waikiki hotels and all the other islands, as well as the food and history of Hawaii and stuff about the war, Fleur smiled. Something about Hawaii had always caught her eye. She distinctly remembered her grandma, years and years before, when Fleur could not have been more than seven years old, watching old Elvis in Hawaii films on repeat. Right from then there had always been something about it calling her, tinkering with a little button on the side of her head, triggering some sort of fascination about a place she didn't know.

Along with Hawaii, she'd always fancied going to Japan, and then, of course, as she turned the pages, there were the usual European places that were a lot closer to home. Walking in the mountains of Norway had tickled her fancy along with visiting Poland and participating in the vodka. Sipping and reading, she decided that she really needed to knuckle down, stop procrastinating and make one of her bucket list travel plans happen, otherwise, another year would go by and she wouldn't have been anywhere at all. Same old story right there in front of her face. Unless you put yourself out there and got on with it nothing would change.

Flipping open her banking app to have a little look at her savings, she looked in her account and was pleasantly surprised. Since she'd been doing the markets, selling her notebooks online, and continuing with her social media postings, the money from her notebooks had continued to trickle into her savings account and had built up quite nicely. It was certainly not life-changing and was never going to pay off her mortgage but the income from her bookbinding was a nice little side hustle that was adding to a nest egg. As the months had gone on and she'd not touched the money, it had accumulated and continued to do so. After years of not having much money put away for a rainy day, Fleur now not only had money for a rainy day but, in fact, money for a sunny day—by way of a trip somewhere else in the world. She'd been waiting for tropical sunshine for long enough. Maybe it was time to take the bull by the horns.

Flipping back to the travel section, she turned another few pages, added a tab, and started to add up the cost of various trips. Popping onto Google to check flights, she calculated the cost of a flight to Hawaii and couldn't quite believe how much more economical they were compared to the last time she'd looked. Clearly, global travel had meant that travelling for the regular person had become more affordable, normal even. She could work with that. As she sat and stared at the figures and looked at the length of the flight, she realised that she could possibly make a trip to Hawaii if she really wanted to. Hoo blooming ray.

Just as she was adding up the figures and flipping through her calendar app on her phone, a WhatsApp video call from Patrick popped up. She pressed the button, propped up the phone on the side of the sofa, and smiled.

'Hey, how are you?' Patrick asked. 'You look cosy.'

Fleur nodded. She *felt* cosy, relaxed, and in the zone. She was cocooned in the corner of the sofa, her hair up on top of her head, dressed in her softest clothes with a tracksuit on, lost in her notebooks and covered in a patchwork quilt. It was her favourite time of the evening, and she loved how the decompression was hitting her in waves. 'Hi, yes, I am. I'm in my happy place. What are you up to?'

Patrick pointed to himself. 'As you can see, I'm not up to much other than chilling in my hotel room waiting for the morning. I have a feeling you're sitting there with your notebooks, am I right?'

Fleur laughed. 'Yes, how did you guess?' She turned her

phone around to show the coffee table and her notebook and panned in on the pages.

'What are you looking at there?'

'Actually, you'll never guess. Have a go.'

Patrick frowned and joked. 'I've no idea. You're not writing notes on the birth of the century are you? '

'Gosh, no. Don't mention Sarah or the birth. It's died a death thank goodness.' Fleur held the book up again in front of the screen. 'I've been looking at my travel section and places I want to go. I've had this section going for years but I've never really made any of them happen. There are so many places on my bucket list.'

'Like?'

'I've always wanted to go to Japan and Norway, and I *really* fancy Hawaii.'

'Alright, not too far then,' Patrick joked. 'No quick trip to Ibiza for our Fleur. You have your sights set on far-away climes.'

'I'd like to go anywhere at the moment, to be quite honest.'

'So, you fancy Japan then?'

'Well, I fancy Hawaii over Japan, but yeah, I've just been looking at the cost of the flights, and it's not as expensive as I thought.'

Patrick raised his hands and then shrugged. 'Let's do it then.'

'What do you mean, let's do it?'

'Why not? You deserve a week off. I'm sure we could manage a trip to Hawaii.'

Fleur frowned. 'Just like that! We can't just take off like that! I think it's a long way to go just for a week, too.'

'Why can't we just take off? There's nothing stopping us. Alright, what about ten days? I'm sure you've got ten days' holiday, and you can do enough at your shop so you've got stuff backed up to keep that going.'

'Hmm. Nah, I can't just jet off somewhere like that at a drop of a hat.'

'Why don't you price it up, and we'll have a proper, serious look?' Patrick leant forward into the screen like a man ready to book a flight that very second.

'You make it sound like booking a cab into town. This is Hawaii, Patrick. You don't just "price it up" and hop on a plane.'

'I don't see why not. I'm the owner of my business, so I can basically do what I want and you get paid holiday from work. Fleur, I hate to break it to you; that is what holiday is for.'

Fleur rolled her eyes. 'Oh, it must be nice to be the owner of a fancy business,' she teased, reaching for her laptop. 'Meanwhile, some of us mere mortals have to check if we actually have enough holiday time to swan off to the other side of the world for ten days.'

Patrick smirked. 'Go on then, let's see what the gods of annual leave have to say.'

Fleur sighed, flipping open her laptop and navigating to her work documents as if she were checking to see if she had won the lottery. She scrolled, tapped, scrolled again, and smiled. 'Yeah, I've got loads.'

'What?'

'I've got loads of holiday left. Like, a ridiculous amount.'

'Excellent. That's one less hurdle. Now, all we need to do is choose the dates, book the flights, and we're off.'

Fleur gave him a long, sceptical look. 'Do you actually think this could happen? Because it sounds like one of those things we talk about at 10 pm with a glass of wine in hand, and then in the morning, we realise it's completely unrealistic. At least that's what I will think tomorrow morning…'

Patrick shook his head. 'Nope. I mean it. You've got holiday, I run my own business, and therefore, I can simply declare that we're going to Hawaii. What our Champo wants, our Champo gets.'

Fleur laughed. 'Right. And what about your clients? Your staff?'

'The world will still be here when we get back. Let's be real, I run an electrical company. I'm not in charge of NATO. Nothing I do is so important that it can't be paused for ten days. I mean, what's the worst that could happen? A few emails build up? Someone has to actually answer the phone? Utter chaos will not prevail. I really am not that important.'

Fleur shook her head. 'This is Hawaii. Not Cornwall. Not the Lake District. It's literally on the other side of the planet.'

Patrick grinned. 'Which is exactly why we should go. If it was Cornwall, you'd just say, "Oh, we'll do it next year." But because it's Hawaii, it's a bucket list thing that we'll actually do.'

'Let's theoretically price this up.' Fleur tapped a few keys, pulled up a flight comparison site, and nodded. 'The flights are actually cheaper than the last time I looked. Either that or I have no concept of money anymore.'

Patrick shrugged. 'Maybe both.'

'Look, if we fly out midweek instead of at the weekend, it's even cheaper. And if we don't mind a stopover in LA—'

'I love a stopover in LA,' Patrick interrupted.

'You love an airport with no fresh air and overpriced sandwiches?'

Patrick shrugged. 'I enjoy the drama of international travel.'

'Alright, well, the drama of international travel could save us a few hundred pounds if we do it that way.'

'And yet, you're still hesitating. What's the issue?'

Fleur bit her lip. 'It just feels, I don't know. Irresponsible? I've never just jetted off somewhere. I've never had the cash for off-the-cuff jaunts, you know?'

'We're not robbing a bank. We're planning a holiday. People do it all over the world, every single day, Fleur.'

'I know, but it's Hawaii. That's *really* special. People go there for special reasons like weddings, big birthdays, proposals, all sorts.'

'It's just a place, with hotels, and people, and food, and will mean that *you* can switch off.'

Fleur couldn't quite believe it was even an option let alone that it could be a reality. 'With beaches, volcanoes, and stunning scenery, and lovely looking cocktails.'

'Which is exactly why we should go there.'

Fleur sighed, looking back at the screen. 'You make it sound so simple.'

'It *is* simple. You have the time off. I have the time off. We have the money. Lucy is okay. Even the baby that has nothing to do with us has arrived safely. We're not waiting for anyone's permission. Why wouldn't we go?'

'You're right.'

'I've always wanted to climb up a volcano.' Patrick grinned.

'I'll mull it over and start a notebook.'

Patrick rolled his eyes. 'I'll take that as a yes. If there's a notebook involved it might be happening.'

Fleur giggled. He knew her too well.

9

Fleur had spent two days at a training conference at a hotel in Essex with Cassy. The pair of them walked out of the door of the hotel, exhausted, and stood by Cassy's car chatting about what had gone on and what was coming up. Cassy kissed Fleur on the cheek. 'I'll see you next week, if not before. You sure you don't want me to give you a lift into the centre?'

Fleur shook her head. 'No, I could do with the walk.' She wiggled her phone around in front of her. 'My step count is pathetic after being holed up in there for two days. Thank goodness that is over.'

'You can say that again.'

'A nice walk will do me the power of good. Get the blood pumping and do all the good hormone things or so they say.'

'Have you heard from Patrick?'

'Yes, he'll be at the pub soon, so that's all good. It's all lined up perfectly.'

'So, what, you're going out for a late lunch now and then staying this way for a couple of nights?'

Fleur nodded. 'Yep, he's been doing that work with the National Trust...'

'Oh yes, that's right. Not a bad weekend on the way for you then,' Cassy said with a smile. 'While I have to get back home and navigate my way through the Friday afternoon traffic and deal with the boys...'

'I feel your pain. The traffic will be heaving.'

'Ahh, well, right, I'll text you. Have a lovely weekend. Send me some pics of the hotel. Let me know if there's any further news on the dancing queen on social media and the baby.'

Fleur shook her head. 'I doubt it. She's gone quiet now she's home and not getting any sleep.'

Cassy rolled her eyes. 'Didn't we know it?'

'Indeed.'

'I'll message you. Enjoy your stay.'

'Yes, yes, you too.'

Fleur stood where she was, watched Cassy pull out of the hotel car park, waved as Cassy turned onto the road then checked the map app. She'd examined her route before and had worked out that basically all she had to do was head in a straight line for about twenty minutes, after which she would arrive in the town centre of a lovely old Essex market town where Patrick would be meeting her in a pub. They'd arranged to meet in the pub for a late lunch and would then drive on to a National Trust property where they would be staying the night. To say Fleur had been looking forward to it was an understatement and Patrick had said the same, too.

As she turned out of the car park and walked along the main road, gazing up at some beautiful old houses and strolling past a church that looked more like a cathedral, Fleur was glad to be done with the training session and with the fact that for once she did not have a lot on her mind. Life was bumbling along nicely, and compared to the few months prior, when Lucy had been in trouble, Fleur felt lighter, as if a physical weight had been lifted from her shoulders. Checking her maps and seeing that she could stroll through a park as a bit of a diversion away from the main road, she turned left through a gate in a beautiful old stone wall, spied a bench in front of a small pond, and stopped for a while. As she gazed at a couple of ducks fluttering around, she let her brain remove itself from all the business stuff she'd been doing for the previous few days and thought about the weekend ahead with Patrick. A few days with no stress, they'd earmarked having a conversation about the Hawaii thing, a lot of good food, country walks, and a big comfy bed where it was someone else's job to change the sheets. Bliss.

About fifteen minutes later, after strolling through the park, she was standing outside a beautiful old whitewashed pub with a steeply pitched tiled roof, looking up at a wrought iron sign and wondering if Patrick had arrived yet. Patrick had told her all about the pub and had shown her some pictures online. As she stood and looked up at it, she could see why he'd blabbered on and loved it so much. With black beams, a heavy timber door with brass fittings and creamy white walls, it looked like something that had been plucked straight from the pages of an old-world storybook. A lantern swung by the door, and through little leaded windows, Fleur could see flickers of candlelight and the promise of a nice, cosy lunch beckoning from inside. Beautiful, heavy pendant lights hung from the ceiling, and gorgeous old-fashioned Chesterfield leather sofas were tucked here and there around an inglenook fireplace and not a slot machine in sight. To the right of the door under a little glass frame, a card displayed details all about the pub's history.

The Oyster Arms, a Grade 2 listed building built in 1540 is one of the oldest pubs situated in the heart of Essex. It boasts a charming Tudor-style façade, featuring black timber beams against whitewashed walls, reminiscent of the town's rich history. The roof is steeply pitched with local classic clay tiles, adding to its old-world charm and the many fireplaces were built by skilled craftsmen ahead of their time.
At The Oyster Arms, you'll be served with fresh homemade food and

ales made right here on the premises. Try our heated beer garden and marquees to keep you warm and book a table for the festive season. Our guest ales and home brews are the best you'll find in Essex.

Pushing open the heavy door, Fleur was immediately wrapped in the scent of cosy comforting things; fires, community, ale, hops, life, smiles and all the gorgeous bits and bobs that made up the pub smell. Inside, the building was the gift that kept on giving; shelves piled with old books, the scent of mulled cider and beer, dark wooden floorboards and a gigantic painting sprawled across the far wall. The place was nothing short of glorious. And breathe.

As Fleur took in a perfect jumble of battered old timber tables and mismatched chairs, each one polished by years of use, she felt her whole body exhale as she walked across the uneven floor in the direction of the bar. Closer to the worn comfy-looking Chesterfields, she took in a tall bookshelf crammed with board games, puzzles, and books as the low black beams overhead, twisted with age, felt as if they were getting closer and closer to her head. Absolute English-pub-get-your-comfy-on, bliss.

As she got to the bar she felt as if she was tucked away from the outside world as the smell of old walls, roast dinner, ale and garlic drifted on the air. If she'd had to put money on it, she would have sworn that somewhere, somebody was baking an apple pie. Smiling when she saw Patrick sitting around the corner at the bar, she walked up, kissed him on the cheek and waved her hand around the room. 'This pub is *so* beautiful.' She gushed as she put her jacket on a little brass hook under the bar and plonked herself down on a stool.

'Yup, I know. We did the electrics for it. The owner in those days was friends with my dad. That's how we got the job.'

'Oh wow, how interesting.'

'They have new owners now.' Patrick nodded towards the

bar. 'They've done a great job with it by the looks of it. Yeah, it's nice in here, which is why when you said you were doing that training course nearby, I was like we have to come here.'

A few minutes later, Patrick had a pint of handcrafted ale in his hand and Fleur had a glass of bubbles. They were scanning the menu, trying to decide what to have to eat, chatting about their weeks and Fleur was enjoying every last second of it. After they'd ordered steak and kidney pie topped with a pastry crust laced with famous Essex salt, Fleur watched her ring catch the sparkle in the lights and sipped on her glass of champagne. For our Champo, life really was rather good.

Patrick smiled. 'So, I have some news.'

Fleur raised her eyebrows. 'Right. I hope it's good news. I'm done with stress news or any other sort of news, really.'

'It is. I've been asked to speak at an electricity conference.'

That did not sound like fun to Fleur. She tried to sound interested as she thought that a conference about electricity was probably the most boring thing she could ever think of. She wasn't really into electricity, it had to be said. 'Right, umm, is that good news? What, err, is good about it precisely?'

Patrick chuckled. 'Ha, don't sound too enthused! I love a good conference. You always learn something.'

Fleur thought about all the business hotels, meeting centres, and conference rooms she'd been to up and down the country, in various hotels here, there, and everywhere. If there was ever anyone who'd seen a lot of conferences and suchlike in her life, it was Fleur—with Cassy up there as a contender too. Fleur would be quite happy not to ever have to attend another one again. 'So which delightful part of the country is it in? I bet you I've been there. Or is it a bit further afield? Scotland? Up north somewhere? Wales? Or in a big venue in London?'

Patrick shook his head. 'Not even close.'

Fleur frowned. 'Further away?'

'Much, much further away.'

'Like where? Ireland?'

Patrick smiled. 'Nope, even further. You have one more guess.'

Fleur shrugged. She couldn't have cared less. She did know she wouldn't be in attendance. 'I've no idea. New York or something like that? No. I know, Sydney, Australia. You can pop in and see my sister while you're there.'

Patrick laughed. 'Nope, wrong country. Los Angeles.'

'Oh wow, that's a long way to go for a conference.'

There was a twinkle in Patrick's eyes. 'And where do you think Los Angeles is near?'

Fleur frowned. 'No idea what we're talking about. I don't know... San Francisco?'

'It's not too far from Hawaii. You can fly there from LA.'

Fleur widened her eyes. 'The same Hawaii that's on my travel bucket list and in my notebook? The one we are discussing this weekend?'

'Yep, the very one. So, what do you think?'

'What do you mean, what do I think?' Fleur frowned. 'I'm not following.'

'Why don't we tack it onto the end of my trip? We could go to Hawaii. We talked about it and did nothing about it. This gives us a reason.'

Fleur felt as if going to Hawaii was something other people did. 'I'm not sure I can.' She screwed her face up.

'Why not? Of course, you can.'

'How long is the conference for?'

'The conference is a week. That's the only sticking point; in that I would be busy working, meaning you'd be on your own, unless you flew out to meet me after it was done, which could be an option. What do you think?'

Fleur raised her eyebrows, took a sip of her drink, and thought about what Patrick had suggested. Now that it was being offered to her, on a plate, she wasn't sure. She'd never really been very far at all, and the thought of a huge flight sounded massive to her, especially on her own. 'I'd have to think about it.'

'Or we can just book it.'

As Fleur went to answer, their pies arrived. They tucked in and smiled. 'On the Hawaii thing. Now push is coming to shove, I'm not sure.'

Patrick slit the top of his pie. 'By the time this weekend is over, we will have our flights booked. We're going. End of story.'

Fleur swallowed and felt a little flutter of butterflies whizz around her stomach. Oh, how her life had changed. One minute the joys of being a single mum and navigating the labyrinth of motorways zig-zagging across the country, the next minute sitting in a pub chatting to a very handsome man about leaving on a jet plane. She most certainly knew which one she preferred.

10

Fleur closed the door on Patrick's car and looked up at the stunning house in front of her—a 15th-century country house turned into what looked from the outside like the most amazing hotel ever. Bring it on. One thing Fleur knew was that this was not some grotty lodge on the side of a motorway trying to pretend it was good at hospitality or even had an inkling of what that was. She knew what the inside of a motorway hotel looked like, through grim experience, that was for sure.

She looked over at Patrick. 'Oh my gosh, this looks amazing. How did you find this?'

'I can't tell you.' Patrick laughed. 'Sworn to secrecy! Nah, it was through the National Trust work we've been doing.'

A few minutes later, after going through a thick timber door with a massive brass handle, Fleur looked around at the low ceilings painted in a beautiful dark green. Panelled walls stretched around to small sitting rooms, with a map room flanked by gigantic lamps and blue velvet furniture was placed just so in every available nook and cranny. She poked her head into the main bar area, wallpapered in a floral pattern, a lush palm plant in a stone pot and a beautiful old white fireplace with a gilded mirror over the top. Beautiful antique furnishings sat around by the dozen—plush embroidered chairs with intricate designs, dark wooden cabinets, and a stunning old bar stocked with a plethora of neatly arranged bottles. A large potted fern reached towards the ceiling and on a picture rail, old photos and paintings jostled for space. Our Champo had arrived.

Deep wallpaper hues and an insulated old-world luxury seemed to welcome Fleur as framed artwork and nautical paintings adorning the walls called out for guests to come and have a nose. Everything shouted history, sophistication, old-school England and elegance. A lit fire crackled away to itself, a low-key warmth enveloped and an odd clink of glassware and quiet chatter from guests here and there created a low, pretty ambience with a slow, easy undertone of classical music playing softly in the background.

Fleur took a deep breath, trying to work out what she was smelling—an earthy aroma from the plants, a faint scent of aged wood, leather feels from the furniture, and a whisper of smoky, dark warmth from the fireplace. A touch of vanilla and oak lingered here and there. She stood still, just gazing at the setting, the quiet luxury, and the feeling of nostalgia wrapping her in a massive hug. Talk about nice. Who needed Hawaii when you could have a slow evening drink beside a crackling English fire in an old 15th-century house?

After checking in at reception and being told that their room was actually in the old servants' quarters, Fleur and Patrick went through a labyrinth of flagstone-floored corridors with very low beamed ceilings until they arrived at a dark timber staircase. Beautiful sconces on the walls let light drop onto the stairs and a huge lantern with small rose-coloured silk tassels hung down from an overhead beam. Our Fleur was in her element.

Opening the door to room number ten, Fleur gasped as she walked in. What they hadn't realised when they'd booked was that the room was a premium room, and after Fleur had stepped through the doorway as Patrick clicked the door shut behind them, she gasped. The room was bathed in the glow of gorgeous bedside lamps, and everything welcomed with an understated, whispered elegance of days gone by. Fleur sighed at the moody warm grey on the walls and how the room seemed to have made the world outside hush and go away for a bit. Crisp white linen and perfectly plumped cushions in tones of slate and dove wrapped the huge bed, a perfectly placed, neatly folded throw graced the foot of the bed, and against the far wall, an old empty fireplace stood beneath a huge round mirror that caught the light here and there. As downstairs in the map room, the scent in the air whispered—a comfy, easy layering of age, lavender and a shed load of care. Beeswax polish on antique furniture, the promise of fresh linen, and something faintly earthy and smoky here and there mingled with a trace of chamomile coming from a small hidden diffuser on top of the dresser. Brass fittings looked back at her everywhere, and as Fleur ran her hand over the bed, she couldn't quite wait to get in and drift off to sleep. All of it was perfect. Patrick had done well. Not grand or ostentatious or gold or glitzy; just beautifully, quietly English, elegant, classy and all around perfect. Stealth wealth oozed from just about every inch.

Patrick wandered further into the room, turning in a slow circle as he took it all in. 'Well, this is better than I expected. I thought I'd booked a nice hotel, not a BBC period drama set. We're about three seconds away from a butler appearing with a candle and some deep, dark family secrets. I'm getting Bridgerton vibes.'

Fleur laughed, slipped off her shoes and padded over to a plush overstuffed armchair in the corner, running a hand over the fabric. 'I'm fine with that as long as the butler also plys me with calories, preferably in the form of scones, fresh cream and homemade jam and ideally, no ghosts.'

'What, you don't fancy a bit of a haunted country house vibe?'

'Absolutely not. I don't have the energy for a four-hundred-year-old duchess wailing about her lost love at three in the morning.' Fleur joked.

Patrick chuckled, making his way to a set of double doors on the far side of the room and reached for the brass handles. 'Hold that thought. Let's see where this leads.'

He swung open the doors, and a rush of fresh air spilt into the room, carrying the smell of salt, the lake, and damp earth. A small wrought-iron balcony stretched out, overlooking a patchwork of rolling fields, distant hills and little copses of trees dotted on the horizon. The only sounds were the rustling of the trees and the occasional bird.

Fleur followed him and rested her elbows on the railing. 'Oh, wow. Okay. You have outdone yourself. You have officially peaked. There is no topping this.'

Patrick grinned. 'I thought you wanted Hawaii, ha. I'll be adding this to my list of greatest achievements.'

'You've excelled.'

'It seems that way. We're here now, and that means no cooking, no alarms, and definitely no responsibilities. Just a couple of days of lounging about, eating far too much, and pretending we belong in this sort of place.'

'Pretending?' Fleur scoffed. 'I was *born* for this level of luxury. I'm going to start carrying around a tiny porcelain teacup and making vaguely condescending remarks about the weather.'

'Speaking of tea...'

Fleur followed Patrick back inside as he started rummaging through the tea-making facilities. 'Do you think they'll have normal tea?'

'This place is fancy. More like hand-plucked artisan leaves infused with the essence of morning dew.' Fleur giggled and flopped onto the bed, watching as Patrick lifted a polished wooden box from the shelf. He flipped it open and groaned. 'I was joking but...' He held up a sachet. 'Organic jasmine and elderflower with a whisper of bergamot.'

'Tragic. That's not tea in my book.'

'Wait, there's hope.' He rifled through the box again and pulled out a more familiar packet. 'Ah-ha! English Breakfast. The one true tea.'

'I was about to start composing a strongly worded letter. Gosh, look at this place. There's a fireplace in the bedroom and the bedding is so crisp, I can actually hear it when I move. Fleur stretched out across the covers, the material cool against her skin. 'It's the sort of bed where you want to merge with it and become one with the duvet. My new identity will be Bed Lady.'

'Well, Bed Lady, your tea is ready. Shall we enjoy it on the balcony, like the posh, refined individuals we are?'

Fleur giggled. 'Shall we discuss poetry? The finer points of literature?'

Patrick handed her a cup of tea. 'I was thinking more along the lines of whether it's socially acceptable to order three desserts at dinner, but sure, we can start with poetry.'

On the balcony, they sat on the iron chairs, the sky a dusky blue, a few streaks of pink and orange fading beyond the horizon. Fleur nodded. 'This was a good idea. We needed this. A few days of pretending the real world doesn't exist. No emails, no stress, just good food, long walks.'

'Yup.'

'I'll be eating all the complimentary biscuits and stealing the fancy soap from the bathroom.'

Patrick grinned. 'A flawless plan.'

Fleur smiled. The hotel was nothing short of glorious. For now, that thing called reality could wait.

∽

The next day, Fleur was sitting in an old vintage lawn chair under an umbrella on a terrace outside the hotel. She'd had a lovely stay so far and was now sitting outside with a pot of tea and a two-tier cake stand filled with finger sandwiches. Patrick had gone for a swim in the supposedly heated outdoor pool. Our Fleur had given that a miss. Sitting with her book, eating cucumber sandwiches and topping up her tea every now and then, she was lost in a bit of a world of her own as she watched wedding preparations in a bandstand-style pergola about a hundred metres away from her. She idly observed a group of mostly men making their way to the bandstand, chatting away, laughing and then standing around with drinks in their hands.

Popping a finger sandwich into her mouth every now and then and pouring from the teapot, she studied a wedding coordinator who clearly had everything under control going about her business. After twenty or so minutes, a jumble of happy guests began to arrive, the men from before now ushers, stood, greeting people and directed them to chairs on a lawn underneath a beautiful old vintage-style canopy. Fleur watched as men in suits with buttonholes and women in pretty English floral dresses and fascinators perched in their hair gathered in twos and threes, chatting and laughing as they waited to take their seats and for the ceremony to begin.

Fleur was thoroughly enjoying herself; having a smashing time enjoying a personal bird's-eye view of the goings-on of a quintessentially British wedding. To her far left, she could see the other side of the party—the bride, and a couple of bridesmaids in pale green dresses with flowers in their hair, and the father of the bride standing, sipping champagne under a similar bandstand-type pergola, clearly getting ready to make their entrance.

It looked like such a lovely occasion, Fleur thought to herself. The pomp and ceremony of it all fluttered around her head, making her feel happy to be part of something she wasn't invited to but just felt like she was. Shifting slightly in her chair, she adjusted her position under the large cream umbrella as she poured herself another cup of tea. The delicate clink of china accompanied the hum of conversation drifting over from other hotel guests scattered across the terrace and little patches of sunshine dropped dappled light on the old stone pavers. Warm, but fresh country air, brought the kind of day where the cut grass smell lingered and a little spontaneous breeze every now and then pushed a swirl of rose petals up from the flowerbeds.

Fleur had an almost perfect view of the wedding unfolding on the lawn below. From where she sat nestled on the terrace with her book, tea and cake stand, she had her own secret vantage point—an observer of a gorgeous day that wasn't hers, her voyeurism radar twitching nineteen to the dozen. The bride and bridesmaids had disappeared momentarily under the white fabric draped bandstand-style pergola, a harpist played something very romantic and Fleur watched as the groom stood greeting a few new arrivals. His best man stood beside him, nudging him now and then, making a joke that Fleur couldn't hear but could guess from the grins was laced with nerves and banter.

It was, in every way, a classic English country wedding; white wooden chairs arranged in neat rows on the lawn, a floral arch at the front where the ceremony would take place, pretty flowers, floral dresses, men in suits and mothers in pastels. Hotel staff moved discreetly around the edges, checking details, adjusting decorations, and ensuring everything was just so.

Fleur took a bite of a sandwich and watched as a few late arrivals hurried across the grass, heels sinking slightly into the ground, clutching tiny beaded handbags and straightening the skirts of their dresses as they rushed to find a seat. She smiled at the familiarity of it all; how very, very nice. She'd been to enough weddings to know how they went—the hushed excitement before the bride arrived, the anticipation, the whispered compliments about the dress, the slight stiffness of the vows spoken in front of so many people, the unfurling of the day into champagne, gossip, laughter, dancing, and someone's uncle embarrassing himself on the dance floor.

Her mind drifted to her own wedding to Ben back in the day. It wasn't a memory she thought about often, not because it was particularly painful anymore, more it was a story she'd long since closed the book on. As if she'd put it away in one of her notebooks. However, watching the wedding unfold, the ritual of it all wiggled her memories and her thoughts drifted back in time.

She had been young, naive and stupid and had believed so very much in the grand idea of it all—the certainty that love was enough, that saying the vows meant something, that it would be forever and ever and ever. Except it hadn't been, not at all. Except it had done nothing other, really, than disappoint. As she took a sip of tea and watched one of the bridesmaids fiddle with the back of the bride's veil, she wondered fleetingly if she would ever do it again. The father of the bride said something, making them all laugh and Fleur felt a pang of something she couldn't quite name. A strange melancholy for a life that hadn't happened mixed with an almost smug realisation of what she had now.

The harpist changed songs, a new tinkle drifted through the air, and the wedding coordinator gave a discrete signal. Fleur sat up straighter and shifted back in her chair, watching as the guests quieted, heads turned towards the pergola, and the bride took a breath and prepared to step into her new life.

'Best of British', Fleur whispered to herself. 'You're going to need it.'

As she sat back, she thought about Patrick and smiled at what she had now. It was good enough for her.

11

Sitting up in bed with a cup of tea beside her that Patrick had just brought up, Fleur had her iPad propped up on her knees and was flicking through Instagram looking at travel recommendations for Hawaii. The more she searched, the more attractive Hawaii became.

She scrolled up and watched a video of a beautiful Airbnb cottage surrounded by blue water, lush palm trees, and hibiscus flowers by the truckload. Another reel played where a woman in a straw hat, bikini, and white shirt strolled down to a secluded beach as if she didn't have a care in the world. Fleur watched the reel, listened to the accompanying tinkling music, and thought that it was high time she treated herself to a proper holiday where she would be the one strolling in a sunhat down to a tropical beach or any beach, really.

It had been a long time since our Champo had sipped a cocktail or skipped through a holiday cottage, or immersed herself in holiday reading. Now that Patrick had firmly planted the idea in her head, she'd come around to it more and more. Why not book something and have a nice holiday to look forward to? After looking at the prices of the flights, she'd hesitated. It was hardly cheap, but it did look very nice. Did our Champo really need, though, to trek around the world to sit on a beach with nice soft sand, a brilliant blue sea, guitars playing in the background, and a lei around her neck? Did she ever? Oh yes, indeed.

Continuing to deep dive and getting lost in a world of mountains, lush green palms, crocheted white hammocks and beautiful white windows, Fleur was sold. Again and again, she scrolled through her feed and lost herself in videos where she couldn't quite fathom how the sea was as blue as it was. It certainly gave Lovely a run for its money, that was for sure. She chuckled to herself as she watched a young girl, completely clad in white, jog in slow-motion through a hotel room to the tune of Hawaiian music, pull her hair back, open her (tanned, slim) arms wide and turn around in a twirl as she got to a private pool outside her room. Fleur chuckled to herself at how the other half lived and continued to scroll, swallowing up other people's Hawaii holiday dreams as fast as she could.

Flicking to a hotel's Instagram feed, she immersed herself in the pictures and imagined herself sitting under the gigantic wicker shade area in what she couldn't quite believe was an open-air reception room. The pictures made even the hotel check-in look magical. On top of gorgeous buildings and lush native landscape, the decor was amazing; beautiful wicker panels on the walls, green palms, views of the mountains, gigantic beautifully dressed beds and just about everything looked like a dream. The boutique hotel was so nice that it felt, just by looking at the images, that Hawaiian history and mythology were in the walls of the hotel itself. The open-air entry and lobby area, with beautiful blinds and plants weaving through the hotel, looked amazing next to reclaimed teak furniture, lava stone walls, and handwoven ceilings made from what looked to Fleur like natural leaf fibre. All of it deliciously nice.

Getting more and more lost in the hotel, Fleur read a few

descriptions, felt as if she wanted to pack her bags right away, and continued to lose herself in a hotel on the other side of the world. As she scrolled through the pictures of the rooms, she laughed at the idea of the handwoven doors, reclaimed teak, and traditional daybeds. A crescent-shaped bay with very blue water made her feel as if she didn't have much choice but to book.

She stopped at a picture of one of the hotel suites, tilting her head as she took in the details; warm, honeyed wood, deep, earthy brown cushions that looked impossibly soft, a woven rattan coffee table, books, bowls of fruit, textured rugs, soft throws, louvred shuttered doors, neutral tones, understated luxury, and lamps, lamps, lamps. A bed beckoned dressed in soft linens, with a headboard of woven panels hinting at island tradition.

Fleur sighed, already picturing herself curled up with a book, the scent of salty air drifting through open balcony doors, a hush of waves in the distance, and yes lamps for days. A little slice of paradise, waiting just for her. The beachfront location, overlooking the beautiful Maui bay with waterfall-streaked mountains in the distance, looked to be one of the prettiest places on the planet and was certainly ticking all the boxes for the magical getaway that had always been a dream in Fleur's head. A swimming pool, a beach at the front, a stunning adults-only pool, a sweet little town nearby for exploring, and lots of walks on a lush, jungle-like mountain track. The cutting-edge spa and wellness offerings weren't too shabby either. No Elvis by the looks of it, but she could cope with that.

Fleur thought about the hotel and the beautiful plants around it; fern palms, coconut trees, birds of paradise, frangipani and grasses. She imagined herself in a swimsuit and snorkel, or shorts and hiking boots in the daytime, and not doing much in the evening at all. She imagined herself every morning opening the louvred shutters, getting back in bed, and just watching the bay almost like she did at home, only the tropical version. Bring it on.

Patrick shouted up the stairs. 'Coffee?'

'Yes, please!'

'What are you doing up there? Are you out of bed yet?'

'No, I'm not. I'm lost on a tropical island in the middle of the sea.' Fleur stretched her legs out under the duvet. 'There's a lot of white linen and coconut cocktails.'

'What?'

'I'm looking at Hawaii stuff,' Fleur clarified, scrolling through another set of pictures.

Patrick's voice carried up. 'Alright, so I take it from that, we're going then?'

'After what I've been looking at this morning? Yes, we are.' Fleur chuckled as she adjusted the iPad on her lap. 'I'm going for the coconuts alone.'

Five or ten minutes later, Patrick arrived with a mug of coffee, topped with squirty cream and chocolate shavings. She smiled as she took the mug. 'I get the best treats when you're here.'

'Make the most of it, because I won't be here tomorrow and you'll be back at work,' Patrick reminded her as he perched on the edge of the bed.

'Don't remind me.' Fleur groaned and turned the iPad around so he could see the screen. 'I've found this fabulous boutique hotel. It looks amazing, but it's really expensive. Like next level expensive. Like I'm surprised they can charge; it's that expensive.'

Patrick rolled his eyes. 'It doesn't really matter how much it costs when I'm paying. And tell me, when was the last time you went on holiday? So, the cost per night isn't really that much if you look at it like that.'

Fleur raised an eyebrow. 'I don't think that's how it works.'

'It does in my world. Trust me, we're going. No more talking about it…' Patrick took the iPad and flicked through the hotel photos. He nodded in approval. 'You're right. This place looks amazing; definitely our kind of thing.'

'So, what do you think? It means we'd have to take another short flight when we got there, I think but we can cope with that, can't we? We might be able to go directly from LA.'

'I'm sure we'll manage,' Patrick grinned. 'We're going to Hawaii, baby.'

Fleur shifted under the duvet and cradled the mug of coffee. 'I never actually thought I'd get to go somewhere like this. It's one of those places you dream about but never really expect to visit, like the Maldives or Bora Bora.'

'Well, we *are* going and I don't just mean in the hypothetical, let's-talk-about-it way. I mean properly. Let's book it today. We said we'd do it in Essex but it didn't happen.'

Fleur's breath caught. She sat up straighter, shifting the coffee onto the bedside table, suddenly feeling as though she needed to be fully awake for the conversation. 'You're serious?'

'Would I joke about something this important?'

'You actually want to book it now? As in *right* now.'

'We've been talking about it for long enough. Why not?' Patrick gestured at the iPad. 'It's the perfect place, the right time of year, and you're clearly in love with it. Plus, you've got the time off work, and I'm going to confirm that conference. What's stopping us?'

Fleur pressed her hands to her face, trying to suppress the ridiculous, giddy grin on her face. 'Oh my God, I can't believe this is happening! You're such an enabler. I love it.'

Patrick chuckled. 'We're getting the best room they've got. The one with the private pool and the outdoor shower.'

'You realise we'll never leave the room, don't you?'

Patrick chuckled. 'That's the idea. Right, well, let's see if it's available.'

Patrick navigated through the booking process. Fleur curled

up against his side, eyes flicking between the screen and his face, trying to read his expression as he scrolled. 'Okay, we're in luck. The suite is available for the dates we want. Ten nights. Sound good?'

Fleur nodded enthusiastically. 'Perfect. Absolutely perfect.'

'Alright, I'm pressing to commit. This is your last chance to back out. Joking, it's fully refundable up to a few weeks before.'

'Ahh!'

Patrick grinned and tapped the screen. A loading icon spun for a few seconds before a confirmation page appeared. Fleur let out a squeal and threw her arms around Patrick's neck. 'We're going to Hawaii! Maui! I cannot believe it!'

'Hawaii and Maui. Tropical islands. Champo and ten nights in paradise.'

Fleur felt as if she was absolutely glowing with happiness and that she'd just made the best decision she'd made for a long time. What she didn't know was that another one was just around the corner.

12

It was about eight-thirty in the morning and Fleur was sitting on a train in a carriage packed to the rafters with a load of head-down-to-their-phones grumpy commuters halfway to London. Her training course bag was wedged into the middle of the seats in the luggage section in front of her, and she was expecting to see Cassy get on the train in a couple of stops' time. As she sat lost in a world of her own and tried as best she could to ignore the man in the seat opposite her who was slurping from a travel bowl of cornflakes, she flicked through the details Patrick had just sent her about the flights to LA. She couldn't quite believe that they were actually going ahead, booking the flights and doing it. Patrick had been adamant that they needed a break and had been to a travel agent and liaised with a woman who had got them really good prices for Fleur's part of the trip, and now it was time to book.

Looking through the details of the flight, Fleur thought about the fact that she would be doing the leg from Heathrow to LA on her own. She still wasn't quite sure what to think about the daunting length of the journey and the many hours she'd be sitting on her own going from her nice, safe little bubble to the

US of A. She opened up Google Flights and checked the exact same flight that Patrick had sent her in the screenshot and on comparison calculated that going through the travel agent saved her twenty per cent on the price.

Deciding to throw caution to the wind and go for it, she phoned Patrick. 'Hi, I got your message. They look great.'

'So, shall I book that one for you on the way there? Then, obviously, for the rest of it, we'll be travelling together.'

It felt strange to Fleur to have someone booking and doing things for her. She'd been on her own for a long time, and now Patrick was taking control. He'd already said yes to speaking at the conference and was booking his own flights to LA. Fleur had been waiting for her holiday to be confirmed and locked in at work and now it had been, he'd been keen to get it sorted.

'Yes, thanks.' She shifted in her seat, ignored the man with the cornflakes and watched the scenery blur past the train window as she held the phone to her ear.

Patrick's voice was clear, in control, and certain. She liked that very much indeed. Hot.

'Right, that's sorted then. I'll book it now, and you'll get the confirmation email soon. They'll be a bit of jigging to make sure we are together on the way back because the first legs are at different times which is another reason to get a travel agent to book it.'

Fleur exhaled, half relieved, half nervous. 'I can't believe we're actually doing this.'

'It's been a long time coming. You need a break, and I need a break and let's be honest, we're going to have a great time.'

Fleur smiled, even as her stomach fluttered at the thought of it. 'You sound very sure about that.'

'I *am* sure. You need to live a little, Champo. The conference in LA will be good and then we're off to Hawaii and Maui. Tell me that doesn't sound like a dream? It does to me.'

'It does. I think I'm just struggling to get my head around it.

Feels a bit surreal. The furthest I've been is Spain and that was on a charter flight that wasn't up to much.'

'That's because you never take time for yourself, Champo. You're always running around after everyone else. For once, you're going to sit on a beach, cocktail in hand, and actually relax. If you continue to stay in my life, things like this are happening for you and *to* you. I aim to please.'

Fleur swooned and laughed. 'I won't know what to do with myself.'

'I'll help you figure it out. So, you're fine flying out on your own? You've checked the times of that Heathrow departure and you're good with it? Speak now or forever hold your peace.'

'Yeah, I'll manage. I mean, it's a long flight, but I'll survive. And you're meeting me in LA at the airport.'

Patrick joked. 'Of course. I'll be there when you land. I'll have a red rose in a plastic cone thingy and serenade you as you walk through.'

'So, remind me about what you're doing in LA? You're at the conference for how many days?'

'Five full days. Shouldn't be too bad, though. Then off we fly to Hawaii.'

'And then Maui?'

'Yep, I'll get the flights booked for that too.'

Fleur sighed. 'This is really happening, isn't it?'

Patrick chuckled. 'It *really* is. Now you just need to stop overthinking it and get excited. We're going on holiday. A proper big fat one to somewhere you've dreamed about for a long time.'

Fleur felt a flicker of excitement. 'Ooh.'

'Before you know it, we'll be on a plane to paradise.'

'Ahh!'

'We're going to drive ourselves mad with anticipation. I'll send over the confirmation as soon as it comes through.'

Fleur looked out at a fully grey-white sky zooming past the

window and thought about palm trees and frangipani. 'Thanks. Really.'

'Don't mention it. I'll see you tomorrow night and we'll check over everything then.'

'Okay, yep, let me know when you've booked it.'

'See you later, love you.'

'Love you, too.'

As she ended the call, Fleur leant back in her seat and stared out of the window as the train slowed to pull into the station Cassy was getting on at. As the doors opened and a few people got off, she watched as Cassy got on with a coffee cup in each hand, headed for Fleur, and sat down beside her. She beamed and smiled, not quite believing what she'd just done. For the first time in a long time, Fleur was doing a bucket list item and boy did the anticipation about that feel good. She didn't know that it was going to get so very much better.

13

A couple of days or so later, Fleur seethed as she walked along a dreary side road in Brighton, weighed down by training materials and two laptops, on her way to a hotel to deliver a training course. The hotel car park had been fully booked, meaning she'd had to park a few streets away and walk. This had not made her at all happy. In fact, it had made her fume because it happened too often; hotels advertised certain facilities, like car parking, and then, once you made the booking and arrived, it wasn't quite true because they had a grand total of ten parking spaces all of which were taken by somebody else. That was exactly what had happened when she'd arrived and she'd driven around the block a few times, finally found somewhere to park her car, felt as if it was a bit dodgy and had hopped out with all her senses on alert. Not a feeling our Champo liked when arriving at a hotel. Ten minutes later, she was walking into the hotel's reception area telling herself by the look of the facilities that it was going to be a long few days.

After checking in, she went to find Cassy who had messaged Fleur to say that she was in the café. When Fleur finally found it tucked down a grotty looking corridor, she tutted at the small room with a bar in the corner and a sullen looking grubby teenager making cups of coffee as if it pained her. She ordered and plonked herself down next to Cassy and rolled her eyes. 'I had to park a mile away. Grr, every time...'

Cassy held her hand up. 'Don't even get me started. It's pretty dodgy around here, too. Sorry, I should have warned you.'

Fleur shook her head. 'I'm emailing work and telling them not to book us in here again. It's not right to have to park that far away. I don't feel safe when my car is down some dodgy side street. I'm not having it, Cass.'

'I'm hearing you. How many times have we flagged this? So many!'

'It makes my blood boil. Anyway, how are you?' Fleur asked, studying Cassy properly and then frowning. Cassy looked tired and drawn, though, as usual, her makeup was immaculate, but Fleur could see beyond the light reflecting foundation and blusher placed just so. There was something off about Cassy, in her expression and the way she held herself. There was a greyness around her face and a dullness that wasn't just about lack of sleep.

Cassy sighed and let out a low groan. 'To be honest with you, Champo, I've had enough. I'm absolutely exhausted. I spend my life running around after the boys, and I don't seem to get a lot of me time; to be quite frank, I don't even know what that is. On top of that, I'm doing all the housework and cooking. You know the gig. Where did it say I had to do all the jobs when I got married?' Cassy trailed off, shaking her head. 'I don't know. It just feels like it's all got on top of me. I'm sick of everything, like to the back teeth sick. I don't want to sound ungrateful. Do you know what I mean, though?'

Fleur smiled knowingly, stirring her coffee. 'I thought you looked a bit off. I know *exactly* what you mean. Believe me, I really do.' Fleur nodded thinking about how she'd experienced her own version of what Cassy was trying to put into words many times before. The feeling of being completely spent, running on empty, wondering how you were supposed to keep going when there was nothing left to give. The feeling had been her daily companion a few times in her life. Thankfully not right at that moment but it appeared that it had transferred to her best friend. Cassy looked as if she'd lost the will to live. 'You need to get away and do a reset, as they call it. Is there any chance of having a weekend off? Even just a couple of nights somewhere, or could you book a family trip away?'

Cassy sighed, rubbing her temples. 'I don't know, not really. Well, I mean, I could, in theory. When I go away on holiday with the boys, I sometimes wonder if it's just work in a different location. It's not a break. It's the same stress, the same responsibilities, just with a nicer backdrop. I need to go somewhere and not do anything at all. Like I mean just me on my own.' Guilt flashed across Cassy's face.

Fleur nodded. 'I know what you mean. Going on holiday with children means you are still playing mum at the end of the day.'

'I just feel exhausted, burnt out, and that everything is on top of me. Who knew my forties were going to be like this? Sorry, I'm grumbling about everything.'

'When was the last time you did something just for *you*?'

Cassy let out a dry laugh. 'You're funny. No idea. Years, probably. The spa thing we went to when we had those seaweed wraps. My birthday but that was me doing all the arranging... I sound so entitled and spoilt, sorry.'

Fleur thought about the demands of their job and the fact that Cassy had three boys on top of that to look after. 'It's not easy doing this job and what with your responsibilities at home.'

'It's all getting too much.'

'Seriously, what is stopping you from booking a night away

on your own? Twenty-four hours just for you to recharge or something like that. Could you manage that?'

Cassy sighed and stared down at her coffee. 'I don't know. Guilt, I suppose. The money. Everything is *so* expensive. Our food bill has more than doubled. Then there are the logistics. Plus, there's always that feeling of I don't know what. I feel selfish.' Cassy's voice lifted up at the end as if she was going to burst into tears.

Fleur shook her head and patted Cassy's hand. 'It's not selfish. If you burn yourself out completely, what good are you to anyone? Put your own mask on first as they say.'

Cassy rubbed her hands over her face. 'Pah! I hate that stupid mask saying. I don't even have a flipping mask. God, I wish I could just disappear to that spa we went to for a weekend and let someone else do everything for once. I'm not being funny but even when I do go away there is so much preparation to do for it, it's not worth it.'

Fleur raised an eyebrow. 'Do it.'

Cassy snorted. 'Easier said than done.'

'You could at least look. Find somewhere, see if it's doable. Even if it's just one night. You deserve it. I don't want my best friend getting burnt out. Or come and stay at mine for a night and do nothing but veg out or we could go to a speakeasy or something.'

'Too late, I'm already burnt out. Maybe.'

'Have a look into it.'

Cassy sighed but gave a small smile. 'I'll think about it.'

Fleur sat back. 'It's a shame you can't pop to Hawaii with me.'

Cassy raised her eyebrows. 'Gosh, have you booked all of it now? Patrick has booked the rest of the flights, has he?'

'Yep, he has. We are officially going.'

'Ohh, I am so jealous!'

'I can't quite believe it myself. It's going to take a while to sink in. Sorry, I don't want to go on about it after what you just said.'

'Don't be ridiculous! Of all the people who deserve to be going on a holiday of a lifetime, it's you. I can't even remember the last time you went away.'

'You and me both.'

'Champo, you are going to have the time of your life.'

Fleur screwed her face up and made little clapping sounds with her hands. 'I hope so, I really do.'

Our Champo was most definitely going to have the time of her life, yup. There were a few very nice things, she didn't yet know about, going to be thrown into the holiday; just for good measure.

14

Fleur woke up to the sound of a car going down the lane and looked over at the blind, where she could see the shadows of the trees outside filtering through the window. Sunshine streamed through and from what she could see, it looked as if it was going to be a nice day.

Remembering it was Saturday, meaning that she didn't have to go to work, she very nearly did a horizontal happy dance; she had the whole day ahead to do nothing but potter about the place, drink cups of tea on repeat, dream about her holiday and read her new book. Did life really get much better than that? Not in our Champo's book.

Padding out of bed, she slipped on her dressing gown, pulled up the blind, and stood looking out in the direction of the sea for a minute. Watching a small pale blue car wind its way down the lane and trundle past the cottage, heading in the direction of the beach car park, she watched as it parked, a woman got out, started to unload beach paraphernalia from the boot, and headed down in the direction of the sand. She loved living by the sea and watching people coming and going from the beach; it put a sort of slow, routine of niceness around her life. A few minutes later, she was down in the kitchen, where, on the worktop next to the kettle sat a cup of tea without any milk. Next to that, on a plate covered in cling film, was a teacake and by the smell in the air, the slow cooker on the side appeared to be filled with curry. She smiled to herself as she picked up the tea and put it in the microwave. Patrick was a diamond wrapped up in an electrician's uniform. Can't be bad to be treated by one. He'd left early to go to a job in Brighton and had a long weekend ahead of him but had made Fleur a cup of tea, left out a teacake, and put a curry in the slow cooker. *I mean, really?* She smiled wryly to herself. *Oh, how things had changed.* Ben, not that he'd been around for a very long time, had barely been able to dress himself and had certainly found it out of his skillset to work out the intricacies of ironing his own shirt.

For years she'd been the one, and only one, to set out the breakfast things, the one behind the brain power and sheer humdrum of thinking about the next morning's tea and breakfast. Blah, blah, blah, whatever. But now, as if by magic, it appeared that somebody else was doing it for her, and not only that, he was wrapped up in a nice shiny ab-filled bow. On a Saturday morning, with peace enveloping her like nothing else that felt really, really, really nice. Very special indeed. Princess vibes for our Fleur by way of a cup of tea and a curry? Yes, indeed.

The smell of washing powder and laundry came from the utility room; Fleur frowned to see washing hanging on the airer by the window – Patrick had hung a load of her work blouses before he'd left, too. The man was an enigma. She noted to herself that not only did he look like a dream, but he was a dab hand at doing stuff at home. He was a keeper, that was for sure. As she pushed the microwave button and opened the door, the diamonds on her forever ring glinted in the sunlight. Patrick had surprised her with the ring when she'd convinced herself that he was about to dump her. Talk about being taken by surprise. She loved the ring and him. However, what she really wanted, but hadn't told anyone and had barely even recognised herself, was to add to the ring by popping a nice gold band beside it lined up like so. *Like, she really wanted it. A lot.*

For someone who'd been married before and had always sworn she would never, ever be stupid enough to do the same thing again, she was secretly sold on getting hitched to Patrick hook, line and sinker. She knew that if the subject of marriage came up—which looked as if it *never* would—she would be there at the drop of a hat, saying 'I do' or whatever it was that was said these days faster than anything. Did she want to be married to Patrick and be happy with him for the rest of her life? *Oh my gosh, did she ever?* And, the bigger the white dress the better. Add a fat diamond to that, too. Plus, a nice tropical beach would be good but she wouldn't say no to the local church in Lovely either. She wouldn't say no to anything. A ceremony in a cupboard would do.

Taking her cup of tea and teacake outside, she sat on the little terrace area by the back door and, for a while, just did nothing but think and listen to the birds chirping away and the sounds of the sea, faintly in the distance. The noise of people on the beach carried on the breeze, and though it was warm there was a definite coolness in the air hinting at colder weather incoming. Sitting and pondering what she was going to do for the day, Fleur thought about the Maui thing and the fact that she had the house to clean and give a good old reset to. Once that was done and dusted, she'd spend the afternoon in her studio creating new notebooks without any sort of schedule or prerequisite for the shop or markets, rather just letting herself play and do whatever she wanted.

As she sat mulling over her day, her phone pinged with a message from Lucy. She read through the message that informed her that the baby had been crying all night, that Lucy had had enough and was coming to Lovely Bay. Fleur chuckled to herself. Real life was starting to take hold in the Ben and Sarah household. She wondered how long it would be before the baby slept through. Lucy had her own bedroom at Ben's and since not going back to ballet school, she'd been working at a job in London in a dance shop three days a week, working for a day in the deli, and living between Fleur's house and Ben's. A newborn's screaming was changing things. The sibling thing had clearly lost its shine.

After answering the text from Lucy, Fleur sat and pondered Ben being closer and decided that it wasn't quite as bad as she'd first thought. Ben's new area had a good regular train service into London, which meant that when Lucy stayed with him, she could commute without any drama. Making another cup of tea, she mused how Lucy was coasting along and had settled nicely into working in the dance shop in London. She'd got the job via a friend who worked there. Lucy had filled in for her one day, had enjoyed it so much, and clicked with the store owner. The owner had been so impressed with Lucy's deep knowledge of dance that she'd offered Lucy a three-day-a-week job which had suited Lucy down to the ground. She was also doing an online course in media studies, which she was enjoying and really everything had worked out well. Lucy was a different person from the one Fleur had watched walk over the railway steps at Lovely Station, frail and tiny and forlorn. She was back to her normal weight and seemed to be happier and more settled all around.

The only fly in the ointment, as far as Fleur was concerned, was the new baby. Fleur wondered how it would go and whether or not once the dust settled if Lucy might be envious or jealous, but so far, so good. In fact, Lucy seemed over the moon about having a sibling and was very excited about the idea of having a brother. She'd even been out and bought things for the baby with her money from her job, and Fleur had been more than encouraging because, really, what was the point of being anything else?

As she sat and pondered what Lucy was going to do with her life, she nodded to herself. Ever since the drama of Lucy collapsing a few times the bumps in the road had smoothed out and there wasn't really much to tell. There'd been the baby's arrival, but that had gone well and even Ben had proved that he was capable of being an adult and had navigated Lucy's part in it all better than Fleur had hoped for.

Fleur made a second cup of tea, wrapped her hands around it and let the warmth soak into her palms as she sat on the little terrace, the morning air soft and still and thought about Lucy. She'd always known that being a mother was never something you finished and that it wasn't a neatly tied-up story or a box you could tick and move on from, but Fleur had found navigating the young adult years tough, gnarly and difficult. She had to admit she'd not enjoyed the challenge. Give her a newborn baby's head to sniff any day of the week. The young adult parenting was an ever-evolving thing, shifting and changing, stretching between joy and worry and all the non-eventful moments in between. Here they were, though, with Lucy back on the straight and narrow and everything going well. There had been a time, not all that long before, when Fleur had worried about Lucy *constantly*, her heart twisting at the sight of how frail, small, and lost she'd seemed. She'd spent nights lying awake, worrying and wondering if Lucy would find her way, feel better again, get back to her old self and ultimately would she be okay?

Now, Lucy very much was. Not only that, she appeared to be thriving, working, learning, laughing again and being part of the world. There was a new brightness to Lucy, a confidence Fleur hadn't seen in her ever, really. A young adult who was starting to find her place in the world. The dance shop job had been unexpected but had come along at just the right time, giving

Lucy a purpose, a routine, something she could pour herself into without the weight of expectations pressing down on her, a little bit of money and someone to answer to who wasn't a teacher standing at the front of a dance class but a small business owner in the real world.

Fleur nodded at how things had turned out and said a silent thankful prayer that the worry had switched off. Lucy was young with loads of time to figure it all out. For now, Lucy could do a *lot* worse. Fleur closed her eyes for a minute and hoped that things weren't about to change and that there wasn't something bad around the corner.

15

Fleur indicated left, turned down a side road, and pulled up outside Cassy's house. She had been delivering a training course on the opposite side of the country and had agreed to pick Cassy up on her way past. They were going back to Lovely so that Cassy could have a weekend to herself and experience a secret chowder evening. Patrick was away at a family event, and Cassy's husband had taken her boys camping for the weekend, which Cassy had definitely not been interested in attending. With all that in mind, the pair of them had earmarked the weekend ready for the taking for best friend therapy, chowder therapy, wine therapy, any therapy, really. Mostly, Fleur had been determined that Cassy have a break.

They'd been planning and cooking up their schedule and were both looking forward to it. Lucy was staying up in London with one of her ballet school friends, and so the pair of them had no parenting responsibilities, no one to annoy them, nothing to worry about, and not even a dinner to cook. All in all, both of them were going to make the most of it. Fleur parked on Cassy's drive, hopped out, and as she got to the front door, Cassy opened it right away with an absolutely massive beam on her face. Cassy was clearly looking forward to getting away. By the looks of it, wild horses wouldn't hold her back.

'Hi, how are you? I'm so looking forward to this,' Cassy rubbed her hands together. 'It's been a week, that's for sure. Let me at Lovely Bay. I'm there for the chowder and the chocolate and one day in the future possibly one of the coats.'

Cassy had had a few problems with one of her sons at school, who had bashed another child over the head with his lunchbox. She'd been in and out of the school office, and then one of her other sons had fallen off his skateboard and cut his arm, requiring stitches. She'd had life stuff up to her eyes and was looking forward to a child and husband-free weekend doing nothing but mooch around Lovely with Fleur.

'No more stitches or lunchbox bashing?' Fleur joked.

'All good. Everyone's fine now. I won't hold my breath. I am hoping for a weekend without stitches!'

'Good. No more trips to the hospital then for you or any of your offspring.'

'I hope not.' Cassy jerked her thumb behind her. 'I made them a huge pack-up. They took sandwiches, a frozen chilli that they just need to take out and dump in a saucepan while they're camping, and I sorted out all their bedding and packed most of the car.'

Fleur raised her eyebrows. 'So basically, you've done it all for them as usual. And here I was thinking you were going to chill out.'

'Well, yes, when you put it like that. Oh well, it is what it is. At least I can relax now. Famous last words.'

'We do that to ourselves, don't we?'

'Yep, we do, but it's easier doing it that way. I think I'll live to regret that though when they're young adults and they won't pick up after themselves.'

Fleur laughed. She knew the young adult thing well. Cassy

wasn't even yet close. 'I'm not saying anything. I'm not exactly a model parent myself.'

Cassy rolled her eyes. 'Says the person with the perfect daughter.'

'Right, yeah, you know what the last year has been like.' Fleur sighed and shook her head.

Cassy chuckled. 'Yes, but she's good, well-behaved, and happy and most of the time, she's nice. So there you are. You've done a good job. Give yourself a back pat.'

'I guess so. I'm never going to win any prizes for parenting.'

'Don't you believe it.' Cassy pulled the front door shut. 'Right, let me at Lovely Bay. I cannot wait. I need my best friend and vodka and not a lot else.'

~

That evening, Fleur smiled as she stood next to Cassy watching a boat chugging up the river. Lovely was showing off to the hilt with light catching on the water, the sound of the river lapping in the breeze and a soft salty sea scent in the air.

Cassy pointed at the riverboat. 'Well, this is better than getting on a stinky old bus, that I know for certain. Ahh, I love it here. I may have to put our house up for sale and join you.'

'Since when did you get on stinky buses? Last time I checked you didn't take public transport if you could help it,' Fleur said with a smile.

'Good point.' Cassy chuckled.

'You have a very nice Audi that's all paid for, and you're getting another new one next year.'

'Wow, you know how to put me in my place and keep me grounded, don't you?'

Fleur laughed. 'Yes, I do. Don't you forget it.'

As they stood looking at the river, a beautiful sunset in the background painted the sky in a flame of pinks, oranges, and reds. The sky stretched above them displaying the kind of colours that made you stop and take it all in no matter how many times you'd seen a sunset before. Vast swathes of pink and deep coral streaked across the horizon, oranges and little hints of lavender popped up as the sun dipped lower, and wispy clouds dusted in rose gold stretched away as far as the eye could see. The river reflected it all, shimmering with the hues from above and little ripples in lazy patterns spread across the top as the boat made its way upstream. The water mirrored the sky in pools of peach and amber as if the whole world had been dipped in the Lovely glow for a bit.

Fleur exhaled slowly. 'It doesn't matter how many times I see the sunsets, when they are like this, they still get me every time. It's this little corner of the world...'

Cassy nodded. 'Same. There's just something about it. It makes everything feel bigger. Like whatever nonsense happened today doesn't really matter in the grand scheme of things. It makes you feel small and forget about making sandwiches and packing a car. Ha!'

Fleur smiled. 'That's exactly it. It just puts everything into perspective.'

The riverboat let out a horn as it approached and Fleur shook her head. Here she was living the dream, standing with her best friend and boy did it feel nice. She had to admit she was happy with her life as it was now. The year before had been a bumpy one with a lot of ups and downs, and at times, she'd wondered if she was going a bit bonkers, but now things were back on the straight and narrow, it felt great to be calm, centred and sorted. Hopefully, it wasn't going to change. Everything with Patrick was fine, apart from the fact that he wasn't thrilled about Ben moving closer. Lucy was good, Ben's arrival had gone okay and as Fleur had settled further into Lovely Bay, she'd made a few friends with neighbours, been to more chowder evenings, and all in all, she was well aware that her move to Lovely Bay had been one of her better ideas. 'I think I did the right thing moving here. I feel pretty lucky, to be honest. Who would have thought, eh?'

'Well, obviously. Plus, you have me as a best friend which makes you very lucky. On all counts you're hashtag blessed.'

Fleur rolled her eyes, but the truth was, she wouldn't have had it any other way.

Fleur looked down at her phone and tapped. 'I just need to find the instructions.'

'Do you have to give a password?'

'Oh yes, I forgot about that,' Fleur replied.

'It's really taken that seriously?'

'Well, I don't know about that, but it's all part of it.'

'So, what's the password for this one?' Cassy asked.

Fleur let out a strange chuckle. 'That's the whole point of a speakeasy and a password. You don't tell anybody.'

'Right. Okay then. That's not weird at all,' Cassy said, laughing.

'Right, okay, here we go. I think the last one I went to, you had to knock three times on the door. This one says you need to go down the path beside the house, and there's an old-fashioned ship's bell hanging off the gate, and you need to ring it twice.'

A few minutes later, they had arrived at the side gate of a beautiful harbourside weatherboard property.

'Looks like this is it, then,' Cassy said, reaching up to a thick piece of rope dangling from a ship's bell. She rang it, waited for a second, and then rang it again.

About thirty seconds later, the gate opened, and they both giggled to see Cally from the chemist smiling at them. She looked down at her phone, then up at them, and said,

'Password?'

'Chocolate, chowder, coats,' Fleur replied.

Cally also giggled, opened the door wider, and gestured for Fleur and Cassy to walk in.

As they walked into the chowder event, Fleur looked around in awe. Everywhere tiny little tealights in blue vintage glass holders flickered softly. It looked as though lots of tables had been pushed together to create special areas, each covered with beautiful tablecloths topped with a white cutwork overlay and vases of fresh flowers. Acoustic guitar music played from a speaker on the side, on the floor a patchwork of rugs in pretty pinks, pale blues, and Paisley patterns had been carefully arranged, and hanging from the ceiling were gigantic white fabric lanterns, casting a glow over the space. At the far end, open doors let in a cool breeze, and the sound of the harbour and clinking of boats carried across the air. All in all, very nice, more than Lovely. Fleur was getting used to the speakeasy events but this one was next level.

'Oh my god, this is amazing!' Cassy whispered. 'Where even are we?'

'Wow, it is.' Fleur looked around and shook her head. Every element seemed to have been crafted to perfection, as though Nina, the speakeasy owner, had spent a lot of time creating a space that made you feel as if you'd stepped into another world. It worked and then some.

Cassy's voice was low as if she were in a library or a church. 'If you'd told me this was happening in some little harbour town, I wouldn't have believed you. Talk about take your breath away.'

'I felt the same the first one I went to.' Fleur pointed to the far wall. 'I think we're over there.'

Birdie approached with a tray of drinks in her hands, smiled, and indicated for them to sit down. 'Evening, our Fleur. How are we? Hoping all is well?'

'Good, thanks.'

'Have a seat, chowder is on the way. Sorry, I'll stop back in a bit and chat.'

Fleur and Cassy sat down, a drink was placed on the table, and about five minutes later two steaming bread bowls of chowder were in front of them.

Cassy dipped some bread in the chowder, popped it in her mouth and widened her eyes. 'Wow, this is unbelievable. Like next level. I thought it was going to be like cream of something or other soup.'

Fleur chuckled, tearing off a piece of her sourdough and dunking it unapologetically into her chowder. 'That's the whole point of the speakeasy. You're not supposed to believe it until you're actually here.'

Cassy took a spoonful of the soup. 'How did you even find out about this?'

'Oh, I have my ways now that I'm a Lovely.'

'Meaning?'

'Meaning I happened to overhear Birdie mentioning it. You'd be surprised how many secrets this town holds. Lovely Bay looks sleepy on the outside, but trust me, there's a whole lot going on underneath. Living near Birdie gives me access to all sorts.'

Cassy laughed. 'Clearly. I feel like I've stumbled into some kind of secret society.'

'You kind of have.'

'Do you get to know who does what?'

'Not really. There's a committee.'

'I wonder if you will get to know what is what.'

'Not a chance. They keep it mysterious on purpose.'

Cassy narrowed her eyes. 'There's something about Lovely.'

'What do you mean?'

'I don't know, it's like it's made to make you forget everything else. All the stress, the chaos of normal life doesn't exist here.'

'That's why I love it and they'll be taking me out in a box.'

'You really have found your feet here, haven't you Champo?'

Fleur nodded and looked around. 'I really, really have.'

'Your life has settled down nicely. No more problems with Lucy, Ben is behaving, even your mum is, well, doing her own thing now. Compared to what, a few years ago, you're great.'

'I am.' Fleur nodded. She didn't know what was coming her way.

16

Fleur was so excited about Hawaii that she'd started a notebook on it. It was one of her special handmade books, with beautiful vintage pages, covered in a light padding, a fabric that said "Hawaii" to her, and bookmarks with shells. In specially marked tabulated sections, she'd noted down all sorts of things now that the flights and hotel were booked. She'd saved things to do, set up a packing list, and made notes about food she wanted to try and places to visit. Together with notes on doing all sorts and seeing some of the things she'd seen on her socials, there was a whole section on relaxing and how to do nothing at all—including a very long list of books she had on her list to read, as well as tips on how to switch off when on holiday and details about the treatments at the hotel's spa. With the amount of money it was costing her, she was going all in.

Sitting on the sofa with a chamomile tea by her side, she relaxed, went through her notebook, and ran her eyes down her packing list. She'd ordered a couple of new swimming costumes, which had arrived and shock horror, she'd actually liked them. She'd bought a nice white shirt-style cover-up and a pair of matching white flip-flops, and she'd treated herself to a white linen strapless dress for the evenings. She did the thing she usually did when she sat with her notebooks; reflected as she turned pages, flicked and pondered. It felt almost surreal to be going away to Hawaii. It wasn't as if she'd never had a holiday, but when she'd been in the cottage and it was just her and Lucy, there had never been spare cash for exotic holidays. Travel had always come under the category of "luxury", it had been something that had been saved up for and had nearly always involved a charter flight to Spain. But now here she was, all these years later, enjoying the sheer pleasure and anticipation of planning an exotic jaunt and milking it to the hilt. Fleur Champion was going on a jet plane, and man, was she looking forward to it.

Checking her phone, she noted that it was time for her scheduled call with Wendy in Australia, went out to pop the kettle on, and made another cup of tea. Then she propped her phone up in front of her on the kitchen table and waited for the WhatsApp call to connect.

A few minutes later, Wendy, sitting on her balcony on the other side of the world with a blue sky behind her that was so saturated it didn't quite look real, smiled. Fleur waved at the screen. 'Hey, Wens! How are you?'

Wendy raised a coffee mug towards the screen. 'I'm good. I'm just having coffee. Glorious day here. How's the weather with you?'

Fleur turned around and looked out of the window. 'Currently overcast but not too cold, so that's good. How is it with you?'

'Yeah, very nice.'

'The sky looks amazingly blue, like it was painted on.'

Wendy turned around to look at the sky behind her. 'Well, it was pouring down here yesterday, so there's that.'

'You sound bright,' Fleur noted.

'I am, actually. I'm doing well, thanks. How are you, anyway? Everything good?'

'Yeah, everything's fine. Have you heard from Mum?' Fleur asked.

Wendy frowned. 'No, I haven't. Should I have? Why? Has something happened?'

'No, no, I was just wondering. Do you know where they are at the moment?'

'The last time I heard, they were halfway down a Turkish mountain.' Wendy rolled her eyes.

'Right, yes, that's as much as I know. Do you know where they're headed next?'

Wendy squinted. 'Croatia, was it? I don't know. I can't remember. There was talk about them staying in Turkey for a bit and heading for Istanbul. I lose track of it all, to be honest. And you know how much I'm not that keen on catching up with Mum if Marvellous Marvin is there. He still grates on me, the poor man. He can do nothing right. Cannot stand the little weasel.'

'I hear you,' Fleur giggled.

'How's Luce?'

Fleur held up her right hand with her first two fingers crossed. 'Fingers crossed she's doing well.'

'The baby and all that? I know she was pretty over the moon about it...'

'Not yet sleeping so Lucy's back here and may or may not have lost the baby glow she was on about having a sibling and how fantastic that was.'

'Hilarious, I thought it might be short-lived, and what about the collapsing and funny turns she had before. Anything on that?'

'Nope, not even a sniff of it. She looks amazing.'

Wendy nodded in agreement. 'Yes, I was chatting to her the other day and I thought how well she looked.'

'The fainting was, hopefully, just because of stress and ballet school. It seems to have left as quickly as it arrived.'

'Hopefully we've seen the back of it.'

'Yes. I'm a bit nervous about going away and leaving her.'

Wendy tutted and narrowed her eyes. 'She'll be fine! You can't put your life on hold forever.'

'Nope.'

'I was going to say to you about your trip, actually. You do know that it's only about a ten-hour trip from here to Hawaii, don't you?'

Fleur frowned. 'What does that mean?'

'It means that that's a short trip rather than having a twenty-four-hour flight to London. I could pop over and see you.'

Fleur beamed on the outside, but inside, she wasn't sure if she wanted Wendy in Hawaii. She did love her sister, for sure, but Wendy had a special kind of way of putting a dampener on things—especially if it involved anything to do with Valerie. She really wasn't keen on the idea of Wendy muscling in on her trip of a lifetime. She shuddered to think what Patrick would think about it. 'Ahh, I, umm, err, yes.'

'So, I could pop over and see you for a weekend or something if you wanted,' Wendy continued. 'But then when I thought about it, I reckoned you probably wouldn't want me to cramp your style and ruin your holiday.'

Fleur laughed, pretending that wasn't exactly what she was thinking. 'No, no, all good.'

'Anyway, have a think about it. I could come for the weekend or something. I wouldn't want to crash your whole holiday, obviously.'

'No, no, of course not. Whatever.' Fleur did not want a guest on her holiday to babysit. She covered a shudder.

Wendy took a sip of her coffee, narrowing her eyes, and studied Fleur through the screen. 'So, are you excited about

Hawaii and Maui? I mean, it's not every day you jet off to paradise, is it?'

Fleur smiled and thought about the fact that she had a whole book dedicated to her holiday. 'I am, actually. It feels a bit surreal, to be honest. I've wanted to go there for years. It's like I've been building up to this big, shiny thing, and suddenly it's almost here.'

'Big, shiny thing, eh? You are funny.'

Fleur laughed. 'You know what I mean. I've never done anything like this before. It's not just a holiday for me. I know everyone goes all over the world now and you live in Sydney where people jet back and forth all the time but for me, it's a proper adventure.'

Wendy laughed. 'I bet you have a notebook on it. You do, don't you?'

'I might have...'

'You and your notebooks. I swear, one day you're going to write a novel just about making lists.'

'Hey, don't knock it. Lists are the backbone of civilisation. Without them, we'd all be wandering around like headless chickens. Ask the Stoics.'

Wendy chuckled. 'Fair point. So, what's on this grand list of yours, then? Sun, sea, sand, cocktails, palm trees...'

Fleur reached for her notebook, flipped it open, and turned it to the screen. 'Well, there's the packing list, obviously. I've got my new swimsuits, a cover-up, and flip-flops. I've been researching all these amazing places to eat. There's this place that does fabulous poke bowls according to Instagram, not that I'm that sure what a poke bowl is but I'll give it a go. There's a store that does fresh coconut water straight from the shell...'

Wendy nodded. 'Very fancy. And what about the "doing nothing" section? I assume you've got that covered too?'

Fleur flipped to a page filled with neatly written notes. 'I've got a whole section on relaxation techniques. You know, like how to properly switch off and just be. Plus, I've got a massive list of books to read. I'm planning to spend at least one whole day just lying on the beach with a good book and a cocktail. I cannot wait.'

'Sounds idyllic. I'm a bit jealous. I could do with a bit of that myself.'

'You should come, then.' Fleur forced herself to say. She was sure Wendy wouldn't actually put her money where her mouth was, anyway. 'Even if it's just for a weekend. It'd be nice to have you there.'

'I'll think about it.'

Fleur laughed. 'To sun, sea, and maybe a cocktail or two.'

'Nah, you don't want me there. You need time for you and Patrick.' Wendy said, raising her coffee mug in a mock toast. 'To Hawaii, Maui and to you finally getting the holiday you deserve. You are going to have a whale of a time.'

Fleur nodded. She really hoped so. What she didn't know was that on a tropical island there were going to be a lot more than a few whales.

17

Fleur pulled the curtains across in her bedroom, tucked them over huge brass tiebacks, and pushed up the beautiful Irish linen blinds. As she did the same on the French doors on the other side of the room, she squinted as bright sunlight streamed in from outside. A gorgeous, clear-skied Lovely day looked back at her, little patches of sunshine made a pattern on her bedroom floor, and sunshine glinted off the leaves on the tree outside her window.

As she pulled the covers over the edge of the bed and smoothed down the top sheet, Patrick came in the door with her phone in his hand, holding its screen to face her, his eyebrows raised. Valerie's name flashed across the top of the screen. Fleur wasn't sure she was in the mood to hear all about Marvellous Marvin's latest escapades, which had taken him and Valerie across Turkey in their van. Resolving to be nice and positive about her mum living her best life, she took the phone, pressed the button, and smiled as Valerie filled the screen. Valerie had her hair scraped up into a clip and a pink chiffon scarf draped over her bare tanned shoulders.

'Hi, Mum, how are you?' Fleur said, injecting what she thought was a cheery, happy, bright tone to her voice.

'Hi, darling. I'm good, thanks. I thought I'd call to let you know what we're up to. We are having such an amazing time! The weather has been fabulous as you can see from the colour on my face. It just does something to you, doesn't it? A bit of sunshine works wonders for everything and now I get to see it every day, not like in the old days.'

Fleur looked at Valerie's overly sunburnt face and thought that "a bit of sunshine" was an understatement. Valerie's face was bright red and she had marks around her eyes where her sunglasses usually sat. Her lips looked cracked and sunburnt, too. Fleur decided there was little to no point in voicing her observations. Her mum was old-school and liked to frazzle herself in the sun; the redder and more sun-damaged the better.

'Yes, sunshine is good. On that note, did Wendy mention to you that I'm going to Hawaii and Maui? She said she was going to.'

Valerie didn't miss a beat in keeping the conversation focused on herself. 'She did. As I said to her, I've *always* wanted to go to Hawaii. There are loads of lagoons there. You can swim in them and come up on the other side in a completely different place. For my whole life, I wanted to travel around and see stuff like that and I never had the chance.'

Here we go, Fleur thought. She couldn't believe her mum was turning the conversation around to the fact that she'd never done much in her life. Rather than being happy for Fleur that she was going to Hawaii, Valerie was rambling on about herself. No change there.

'You see, I always wanted to go places and explore. I've always been a bit of a wanderlust, but, well, you know, there never really was the inclination. But now I've got Marvin, he wants to do everything, just like me. I'm so pleased I met him.'

Fleur felt sick at the mention of Marvin and the passive-aggressive digs at the fact that her dad had never taken Valerie to places like Hawaii. She tried not to think about it too much and told herself that her mum didn't realise what she said was hurtful. All of it was getting a bit old, though. Valerie needed a good talking to. 'Yes, true,' was about all she could manage.

Fleur sighed, rubbing her temple as her mother's voice droned on and on about all the places she'd wanted to visit but had always missed out on. Holding her phone in front of her, she padded downstairs, the thud of her bare feet against the wooden steps the only sound besides Valerie's never-ending monologue all about herself. Talk about boring and self-centred. It was the same old story every single time Valerie got on the phone.

'I mean, I always thought I'd go to America one day,' Valerie pontificated as Fleur reached the kitchen. 'Not just Hawaii, but all over. Route 66, New York, the Grand Canyon. You know, really experience it. It's just well, you know how life was then. Some people get to go places, and some people don't, was what I always thought, but now obviously I know because of Marvin that life is what you make it. You have to lead your life in places you want it to go, Fleur.'

Fleur rolled her eyes and flicked the kettle on, putting her phone against the bread bin so she didn't have to hold it. She thought about how hard it had been as a single parent; there'd not been many options for leading her life anywhere other than coping. 'Mm, yes you do.' She reached for a mug and felt her nostrils go wide in irritation.

'I mean, it's not like I didn't want to go,' Valerie continued as if Fleur had disagreed. 'I always had the spirit for it. The adventure was there, Fleur. But you know how it was with your father. Always working, never much for holidays. Never one to just pack up and go, was he? Spontaneity! Ha, I ask you!'

Fleur clenched her jaw as she reached for a teabag. The way her mother spoke about her dad as if he'd kept Valerie locked away and stopped her from living her life set her teeth on edge.

Especially now, when he wasn't even here to defend himself. Fleur felt sad about Valerie, but not because of what Valerie had supposedly missed but more because of the big deal Valerie always made about it. It was as if Valerie was mourning a person Fleur believed had never existed in the first place anyway.

'Well, at least I've got Marvin now. He's just like me, you know. Free-spirited. Doesn't need everything planned down to the last detail, doesn't worry about whether the bins have been taken out or if the hotel has good reviews. He just goes with it. Go with the flow and that's what I've always wanted—someone who just goes with it.'

Fleur let the tea bag steep in silence, pressing her lips together. She didn't want to argue. She didn't want to remind her mother that her dad had worked hard so they could have a house, a life, security, nice things, safety. That not everyone had the luxury of "just going with it". How, in her opinion, Marvin didn't have a pot to do anything in and was happily living his best life because Bill had worked to leave Valerie in a very nice position. It just wasn't worth Fleur's emotional bandwidth to say anything so she sucked it up and continued to listen as her stomach felt as if someone had poured bile into it and was stirring it with a giant wooden spoon.

'Oh, and the food in America, my gosh, Fleur, you'll have to try everything! The portions are huge, apparently. I mean, not that I could eat all that. I don't know how they manage over there. But you, oh, you'll love it, I'm sure. You'll have to watch your waistline, though, you do tend to put it on, don't you? You get that from your father.'

'Mmm.'

'Anyway, tell me more about it. Where are you staying? Have you got excursions booked? Oh, you must go snorkelling! You've never been very adventurous, have you?'

Fleur's jaw twitched, if jaw twitching was in fact a thing, and closed her eyes for a bit. As her mum continued without drawing breath, she opened her eyes, stared out of the kitchen window, and watched the way the sunlight dappled across the garden. She told herself that she had a choice; she could rise to what her mum was saying and snap or she could do what she mostly always did and just let her mother talk. She took another sip of tea. 'Mmm.'

'Well, honestly, Fleur, it's good to see you actually doing something. Life just passes you by if you don't push yourself a little bit.'

'Yep.'

'I mean, you never were the adventurous type, were you? At least you're going somewhere...' Valerie sighed, a long, put-upon breath that made Fleur's teeth clench as the bile continued to turn.

Fleur leant back against the worktop, cradling her tea. 'I'm literally going to Hawaii and Maui, Mum. That's quite adventurous.'

'Yes, but will you *do* anything? Or will you just sit on the beach writing stuff in one of your books?' Valerie sniffed. 'I always said, you've got to *experience* life, Fleur. Feel it! Taste it! You'll regret it if you don't. I spent years waiting for things to happen, and then, well, you know how that went. Some people just don't take you on adventures, do they?'

Fleur's grip tightened around her mug. There it was again. The not-so-subtle dig at her dad. 'Right,' she said flatly.

'Oh, don't be like that, love,' Valerie tutted. 'I'm just saying, I know what it's like to look back and wish you'd done more. You don't want to be my age thinking, why didn't I ever just pack up and go? You know? That's why I'm making up for lost time now. I mean, Marvin, he's just such a breath of fresh air. Always up for anything, always pushing me to be a little braver. It's just so *freeing*, Fleur. You wouldn't understand until you've had someone like that.'

Fleur turned and pressed her forehead against the fridge,

inhaling deeply. She wanted to tell her mum that she had done things, like looking after Lucy on her own, like starting her little Etsy business, like holding down a full-time job. Like travelling up and down the country making ends meet. That she was more than capable of having an adventure without Marvin-style chaos and a boho-style striped bandana tied on her head. But there was no point. Valerie had already made up her mind about the kind of person Fleur was.

'I mean, it's just a shame, really,' Valerie continued. 'Your dad never really had the imagination for it. He was always so practical in that sense. Or would we call it sensible? Oh, I don't mean that in a bad way, Fleur, don't get upset—'

'I'm not upset.'

'Good. He was a home bird, wasn't he? Never wanted to go anywhere, never wanted to explore. I spent years trying to get him to just live a little, but no, it was always, "maybe next year, Val," or "we should save for something more important, Val."'

Fleur turned around, her jaw set. 'You mean, like a house? Or putting food on the table? Or making sure we were okay?'

Valerie waved a dismissive hand past the screen. 'No need for the amateur dramatics. I'm just saying, he wasn't exactly spontaneous. Not like Marvin. Do you know, last week, Marvin just decided we should go to a hot air balloon festival? Just like that! And we did! That's what life should be. Loads of fun! Excitement is what you need, not talking about pensions all day long...'

Fleur exhaled sharply through her nose. 'Right. And how did that go?'

'Oh, well, we ended up in a bit of a pickle because Marvin lost his wallet and then we had a bit of a tiff over whose fault it was, but that's not the point here. The point is we went and tried something new.'

'Of course you did.'

'And that's what I love. There's so much possibility in the

world and freedom, yes, that too. I mean who wants to sit around waiting for their pension day to come around again? Honestly, Fleur, that's about the extent of some people's lives. I'm well out of that.'

Fleur took a long sip of tea and stared out of the window, trying to let the irritation slide off her like water.

'Anyway. We don't need to talk about me the whole time. Tell me more about Hawaii!'

Fleur arched her brow. 'Do you actually want to hear about it, or are you going to tell me all the places you wish you'd gone instead?'

'What? Gosh, you can be so prickly sometimes. Just like your father.'

Fleur clenched her jaw so tightly she could feel it in her temples. She took another sip of tea, closed her eyes for a second, and pretend-smiled. 'I'm fine.'

Valerie sighed dramatically as if Fleur was being difficult. 'Honestly, I don't know why you get so funny with me. Your sister can be the same. I'm just excited for you! I'd love to go to Hawaii and Maui. Oh, imagine it, white sand, crystal-clear water, all that exotic fruit, and the volcanoes and stuff. I was born for it. I often wonder why I landed in some godforsaken boring, grey, English town when I was clearly meant for different climes. Anyway...'

'Yes, it's exciting.'

'I just wish I'd had the chance, that's all. But it's not about me. It's just lovely to think about. I deserved a bit of adventure, didn't I?'

Fleur closed her eyes briefly, willing herself not to give her mum a short, sharp dose of two very blue words. She took another sip of tea as irritation crawled up her spine.

'You know, I was meant to go to America once,' Valerie continued as if Fleur had asked. 'Way before you were born. My friend Debbie and I had it all planned—six weeks backpacking across the States! Imagine! But then, well, life happened as it does.'

'Right.'

'Things just didn't work out and then I met your father, and you know what he was like about travel. Honestly, Fleur, it's a miracle we ever left the country at all. I mean, one week in Spain every other year doesn't exactly count as seeing the world, does it? And would you call Marbella, Spain? Pah, hardly a local in sight!'

Fleur exhaled through her nose and pressed her fingers to her temple. 'I liked those holidays.'

'Oh, sweetheart, of course, you did, you didn't know any better.'

Fleur's stomach tightened. 'That's not what I meant.'

'All I'm saying is, I never got the chance to do what you're doing. I always wanted to go to India and America. I don't suppose you could squeeze me into your suitcase, could you?' Valerie let out a tinkling little laugh as if she hadn't just spent the past ten minutes making Fleur's trip about herself.

Fleur forced a tight smile and attempted a half-hearted chuckle. 'Not unless you meet us at Heathrow and fold yourself up very small.'

Valerie went on, in the saintly, martyred tone Fleur knew only too well. 'I don't mind that I never got to go. Really, I don't. I suppose some people just aren't meant to have those experiences, are they? Some people just have to stay at home while everyone else goes off having adventures. Until now.'

Fleur shut her eyes. Her mum seemed to be getting more and more unbearable by the minute. It was as if she was now using any opportunity to tell Fleur and Wendy how much she'd missed out.

'Your dad never cared about travel and he never wanted to go anywhere. And he certainly never wanted *me* to go anywhere. Maybe that was the real problem all along.'

Fleur's eyes snapped open. 'He's dead, Mum and I won't have you saying anything else about it. Stop it! Just stop it!'

Silence. For the first time in the entire conversation, Valerie had nothing to say.

Fleur's heart pounded in the quiet. She hadn't meant to say it like that, hadn't meant to sound so sharp, but goodness, was she tired of listening to the same old sob story.

'You don't have to be harsh. I did not spend my life raising you to be rude, Fleur.'

'I'm not, but just because Dad didn't want to spend his life gallivanting around in a campervan doesn't mean he didn't have imagination. You sound nasty and bitter. It's not nice.'

Valerie sniffed. 'Well, there's no need to attack me.'

Fleur pinched the bridge of her nose. 'I'm not attacking you.'

'Right. Well. Good.' Valerie cleared her throat. 'Anyway, I should go. Marvin and I have a walking tour in an hour. He loves those, you know. Such a curious mind. So open to new experiences.'

Fleur closed her eyes again. 'Of course. Right, well, bye. Have a lovely week. Enjoy the walking tour.'

'Bye, darling!' Valerie trilled. 'Love you!'

And with that, Fleur's phone screen went black. She let out a huge long exhale of air through pursed lips and put her mug down on the worktop with a clink. Every single time she spoke to her mum she ended up wound up. She didn't know why she still let herself get worked up. It was always the same; the guilt trips, the backhanded comments, the constant, endless self-pity, and the Marvin worshipping.

Fleur was over it but really these days it was just at the other end of a phone screen. She sighed and closed her eyes. Thank goodness Valerie no longer lived in England. A recharge and reset in Hawaii couldn't come soon enough. Valerie Champion would not be in sight.

18

Annoying calls from Valerie notwithstanding, Fleur's life was back on an even keel, and she was now on the countdown to going away. Even though it was still a good while off, it was close enough for her to *feel* and *be* ready for it. It couldn't quite come soon enough. She had been telling herself for ages that she would be fine flying to LA on her own, but in the back of her mind, she was a little bit nervous. It was ironic, really, considering she'd spent the best part of the previous ten or so years driving around the labyrinthine network of motorways in the UK and staying in hotels on her own that getting on a gigantic box to fly up over the clouds scared her a little bit.

The travelling and quality of the hotels had, to be quite honest, often left a lot to be desired and put her in situations where she'd had to think on her feet. Therefore, she told herself that getting on a plane at Heathrow and hopping off at the other end in LA, where Patrick would be waiting for her, was actually safer than some of the places and situations she'd found herself in. So she stuck with that thought and tried to focus on the fact that everything would be fine.

Everything about the trip had been planned and arranged in

typical Fleur style; her passport was double-checked and up to date, her travel insurance was in place, her bag was planned, and a special notebook had been made—not just the pre-holiday one, but another for when she was away. Everything was organised and scheduled to within an inch of its life. Our Champo was raring to go.

As she sat on the sofa, flicking through what she was now calling her Maui notebook, she soaked a cotton wool pad with toner, wiped the pad onto her face, did the funny little dabbing and tapping under her eyes thing that a beautician had told her and Cassy to do and waited. After she'd let that sink in for a bit, she opened a sheet mask, a gift from a spa she'd been to with Cassy, flicked it out, plonked it onto her face, leaned back, and settled into the cushions. Keeping her head tilted, she could feel the mask doing something, she wasn't sure what, but assumed that the tingling was a good thing that was injecting vibes of health and glow into her face.

About twenty minutes later, the special ringtone which indicated that Ben was calling started going off. Frowning, Fleur shook her head, wondering what he could want. She hadn't directly heard from him for ages. Probably money. Since the baby had arrived, anything to do with Lucy had more or less been refused payment, which wasn't really much of a problem anymore because there were no school fees, and Lucy was obviously an adult, but Fleur had noticed Ben was no longer as keen to spend money on Lucy. For a good few seconds, she contemplated not answering, but he rarely called her, so she assumed it might be something important.

As soon as she heard his voice, she panicked, sitting bolt upright and listening. 'We're in Accident and Emergency. You need to get here.'

Fleur's first thought was that something had happened to Sarah and the baby and, for some reason, Ben was calling her because he had no one else. 'What's happened? Is the baby okay?'

'Not the baby! It's Luce! She just suddenly collapsed, and we called an ambulance and—yeah—you just need to get here, Fleur, as quickly as you can.'

'What do you mean? Oh my God!' Fleur screeched. 'Get where?'

'I just asked them but they're not sure. She was out cold. Sorry, they think she's fine...'

'You're not making sense! What happened? She's fine, she's not, where are you?'

'She kind of—I don't know—lost consciousness. Is that it? I don't know, I don't know. Just get here!'

'Ben! Slow down. Where are you? Which hospital?'

'Sorry. St. Alexander's. Do you know where it is?'

Fleur had parked in a multi-storey car park near the hospital many times because it was near a business centre where she'd delivered training courses. 'Yes, okay, I'll be there. I'll text you.'

'Try not to panic. I think she'll be okay, right?'

'Okay? No, I'm not okay! You are the one who is panicking!'

'Yes, sorry. Look, I should have been calmer. Sorry, she's okay but you need to come. Just get here.'

Fleur whipped off the sheet mask, ran upstairs, and started pulling on clothes. She quickly went to the toilet, opened the vanity unit, grabbed a toothbrush, some toothpaste, and deodorant, then hurriedly threw some clean underwear and a plain top into a bag along with a flannel, grabbed a jacket, and ran out of the cottage, pulling the front door shut behind her before getting into the car.

As she reversed off the drive, she repeatedly told herself to keep calm. The last thing she wanted was an accident. What had really scared her was the tone in Ben's voice—he'd sounded petrified. A strange, unheard of voice, full of trepidation. She'd never heard fear like that in his voice and never wanted to again.

Driving along the lane, taking the route she knew well, she stopped at the 'Keep Right' sign at the end, drove out of Lovely, made her way out onto the dual carriageway, and tried to remain on an even keel. Ben had never been good in a crisis and despite his thinking that he was the capable one, in actual fact when things got iffy, he panicked like nobody's business. She'd seen it happen with him before. Pressing the button on her steering wheel, she called Patrick. He answered on the second ring.

'Hey. How are you? Thinking about our gallivanting off to Hawaii yet, sunning ourselves on a beach?'

'I'm not good,' she said quickly. 'I've just had a call from Ben. Lucy's in Accident and Emergency. That's all I know. Ben sounded terrified. I'm on my way there now.'

'What? What hospital?'

'St. Alexander's.'

Patrick swore but he sounded calm. 'Where are you?'

'Just pulling onto the dual-carriageway.'

'Do you want me to meet you there? I can be there in about half an hour. An hour, I don't know.'

'I really don't know. Ben sounded panicked but he's *not* good in a crisis. He said she was out cold.'

'I'll call him. Don't drive too fast. Just stay calm. I'll phone Ben and make sure everything is okay. Don't worry, you just get there. I'll take care of anything else.'

'Okay, thanks, yes.'

Patrick clicked off the call. Fleur pushed the button to end hers and focused on the road as her mind felt not like it was going at a hundred miles an hour, more like it was in a vortex of numbness. She kept her hands steady on the wheel, her fingers tight as she sped along. The familiar stretch of road blurred past as she barely registered it at all. All she could think about was getting to the hospital. All her mind could see was a vision of Lucy collapsed. What did that even mean? Was it exhaustion? Something more serious? Was she breathing when they found her? Was she awake now? The questions piled up in her head, none of them with answers, and she *hated* it. She could have wrung Ben's neck, too.

Her phone rang again: Patrick. She pressed the button on the steering wheel. 'What's happening?'

'I just spoke to Ben. He hadn't heard anything else. I think she's okay. I couldn't get much sense out of him. He said that they said they were doing tests.'

Fleur's stomach twisted. 'Did he say why? What's wrong with her?'

'No. They wouldn't tell him much, just that they needed to do routine stuff but that overall, she's okay and they think she will be fine.'

Fleur shook her head. Surely, they wouldn't have taken her to the hospital for exhaustion. She swallowed hard. 'Okay, I'll be there soon and will get some sense. Ben is a nightmare.'

'How far off are you?'

Fleur glanced at the satnav. 'About twenty minutes.'

'Right. Look, the traffic is at a standstill where I am. You get there and then if you want me to come, I will.'

Fleur nodded, even though he couldn't see her. 'Okay. You don't need to. I'll be fine.'

Patrick's voice softened. 'Try not to panic, okay? We don't know anything yet and it sounds like she's okay. I hate to say it but I think Ben put the willies up you for no reason. For someone quite as arrogant as him, he was, well, I can't even describe it...'

Fleur sighed. 'Yeah, tell me about it.'

'Just get there safely.'

'I will.'

'I love you. Keep me in the loop.'

'Yep, love you, will do.'

Patrick hung up. Fleur reminded herself that she needed to stay calm for Lucy's sake. She pressed her foot harder on the accelerator and shook her head. Just when things had been going so swimmingly, too. There was always, always, always something that came up when she thought her life was going well. Every little part of her, every cell, every fibre wanted to curl up into a tiny ball.

Fleur slowed down in the middle of the access lane to the hospital car park and looked up at the huge building towering over to her left. She couldn't work out which way to go—whether to go straight on or right to where another bank of barriers led the way to what appeared to be thousands of parked cars. It seemed as if there were barriers everywhere and her brain couldn't quite compute where she needed to go. Peering up through the windscreen, she squinted and then jumped as an angry, heavily bearded driver behind her beeped on his horn. She couldn't have cared less about him as she glanced in her rear-view mirror and caught him waving his fist out the window of a bright yellow sports car. All she wanted was to make sure she went the right way so that she could get inside the hospital as quickly as possible.

Plumping for the short-stay car park aisle, she pulled up to a barrier, pressed her window down, and waited for the machine to do its thing. It seemed to take ages. Finally, she pulled out the ticket and drove in as signs here, there, and everywhere went left, right, and centre. Red signs, green notices, yellow posters taped to posts appeared to swim in front of her eyes. Taking the first right that she could, she drove past what felt like thousands of cars lined up in rows until she reached the very back of the car park, where there was half a row of unoccupied spaces. The man in the yellow car zoomed past her angrily as she slowly tried to reverse park into one of the gaps. Shaking her head, she completely ignored him; as if she was remotely bothered about an angry man in a stupid yellow boy racer car who had clearly forgotten to take the module at school that dealt with manners.

Once she'd manoeuvred into the space, she forgot all about her resolve to stay calm, grabbed her bag off the seat, locked the car with the remote locking system, and started to leg it through the car park, her cardigan and bag flapping behind her. As she passed the bearded man in the yellow car, he recognised her, shook his head, and called out something rude. Fleur registered his menacing looks in seconds; thick black beard, overworked gym body, tight shiny jogging bottoms, together with huge tyres on the lurid yellow car, and a spoiler on the back. Refraining from giving him the finger and shouting the worst swear words she could think of, instead, she put her head down and continued to sprint towards the hospital reception. No need to participate in acknowledging the dregs of the earth.

A few minutes later, she was standing at the entrance, looking up at a board, wondering why she couldn't see Accident and Emergency anywhere. It appeared that just as she had thought when she'd slowed in the middle of the road by the barriers, she had gone the wrong way. She stepped to her left and peered at another sign that was very clearly telling her that Accident and Emergency was on the north side of the campus. Shame no one with a brain had thought about putting that on a sign by the car parks. Squinting at the map, she realised it would be quicker to go back outside, run along the walking track, and enter Accident and Emergency that way. Just after she'd gone back out the entrance she'd come in, had found the walking track marked by way of a blue line, and had started to half-jog, a text arrived from Ben.

Ben: *I've just spoken to the doctor. She's okay. They're not sure what's wrong with her. Where are you?*

Fleur: *I've just arrived, but I was on the south side, so I'm on my way now.*

Ben: *Thank God she's okay by the sounds of it. Don't panic.*

Don't panic! Bit late for that. Fleur rolled her eyes as she jogged and thought to herself that it was a bit rich now for him to be saying not to panic. Her legs felt like they were going to give way and she felt as if her top was sticking to her back. As if she wasn't panicking, duh; her only daughter was in hospital. That was enough to make anyone panic. She typed as she ran.

Fleur: *See you in a minute.*

Finally arriving at the entrance, hot and most definitely bothered, again the signs seemed to pulsate in front of Fleur's eyes. Why did it all have to be so complicated? Why were there so many signs? As she looked around, she inhaled and swallowed; everywhere she looked, sick, unwell people seemed to be multiplying in front of her eyes. A woman in a wheelchair with a pink blanket, a man hobbling with a stick, and two nurses on either side of a young boy who was holding a sick bag up to his mouth. A heavily pregnant woman stopped by a barrier, clearly in the middle of a contraction, let out a small, tight wail.

Fleur ran past them all, waited for the automatic doors to open, stepped inside, and nearly keeled over from the revolting smell. A mix of stale bodies, antiseptic, and sickness together with a healthy sprinkling of grot and grime. She didn't like it. Not at all. The lights were horrible, too bright strip lights shining down on marked, grubby floors, and walls covered in old posters barking instructions left, right, and centre. To say Fleur was out of her comfort zone was an understatement.

She spied Ben launching himself out of his seat and striding over to her. His face looked like nothing she'd ever seen before. Completely drained, pale, and as if he'd aged by many years. He was the epitome of worry, standing right there in front of her eyes.

'Is she okay?' Fleur asked.

Ben pointed to a set of wide, grey, scuffed double doors. 'She's gone to an observation area or something. I was in there, but then they took her through and asked me to step out here to the waiting area again because they've got an emergency trauma case from a road accident and it's chaos in there.'

'Right, so, what happened?'

Ben shook his head. 'Everything was fine. We were going out for a walk with the baby, and she just suddenly looked really unwell, and I don't know, it went so fast. Like she fainted and we couldn't get her to come round, she was just lying there. So, I called an ambulance, but by the time we got here, it seemed like she was better. Well, not better, but she'd come round and they said her vital signs were fine. And that's all I know, really.'

Fleur sighed. 'I don't know what to think. She's been great. I was only just thinking yesterday and Patrick mentioned that she's much better. Now this out of the blue.'

'I know, Sarah and I were saying the same.'

'Thank God she was with you,' Fleur noted. 'It would have been worse if she'd been up in London.'

Ben frowned. 'I hadn't even thought about that. You're right.'

Fleur looked at the double doors and then sat down heavily on a plastic chair and Ben plonked himself next to her. 'So, now what?'

'I suppose we just wait. I'm sorry, I think she'll be okay. I panicked like crazy there. Maybe I shouldn't have phoned you in that state.'

'You never were the best in a crisis.' Fleur stated drily. She knotted her fingers together in her lap and looked around; it wasn't a pretty sight. The whole waiting room smelled of disinfectant, sweat, and the faint, stale tang of something she didn't want to think too much about. A baby cried somewhere down the corridor, a thin, reedy wail that set her nerves on edge and every few seconds, the sharp bleep of a machine sounded from behind the double doors, followed by the muffled sound of voices and machinery. She didn't want to be ungrateful but from where she was sitting the NHS wasn't looking very good. Fleur swallowed, her throat dry. 'So, she just collapsed? No warning?'

Ben exhaled and scrubbed a hand through his hair. 'Yeah. We were just walking, and she said she felt a bit dizzy, but I thought it was nothing, you know? She's been so much brighter lately. I was literally saying to Sarah last night how much better she seemed.'

Fleur's stomach twisted. 'And she was okay this morning?'

'Yeah. A bit tired, I suppose, now that I think about it, but nothing unusual.'

Fleur looked down at clammy hands and watched as a nurse walked past. 'I should've realised something was wrong.'

'You couldn't have known. None of us did. She was fine.'

'Obviously not if she collapsed, Ben! That's not fine.'

Ben sighed, rubbing his hands up and down the side of his face. 'I know. But we didn't see it coming, there was nothing to suggest anything. I don't know what to think.'

Fleur stared at the scuffed floor, dirty marks, remnants of a packet of crisps and a dirty paper coffee cup making her stomach turn. 'Did she hit her head?'

'No, it wasn't like that.'

Fleur nodded. 'That's something, at least.' Fleur's throat felt tight and she could feel a sting of tears, but she forced them down. 'I don't understand. She's been great, glowing even. She's been happy. I thought we were past all this.'

'She'll be okay.'

Fleur didn't say anything as she watched the hands of an oversized clock above her head tick around. It was going to be a very long, horrible, drawn-out day.

19

The house felt too quiet as Fleur opened the front door to the cottage and sighed. She was very glad to be home. As she stepped inside, shutting the door behind her, the familiar scent of home wrapped around her—fresh laundry, the faint trace of Patrick's aftershave maybe, the lingering hint of the slow cooker from the night before and the smell of lavender from a room scenter sitting on the dresser at the bottom of the stairs. Normally, the cottage smell felt comforting, warm, and good like home. Tonight, though, after the day Fleur had had, everything felt a bit off. Just like she did. She dropped her bag by the kitchen table, scooped her hair up in a band, and let out a long breath. What a day: all that mattered though was that Lucy was fine.

Popping the kettle under the tap, Fleur thought about what had occurred; she had sat in the hospital for what had felt like a lifetime, her mind cycling through every possibility, heart tight in her chest, waiting for someone to tell her something awful. But in the end, it had been fine and that hadn't happened at all. A fainting spell, exhaustion, low blood sugar, dehydration. Nothing more, nothing less according to the powers that be, but still, panic had settled into Fleur's bones, the way it always did when it came to Lucy. It didn't matter that Lucy was a young adult living half here, half there, working, independent, grown up doing her own thing. She was still her daughter and when Fleur had seen her in the hospital bed, she had felt something inside her shatter. A sight no one ever wants to see whatever the circumstances.

Running the tap and pouring herself a glass of water while she waited for her tea to brew, Fleur took a slow sip of water and pondered the horrible day and how it had finished. In the end after a few discussions, Lucy had gone back to Ben's after the hospital. It had made sense because it had been getting late —his place was closer, and if Lucy needed to go back to the hospital it would be easy. Meaning Fleur had driven home alone, telling herself it was fine and all was okay. That she would see Lucy the next day and they would laugh about it, make some sarcastic comment about hospitals and dramatic episodes, and move on. However, despite what any doctor had insisted or what the words on a discharge note said, Fleur still felt exceedingly unsettled as if someone had grabbed onto her cage and rattled it for a while just to see what happened.

After making her tea, she walked through to the living room, flicked on a lamp, and curled up on the sofa, pulling a blanket over her lap and just sat there for ages, listening to the hum of the house, staring at nothing in particular. She wasn't even sure what she was feeling. Her emotions had moved on from the original dastardly, throat-grabbing panic in the hospital to a different feeling. Not relief really, because the weight of what ifs and the not knowing lingered, nope, it was something else. Something quieter, heavier, harder to explain. A weird, odd sensation of exhaustion and a come down from an emotional adrenaline-fuelled rush.

A tap on the front door made her nearly jump out of her skin. She heard Patrick's voice from outside. 'Sorry, I left my other bunch of keys at home because I brought the car, not the van.'

Fleur got up, unlocked the door, stepped back as Patrick walked in, already frowning slightly. 'How was it? You okay? You look dreadful. What a nightmare. Sorry you had to go through that. How's Luce?'

Fleur nodded automatically. 'Yeah, she's fine. I think we're all just tired now.'

Patrick studied her for a second, then did what he always did and squeezed her shoulders and just like that, she felt the worry drop a fraction, the rattly cage stilled a little bit. 'Talk to me, Champo. Tell me all of it.'

'You know it all, really. There's nothing much else to say. I feel so exhausted, so goodness knows how Lucy is feeling. I'm fine.'

Patrick raised an eyebrow. 'You don't sound fine. Have to say you don't look fine, either.'

'It's just seeing her like that and Ben totally overreacting. It's made me feel *very* out of control. Even though she doesn't seem to have anything wrong with her, even though I know she's fine, I keep thinking—what if she wasn't? What if next time it's worse? What if they've completely overlooked something? Who really knows? You hear these stories, don't you?'

'Yeah, I've been thinking the same.'

Fleur squeezed her eyes shut for a second. 'I still feel like I'm waiting for something to go wrong. She's so much better now, but every time she seems okay, I get this nagging feeling in my gut. Like it's all too good to be true. Like something's going to come along and upend us, if that makes sense?'

Patrick nodded and flicked his eyes a few times. 'You've been on high alert all day, anyone would be. It's going to take a while for your brain to realise she's okay. That *you're* okay. Not being funny but Ben didn't help. He catastrophized right from the word go. Funny bloke, really.'

Fleur let Patrick's words sink in; they made sense, of course. For so long, Lucy had been her entire world. Every decision, every thought, every worry had revolved around making sure she was alright and she hated with a passion anything that rumbled that. Plus, Ben had made things a whole lot worse.

'You don't have to be on edge anymore from what you've told me.'

'How do I do that?'

'For starters, you finish that tea. Then, have a nice bath and go to bed. We'll keep our phones on. Ben will be in touch if he needs to. I think we all need a good night's sleep here. Everything will look better tomorrow. You don't worry. I'll do everything.'

Fleur loved that. Someone else to just take over. Someone to run her a bath and make her feel okay. Fabulous. 'Right. Sounds easy enough.'

Patrick joked and broke the very tight, horrid tension in the air. 'I can supervise the bathing ritual, if you want.'

Fleur smiled. Patrick was right. She had to put the Lucy thing down to the fact that it was a blip. She couldn't spend the next few months waiting for things to fall apart again. She'd done enough of that in the past already.

Patrick patted her knee. 'I'll go up and run the bath. Trust me on this Champo. Everything is going to be okay.'

Fleur felt the cage come to a complete standstill and loved having someone on her side. It had been a long time coming.

20

Fleur sat in a café not far from Ben's house and watched as a tall, black fan moved from left to right blowing warm air around the back section of the room. An old couple in front of her were finishing their coffee and lunch, and to her left, floor-to-ceiling cubbyholes held so many bottles of San Pellegrino it looked as if they were multiplying in front of her eyes. Just to her right a little Buddha sat surrounded by various gifts and offerings including a cup of coffee and a huge vase full of faux flowers. Fleur nodded to herself as she looked around and made herself comfortable. It was a lovely little hole-in-the-wall café, the sort of place she loved to find—full of regular, everyday people doing their thing, and not a fancy squash and sage challah bread sandwich in sight.

As Fleur dipped into her salad, half tabouli, half Greek, she thought about how much the episode with Lucy had rattled her. The same had happened when Lucy had come home from ballet school, the hospital visit had completely and utterly taken her by surprise. At the end of the day, though, there had been nothing wrong with Lucy. In fact, the doctor Fleur had ended up speaking to, had confirmed that there was nothing to note, at least not that they could find or that anyone could see. As far as the results went, Lucy was in optimum health. But what was causing the fainting, though? It was a question yet to be answered. Rummaging in the salad for the elusive feta cheese, Fleur thought about what had happened and hoped that the doctors were correct. Really, what else could she do but hope? She'd asked for a second opinion which had reiterated that they couldn't find anything wrong. What more was there that a mother could do?

She was now near Ben and Sarah's house waiting for Lucy to collect her things. Instead of making things awkward, mostly for herself, she'd avoided having to go in and be in the vicinity of Sarah and had parked her car not far from Ben's house. She'd then strolled down the road to the little café, using the excuse that she needed to go and get a bite to eat. Tucking into the salad, she thought how being a mum right from the word go had changed everything in her world and perused how funny it was that being a mother affected so many things in life—things that were really out of your control, but you worried about anyway. Like Lucy having her funny spells, which was what Lucy had started to call them. Ultimately, there was nothing Fleur could do about it or them but despite that, she still worried, a little bit out of her mind.

She tried to push it to the back of her brain and get on with her salad, but all she could think about was how life was always on the edge. The Lucy hospital episode could have been a completely different scenario altogether. Musing and picking at her salad, she thought about a woman she'd met on one of the training courses who had received terrible news about one of her children right in the middle of one of Fleur's sessions. It was news that had literally changed the woman's life in a flash and not for the better. Fleur was well aware that it could have happened to her just as easily and she did not like that thought in the slightest.

She forced herself not to pick up her phone and Google, for the tenth time that hour, the symptoms Lucy had displayed—asking Dr Google what was wrong with Lucy had not been one of Fleur's better ideas. If she searched for fainting or losing consciousness one more time, it would be one time too many because Dr Google gave no conclusive answers.

She must have googled Lucy's symptoms a million times since she'd been sitting in the waiting room and all to no avail. All of it, in some form or another, only haunted her with the fact that it could be a multitude of things. She'd read through every possible option, and in the end, her mind had convinced itself that Lucy had all manner of conditions—each more bizarre than the last. The incessant googling of symptoms helped nobody, made her worry more and left her brain even more saturated with the fear that something was seriously wrong with Lucy.

She tried to stop thinking about it and instead focused on her salad and called Patrick, who picked up on the second ring.

'Hey.'

'Hi.'

'Everything okay?'

'Yep, I'm in a café around the corner from Sarah and Ben's waiting for Lucy to get some bits together.'

Patrick chuckled. 'What? You didn't want to go in?'

'Goodness knows, the last thing I want to do at the moment is go in there and baby worship. Sorry, my inner bitch is coming out. I really wasn't up for going in there and having Sarah lecture me on parenting now she's been a mum for all of like five minutes.'

'Yep, I'm sure she knows everything about parenting now.'

'Yeah, for sure. Anyway, Lucy seems fine. It's the weirdest thing. She's just going to pick up a few bits, and then we'll drive home.'

'Okay, that's a good thing. Did you find out anything else?'

'No, they just said she's fine. They said to keep an eye on her. I don't know what to think, really.'

'Hmm.'

'I must've googled the life out of Dr Google, asking for something with her symptoms but to no avail really. Although, on the other hand, it could be any number of things that freak me out.'

'Well, that's pretty pointless googling it.' Patrick stated matter of factly.

'I suppose it is. It's not brought me any closer to anything.'

'So, Lucy's fine now?'

'Yeah, she seems it. Almost as if nothing ever happened. It's the strangest thing.'

'And the doctors found nothing at all? Run me through that bit again.'

'Nothing. Ran all the tests. Blood pressure, this test, that test, blood sugar, neurological stuff—everything came back normal.' Fleur shook her head. 'Which is obviously a good thing, but it still doesn't explain why she keeled over in the first place. I don't know what to think for the best.'

Patrick exhaled slowly. 'So, what are they saying? Just one of those things?'

'Pretty much. They think it might've been a mix of dehydration, maybe a bit of low blood sugar, maybe just one of those weird childhood things that happen for a period and never happen again. Though she's a young adult not a child. Not exactly reassuring, though, is it?'

'Not really,' Patrick admitted. 'But I suppose, like we discussed last night, if they've done every test under the sun and she's fine, that's got to count for something. What else can they do?'

'That's what I keep telling myself. But you know me, I then proceeded, in my wisdom, to go down a rabbit hole, and convinced myself she had every condition under the sun. Absolutely no help, whatsoever.'

'Classic move. Let me guess—you started with something mild and ended up diagnosing her with something so obscure only three people in the world have ever had it? Ask me how I know.'

Fleur groaned and dropped her head into her hands for a moment. 'Exactly! I know it's pointless. But when it's your child, you can't help it, can you? One minute I was reading about normal fainting episodes, and the next I was convinced she had some rare neurological disorder that only specialists in Switzerland know how to treat.'

Patrick chuckled. 'Sounds about right and how's she taking it all? Scared? Confused?'

'Oh, not at all. She's calling them her "funny spells" now like she's some kind of Victorian lady swooning onto a chaise longue with smelling salts.' Fleur rolled her eyes.

Patrick laughed. 'I can just picture her. "Oh, Mummy, I'm having one of my funny spells!"'

'Exactly. Meanwhile, I'm quietly losing my mind in the background, trying not to smother her in bubble wrap.'

'Kids, eh? No fear whatsoever.'

'None. Not an ounce of worry in her. Which, to be fair, is probably better than her being terrified. But I'd like a happy medium, you know? Just a little concern would be nice.'

'I think you're asking too much there.'

'Probably,' Fleur admitted with a sigh and glanced at her watch. 'Anyway, I should get going. Heading back to Lovely in a bit once I've got her in the car.'

'At least you'll be in your own space, and you can try and get some proper rest.'

'That's the plan. Not that it ever works that way, but I can dream.'

'You driving straight back?'

'Yeah.'

'Well, drive safely and try not to overthink it all too much. She's okay, that's what matters.'

'Yeah. You're right. Thanks.'

'I'll go straight to yours and sort out dinner and stuff. For God's sake, stay away from Google.'

Fleur laughed, standing up and gathering her bag. 'Fine, fine. I'll try. No promises, though.'

'Message me when you're fifteen minutes away and I'll get the tea in the pot.'

'I will. See you soon.'

'See you.'

As Fleur said thank you to the people behind the counter and then walked off in the direction of Ben's house, she felt a little bit lighter. Lucy was fine according to the doctors who had said so and for sure Patrick had her back. That would have to do for now.

21

It was a day or so after the fainting episode and Fleur was in the studio, but not in her usual spot at her desk by the window. Nope, instead, she was sitting on the floor, surrounded by her notebooks. She'd gone to the bottom bookshelf and pulled out an old notebook to look at a binding technique she'd used a few years prior and had ended up bobbing down on the floor flipping through the old book for ages. That had led her down a rabbit hole of looking through her books where she had spent way too long sighing, flicking through pages, smiling, and letting memories flood her mind as she looked at some of her old lists, doodles, words and notes. There had even been the odd tear here and there as basically she'd perused her own life laid out in the pages of her notebooks. A strange mix of memories, melancholy, happiness and reflection all rolling around her head at once.

It felt bizarre as she flipped through one of the books, feeling as if she was reading about someone else, someone who didn't sound like the Fleur she was now at all. Landing on an entry from when she and Lucy had first moved into the cottage on the green, she smiled as she read through a note she'd made about a neighbour. The woman had popped around with a homemade cake to say hello, had chatted away and welcomed Fleur to the village. Fleur remembered how, in that moment, she'd felt that maybe everything would be okay. As her mind flicked back to that first week in the cottage, when her dad had been around every day to help, she was utterly flooded with emotion. She wasn't sure whether to laugh, cry or what to feel or do as she sat on the floor of her study with memories and thoughts seeping out of her by the dozen. A prickle of emotion in the lining of her nose and a strange static fuzzy feeling in her ears. All in all, not that nice.

The most striking thing was that so much had changed since the notes had been written in the book. Now, here she was in a completely different place, her dad no longer on the planet, Wendy in Australia. Her mum was definitely on another planet, with someone else entirely. Lucy was grown up and Fleur was in the cottage in Lovely Bay, in a different relationship altogether. So much had changed in what was ultimately quite a short amount of time that Fleur felt as if she was making things up. She shook her head as she pondered the changes and felt as if the person in the books wasn't her at all. As if that person had lived in another life, in another universe, in another place. The person all that time ago nothing like the person she was now.

Musing how much had changed, she knew that despite her dad no longer being around, the place she was in now was a good one, just not as good as it would have been if he was still in it. Shifting from her spot, one leg half asleep, she thought about her dad, how much she still missed him every day and how despite what numerous people had told her, it was not getting any easier in any shape or form. The heartache had never really gone away and didn't look as if it would anytime soon. To be fair, it wasn't quite the same as it had been at the beginning. It wasn't as raw and didn't feel as if she would never be happy again. No, now it was more of a resigned feeling and an acceptance as such. Half happy memories, half full of sadness, all mixed up with the daunting realisation that our Champo was never, ever going to see her dad again. He would never be there to say, "Way to go, Champo, you'll be okay".

He would never hold his two fingers together and tap them against his temple, repeating one of his classic phrases. He would just never be there to have her back. The reality yet again whipped her around the head and made her feel as it always did; awful, dreadful, horrible, all the words.

So many things still reminded her of him, and it was funny how they seemed to suddenly drop into her mind at random moments. Even in the cottage, somewhere she'd never been to with him, she felt as if there were reminders of him everywhere. Feeling a little prick at the side of her eyes, she wondered what Bill would think about her life now. About what had happened to Lucy and the fainting episodes. About Wendy being in Australia. About his wife, Valerie and what she was doing. That part, the Valerie thing, she still couldn't quite fully wrap her head around, and there was no doubt that Bill would have found it challenging too. However, he'd always had something pragmatic to say about everything in life. Regarding the fact that his wife was now with Marvin and spent most, if not all, of her time telling everyone what a grand time she now had and how unhappy she'd been before, Fleur wasn't sure what Bill Champion would think about that.

Deciding that she didn't have time to reminisce, she put the notebooks back in their neat order, got up, dragged her half-asleep leg over to the desk, and sat down. For a minute she rested her chin in her hand just thinking about her dad as images and memories flooded her brain. She remembered him on her wedding day, how he'd been there at her side, squeezing her hand all the way down the aisle. How, when Ben had left, he'd phoned her every day and been around, just to make sure she was okay.

As she sat, thinking, pondering, and musing, she recalled what she now knew were the five or was it seven stages of grief and how they'd affected her. It had come and gone with her in waves. After the utter shock and then the pure sadness, she remembered feeling so angry that Bill Champion had left the Earth. Together with the anger and sadness, despair had been her constant companion in the early months, but now, the despair had worn off, and something else had taken its place. Not quite acceptance, more a quietness, really. A resignation that he'd never be back and she'd never be the same again.

Getting up again, she pulled out another one of her notebooks, the one she'd written in when grief had had her by the neck. Inside were all sorts of photos of Bill, tucked into little handmade flaps she'd created here and there. She stopped at one in particular; a picture of her walking with Bill on the way to get married. A snap taken by Wendy as they were leaving the house. Fleur stared at it for ages and traced her fingers over the glossy edges. In the photo, she was looking at the camera, her veil caught up behind her in a gust of wind. Bill had his head back, laughing, his face tanned, his suit not quite fitting as well as it should have, so happy, so full of life, so pleased with himself and his daughter, too.

Fleur looked at herself in the picture—her dress pure white, a simple fitted style with a high neck and slim silky skirt. Her bouquet a tumble of pale pink and white flowers, her hair twisted at the nape of her neck, and a little white bag hanging off her left arm. She stared at the image for ages and ages letting it settle in her head. The person in the picture didn't really look like her at all. This person appeared to be younger, freer, and prettier but somehow it all felt strange, odd, fake, and wrong. It wasn't hard to work out why; the picture wasn't true, especially the happier bit. She was so much happier now and freer, too. Really, she was happier than she'd ever been.

As she sat and pondered a bit more, she shifted her gaze

away from the way-too-young bride with her dad and looked out at the sea. Watching the goings-on down Lovely Pott Lane as a car made its way in the direction of the town, she realised what she had now, how she felt, and the things around her she wanted forever. She never wanted them to change. The scariness of the Lucy episode had also reiterated that.

She traced the edge of the old photograph with her fingertip, her thoughts turning over themselves in slow circles. The person in the picture, the girl in the white dress, the veil caught in the wind, felt like someone she used to *know* rather than someone she used to *be*. She had been happy then, at least she'd thought she'd been. In the way that you're happy when you don't know what's coming next. When you've followed the rules because they're the only rules you know and have been laid out in front of you by somebody else. The kind of happiness that isn't really tested, that hasn't had to prove itself against anything properly hard.

Sitting and reflecting, Fleur thought about Ben. She supposed it hadn't been a lie then to think and say that she'd loved him. She had loved him, but now realised that she'd loved the life they were supposed to have. But looking at the picture now, with the distance of time and everything that had happened since, she realised that none of it had been true anyway. She had been more in love with the idea than with him. All of it was weird and disjointed and ugly and just felt wrong. It didn't even hurt as it had. Sitting there, she put the notebook down, shifted in her chair to ease the ache in her leg, and watched out the window as the sea stretched out in front of her, the afternoon light catching on the water.

Shaking her head, she sighed as she realised she had been so many different versions of herself in the previous years. There was the version of her who had been a wife, living in a house she'd thought would be hers forever, planning a future that had never actually arrived. The single mum version where she'd forced herself to try to do everything right. The version of her who had moved to Lovely Bay, exhausted, brittle, trying to hold everything together with her fingernails, hanging on for dear life. The version of her who had cried in the kitchen when Lucy had left ballet school and fainted in the deli. The version of her who had picked herself up and decided that if she was going to have a new start in a small town, she might as well make something of it.

And now here she was, another version. This version had built a life for herself that was entirely her own and just what she wanted. This version spent her mornings looking out at the sea, had a studio filled with things she had made with her own hands, and had good people who made life better around her. This version was in love. Oh-so very much in real, actual, heart-palpitating, cry-over-your-pancakes, top-to-toe love.

Exhaling slowly, Fleur rubbed her thumb over her palm. It was funny really; it was almost as if what had happened since moving to Lovely had been meant to be. Patrick had just been there, from the moment she'd arrived more or less. In the background, in the foreground, somewhere in the middle. And then, at some point, it had shifted to something so much more important.

Staring out at the sea, Fleur looked down at the picture of the bride again and nodded as a realisation dropped slap-bang into the middle of her head. She wanted to marry Patrick like for actual real and she wasn't prepared to wait. No more of this dicking around, forever ring stuff. The thought came out of nowhere, landing solidly as if it had been waiting all along to lodge itself in her head. Ready for a gap to squeeze itself into. She had, yes, wistfully thought to herself that if the opportunity had arisen, she would say yes to Patrick and that she wanted a wedding band on her finger, but she'd not actually properly thought about it as something that could be real. Fleur frowned and sat with it for a second. It didn't feel strange or like a big, dramatic realisation, more that it was so very obvious, as if she had always known, right from the day she'd first laid eyes on him, that she'd wanted it but just hadn't let herself run with it.

Shaking her head, she tutted. *Getting married, really?* Sure, she'd thought she'd quite like a nice gold band next to the diamond forever ring, but really, really, really? Yes. Not that she would be announcing her thoughts to anyone and definitely not in some grand, over-the-top way. But the thought of actually *making* it happen was there now settled into her head, and she could tell that it wasn't going anywhere anytime soon.

What our Champo had realised, sitting at her desk and reminiscing about a white dress, was that she wanted to make the Patrick and Fleur story a more permanent one. *What did that even mean?* She didn't even know. Was it the actual marriage certificate and vows stuff that she wanted? She knew she wanted more than what they currently had, which always felt a bit of a half-and-half affair. They lived in each other's houses, both did their own independent thing and came together at a meeting point somewhere in the middle. Like good friends, who loved each other with very good sex thrown in for good measure. All of a sudden, for our Champo, that wasn't enough. Something about the bride in the picture had triggered that.

Did she want to get married? Did she want to just move in with Patrick—or him with her? Did she want to do what was now called a companion ceremony or something like that? She wasn't really sure. All she could think was that the first time she'd made things permanent by way of marriage to Ben, the woman in the white dress had not been true to herself. She had not felt as she did now. That woman hadn't even known what she was doing. She'd followed protocol and rules and what everyone else had done at the time. Hadn't everyone just wanted to put a diamond ring on their finger, create a home, get married, have a baby, and do all the things?

Fleur realised as clear as day that she'd unwittingly slipped into that scenario of life, the one predetermined by a lifetime of tradition and ideals. And it had, in her case, fallen onto the floor like a toppling of cards around her, suffocating her as they fell. However, now here she was, thinking about how much she wanted to do it all again, but this time, on her terms to someone she actually loved. How it was meant to be and feel.

Now all she had to do was work out how she was going to make it happen and put it all into place. Our Champo was on a mission to *really* be okay. She was going to propose.

22

As Fleur drove along a dual carriageway behind a lorry that was clearly on its way back home to Germany via Dover, she kept her required distance and thought about what she was going to do about the mad proposal idea that was beginning to form in her head. Her brain played a game of Eenie Meenie Miney Mo, back and forth, over and over again. Would she be doing it? Oh yes, she would.

She let herself imagine what it would be like to get married again, to anyone, let alone Patrick. How had she even got to this place where it was a thing in her head that she wanted to do? She'd sworn off being in a serious relationship after her disastrous dabble with dating, and now here she was locked in a world of her own considering marrying someone. *Stranger things.* Would she wear a white dress, a trouser suit, a ball gown with a pink sparkle? Would she not even care if it was a local registry office or a country house somewhere? So many questions in a lovely, big, frothy, happy swirl.

As she stared at the German number plate in front of her, a thought suddenly popped into her brain—she knew a place where she would really like to make things *forever*. Somewhere she would like to marry Patrick. A place that had been in her mind for a long time, but she hadn't really realised it, until now. Driving along a dual-carriageway in the southeast of England in the direction of the White Cliffs, topped by grey skies and a smattering of drizzle on her windscreen, she realised that a wedding ceremony, surrounded by tropical flowers, on a beach, waves swaying, guitars playing, marrying someone she loved to his core was top of her list. Fleur Champion wanted to marry Patrick in Maui. A vision of it swam in front of her eyes. All she had to do was make it happen.

As she drove and continued to keep an eye on the German number plate, the thought settled in her mind like a book slotted into the right place on a shelf. She wanted to marry Patrick, hook, line, and sinker. That part wasn't up for debate, but the *how* was where her brain got stuck. Because if she really thought about it and was honest with herself, she knew that if it was going to happen, *she* would have to be the one to ask. It wasn't as if he was going to suddenly pop the question just because it was now very important to her. As far as she could tell, it wasn't on Patrick's radar.

The notion of her doing the asking messed with her head more than she cared to admit. It felt as if doing that was upside down. It wasn't as if Fleur was traditional and sentimental – well, not really, not anymore. Nope, she'd seen too much, lived through ups and downs and quite frankly been a bit scarred by life to cling to outdated ideas about how things were supposed to go and be done, but still in some obscure dusty corners of her mind, old narratives lingered. They whispered and sniggered; he proposes, she waits, that's just how it's done.

The whole thing was ridiculous when she picked it apart, but it was still there, front and centre. She huffed a little bit and shifted in her seat, keeping her eyes on the road and mulled over how it might go and what she would do and say. It wasn't about waiting for Patrick and wanting some over-the-top, down-on-one-knee moment. It wasn't about expecting Patrick to prove something or anything like that. But a part of her, some deeply ingrained old-fashioned part, had always assumed that if she ever got married again, it would happen to her, not because of her.

Yet, here she was, driving down a dual-carriageway, actively scheming to be the one who asked a man to marry her on a tropical beach. She'd have to have a plan, maybe start a list in one of her books. Or maybe even do it right on the spur of the moment and wait until they were in Maui, standing in the very place she could see in her mind—a beach at sunset, warm air, soft waves, a feeling of absolute rightness, perhaps a rainbow. She could just say it then and there and totally surprise him. Her stomach fluttered and turned over in sheer disbelief at herself. Who even was she?

Percolating the whys and wherefores through her mind, she watched the traffic shift around her; cars slipping into different lanes, people going wherever they were going, no doubt none of them agonising over the gender politics of a marriage proposal they were cooking up in their head. One that had come from nowhere and no one else on the planet had an iota of an idea about. One that she was now so fixated on, it was driving her a little bit around the twist.

Thinking about the bride in the picture on her desk, she perused the traditional way she'd been married before. The ring, the wedding, the life that was supposed to follow, and look how that had turned out. Absolutely dreadful. She wasn't the girl in the white dress anymore, though. She was someone so very different, grown up and out of that old life and had built a new one.

She tapped the steering wheel and nodded, feeling ridiculously happy with herself and excited at the same time. Not that long ago, she'd thought that Patrick was going to dump her. Now, here she was, the decision settled. *Ding-a-ling.* She was going to ask him to marry her to make the forever ring really true and cement it with the law.

Fleur flicked the indicator on and overtook the German lorry, barely registering the movement as her mind continued its circling. The reality of what she was planning was settling properly, digging its heels in and making itself known. She was actually going to do it, of that she was adamant. It wasn't just a passing thought, not some vague idea she'd toss aside in a few days. It was real, and all she had to do was work out how. The clarity felt amazing.

How did one go about proposing when one had never, in all their years, even imagined doing it again, let alone being the one to do the asking? Did she need a ring, a speech, an occasion? Would Patrick want a ring? He wasn't exactly the jewellery-wearing type. Perhaps a watch, but that didn't seem quite right. Or maybe something different entirely that meant something to them, what, she had no idea. It wasn't just about a ring, though. That was the easy bit, really. It was the moment and how she was going to deliver it that tripped her up the most.

It wasn't as if they'd sat down and had long conversations about marriage. They were good together, steady, solid, but marriage hadn't ever been on the table. At least not in the sense that she knew Patrick had given it any serious thought; she was fairly sure he hadn't. She could almost hear his voice now, half amused, half incredulous. "You're asking me?"

Fleur groaned at the possibility that Patrick might not say yes. Not because he didn't love her or want to be with her, but because it simply wasn't on his radar. Her stomach flipped at the thought, but she batted it away. Nope. She wasn't going to let herself get worked up over that part, she was doing it, end of.

Checking her mirrors and merging into the left lane, traffic thickened slightly as they approached a service station. She wasn't stopping, but the sight of cars pulling in, people getting out, stretching their legs, grabbing overpriced coffee all made her suddenly aware things were different in her regular old humdrum commute to a business centre in some obscure part of the country. Today, here she was perusing the ins and outs of a marriage proposal; hers. Gulp.

About twenty minutes later, she'd arrived in the car park of the hotel, pulled out her day-to-day notebook and started a list.

1. Decide how to do it. (Big moment? Casual conversation? Blurt it out?)
2. Figure out the ring situation. (Jewellery? A watch? Something symbolic?)
3. Pick the right time. (where?)
4. Don't overthink it. (already failing spectacularly, hahaha.)

Fleur chewed her lip as she looked down at her notebook. The reality was, she could plan it to within an inch of its life, but at the end of the day, it would be what it would be. Patrick loved her. That part wasn't in doubt. And she loved him enough to want to say this is forever, let's make it official. Simple. That was all that really mattered, and she'd figure it out as she went.

The thought sent a weird tingle of nerves and exhilaration through her. All she had to figure out was how, when, and where to do it. She wanted to marry Patrick; that part wasn't up for debate. Our Champo just needed to make it happen. She tapped the side of her head with the first two fingers of her right hand and laughed to herself at what her dad would have said. He'd probably tell her she was off her rocker. Would he have been that wrong?

23

An hour later, Fleur was standing at the podium of a small training room with one of the staff from the hotel—a roly-poly woman, whose hair looked as if it had a life of its own, who was trying to work out what was wrong with the connection between the screen and Cassy's laptop. As she stopped herself from sighing and shaking her head, she realised she was going to have to deliver the training session without the aid of her slides, which made the whole thing a whole lot harder. Not that she hadn't been there before; she had, a few times over the years. It wasn't *that* bad as long as Cassy was there to back her up, which, of course, she was. It was just irritating how so many facilities bragged about what they could provide and many times the actual places themselves didn't match what was on offer.

As she stood there watching the woman, who clearly had no idea what she was doing, fiddle with the cables, Cassy came in through the double doors at the back with another man from the hotel. The tall, skinny man in drainpipe trousers and a grubby shirt looked harassed, and Fleur watched in bemusement as if observing some kind of strange, not-very-funny play, as the man, who looked as if he needed a good wash, tried to mess with one of the wires. He said it was probably something to do with the Wi-Fi and that an extra cable would help. All Fleur could think about as she stood there observing was the fact that she was going to ask Patrick to make things more permanent. Wedding bells pealed in her ears. White veils flapped in the wind.

Precisely nine hours later, Fleur was sitting in the same hotel, but this time in the bar—a grotty-looking affair that appeared not to have had a lick of paint since the 90s, and where someone in their wisdom had designed an entire wall of tinted grey windows looking out onto an industrial estate, the only view being piles of shipping containers. Fleur grimaced as she took a sip of the packet-mix made margarita in her hand cobbled together by someone without a clue. Nodding as she listened to Cassy telling her about her middle son's birthday list, which included a video game that was far too old for him, she could barely concentrate on what Cassy was saying and was biding her time until the opportunity arose to fill Cassy in on her plan.

She'd waited until they were a couple of drinks in, had thoroughly debriefed about the day, and had spent a significant amount of time decompressing about how the session had gone before gearing up to mention what was really on her mind. She waited for Cassy to finish going on about her middle son's birthday and smiled as she took a sip of her drink.

Cassy frowned. 'What's that look? I haven't seen that look for a long time.'

Fleur started to giggle, the effects of the margaritas, although they were not particularly nice, they were potent, clearly taking effect. 'I've been thinking about something...'

'Oh wow, that sounds dangerous,' Cassy giggled and took a huge sip of her drink, licking the salt off the edges of the glass and making a face. 'God, this stuff is disgusting. Why are we drinking it?'

'Ha, ha, yes, you're right. Anyway, anyway—'

'Yep. What have you got to tell me? Let me guess. Hmm…'

Fleur pressed her lips together and shook her head. 'No, no, you'll never guess.'

'What are you up to?'

'So, what would you think about coming to Hawaii, to Maui, in fact?'

Cassy frowned. 'What are you talking about? What on holiday? Yeah, right. Pigs might fly. What are you saying?'

'I'm saying, do you think you would be able to get to Maui, with Patrick and I?'

Cassy blinked. 'Fleur, you seem to have forgotten that I have three children and a husband.'

'Yes, yes, I mean, you know, you could come with them or without them.'

'Why would I want to come on holiday with you?' Cassy shook her head. 'This margarita is laced with something that is messing with your head.'

'Well, because it's not just going to be a holiday.'

Cassy side-eyed. 'You're not making any sense. You're speaking in riddles.'

'I'm going to ask Patrick to marry me. Or at least make things permanent with me. And the more I have thought about it, the more I've decided that I want to do it while we're away.'

Cassy nearly fell off her stool, spilt her drink, and shook her head as she plonked herself back down again. She stared at Fleur, wide-eyed, shaking her head back and forth, not saying anything for a moment, blinking over and over again, and then she coughed. 'I literally don't know what to say. I've never been more floored or wrong-footed in my life. Where on earth has this come from? You are going to ask him to marry you! You? Like really? Wow!'

Fleur giggled and downed the rest of her margarita in one. 'I don't know. The other day, I had my notebooks out, then everything that's happened with Lucy, and then I started thinking about Patrick, and the fact that we don't live together, etcetera, etcetera, etcetera. The more my mind went on, the more it tumbled further and further and further, and I thought, I'm going to ask him before it's too late. I might be dead tomorrow...' She held out her hand with her "forever ring" as Patrick had called it. 'I want to do something more than this. I want to live with him. I just love him, Cass.'

Cassy shook her head in disbelief, still staring at Fleur as if she had grown a second head. 'Right, well, this is mad, but I love it.' She waved at the bartender and pointed to Fleur's drink. 'Another one?'

Fleur chuckled. 'We shouldn't, they're awful.'

'They *are* awful,' Cassy grimaced. 'Like a weird lime-flavoured cleaning product, however this conversation requires alcohol.'

The bartender, a bored-looking man in his late twenties with a crooked tie and the general air of someone who wanted to be anywhere but behind the bar, wandered over.

'Two more margaritas, please,' Cassy said, resting her elbow on the sticky bar.

The bartender barely nodded before shuffling away to assemble more of whatever packet mix monstrosity they were drinking.

'So, you're serious about this? Like, actually serious?'

'I think so. I don't know, Cass. I want something more than what we have now. I don't want to just drift along and then suddenly look back and think, "Oh, I should have done something."'

Cassy studied Fleur. 'Yeah. Yeah, I get that but I am shocked. I didn't see this coming.'

'And it just feels right, you know?' Fleur shrugged. 'I don't want some big, fancy thing, but I *do* want it to mean something. The more I think about it, the more I think I want to do it in Maui. I mean as settings go, it's pretty up there and we've got the flights booked and hotel sorted. It just means I would need to get our nearest and dearest out too.'

The bartender returned, putting down two more margaritas that were the exact same radioactive green-yellow as the previous drinks. Fleur and Cassy exchanged a look before clinking their glasses together.

'To whatever this is, cheers.' Cassy took a sip and immediately winced. 'Dear God, it's worse this time.'

Fleur laughed. 'I think he must have forgotten to put in the tequila. It just tastes like sugar-y toilet cleaner.'

'Fitting, really for this place. Cheers.' Cassy tapped her fingers against her glass. 'So, I'm going to ignore the fact of how you're actually going to ask Patrick to marry you and go straight to Hawaii, Maui.'

'Maui, yep.'

'Technically, we could come. I mean, in theory. But I don't know if we'd have the money for flights, and I don't know if we could get the boys looked after.'

Fleur nodded, stirring the sad, artificial-looking lime wedge in her drink with the end of her straw. 'Yeah, I did think about that. I mean, you could bring them? Make a holiday out of it? Your mum could come to help with them?'

Cassy let out a short laugh. 'The idea of taking my mother on a long-haul flight with my children is *horrifying*. She'd moan about everything. It's a flat no from me.'

'But she would do it?'

'Oh, she'd do it. She loves an excuse to tell me how much she's doing for me.' Cassy pulled a face. 'I'll have a think. It would be amazing, but it just depends on logistics.'

Fleur nodded again. 'I get it.'

'And Wendy?'

'She's already mentioned maybe coming for the weekend. It's not so far from there.'

'And your mother?' Cassy raised her eyebrows.

'Yeah. Well. That's the thing, isn't it?'

Cassy cocked her head to the side. 'Would you even want her there?'

'I don't know.' Fleur traced the rim of her glass with her finger. 'I wouldn't have any choice, but I also think she'd make it all about her. She's good at doing that. Very good.'

'Oh, she definitely would. She'd tell everyone how she'd always wanted to get married in Maui but never got the chance and how marvellous it was that her daughter was finally doing something exciting with her life.'

Fleur groaned. 'God, you're right. You nailed it. She'd spend the whole time talking about Marvin and his deep, existential connection to the ocean breeze or some rubbish.'

Cassy cackled. 'Shame if she couldn't come.'

'She's still my mum, Cass.'

Cassy nodded and looked apologetic. 'Sorry, I know.'

Fleur took another sip of her drink, ignoring how utterly awful it was. 'It's a lot to think about.'

'Yeah, it is, but for what it's worth, I love this for you.'

Fleur smiled. 'Yeah?'

'Yeah.' Cassy raised her glass. 'To you, making a completely uncharacteristic, impulsive, slightly chaotic decision and for me going along with it. I am *so* glad we're friends.'

Fleur clinked her glass against Cassy's again, grinning.

'To me and you and a very cray-cray idea.'

24

It was the next day, and Fleur felt as if she was in the same scene twenty-four hours later, only the roly-poly woman had been replaced by another woman with unwashed hair which jutted out in odd shapes all over the place, deep rings under her eyes, and smelling of two-day-old smoke. Fleur took a couple of steps away from the woman and flicked her eyes up at Cassy, who was rummaging through her huge work folder, looking for the backup handouts they always kept in case the laptop didn't work. Which, today, it wasn't. The woman with the unwashed hair called over, 'Why don't you go and get a coffee, and I'll see if I can call Martin from the office to see if he can sort it out?'

Fleur smiled and muttered under her breath to Cassy that she didn't think Martin from the office would be able to do anything since the day before, he had been more than useless. The coffee sounded nice, though. Following the woman's instructions, they walked out of the function room and made their way down a narrow corridor to the same bar they'd been in the night before, which had now been repurposed as a place where people sat with laptops, drinking coffee. After ordering, they sat down by the windows, looking out over the shipping containers.

'So, any more thoughts on what we discussed last night?' Cassy asked, raising her eyebrows. 'Or was that just because we were a few margaritas in and were looking out over the pits of the earth so you thought you'd throw something mind-blowing into the mix?'

'I haven't changed my mind, nope. I don't know how I'm going to ask him, though, and I need to get a wriggle on. What do you think?'

Cassy narrowed her eyes and made a wincing face. 'I really don't know. I don't think I'm the right person to ask about how you're going to ask your partner to marry you.'

'Maybe I'll just do it casually. I mean, it's not like I'm going to get down on one knee or anything like that, am I?'

'Well, you could either go one way or the other, as far as I see it. You could go full proposal, or you could just serve him up a round of beans on toast and suggest it.'

'I don't know if I like the sound of either of those.' Fleur giggled. 'Beans on toast is not quite what I had in mind.'

'How about you do it over dinner or something?' Cassy took another sip of her coffee and glanced out at the grey-tinted windows overlooking the shipping containers. 'Honestly, this has to be one of the worst views I've ever had while drinking coffee.'

Fleur smirked. 'It's a real aesthetic choice, isn't it? Whoever thought about putting the windows on this side. At least there are some trees on the other side. Industrial chic meets post-apocalyptic wasteland.'

Cassy chuckled, shaking her head. 'Anyway, back to you. What about Lucy?'

'What about Lucy?'

'Last night you said I was the only one you've told. Are you going to tell her first or wait until it's done?'

Fleur stared at the uneven foam on top of her coffee. 'I don't know. Part of me thinks I should run it past her. Like, get her thoughts on it, however, another part of me feels like *it's my life, my decision*. I don't need permission. Then there are the funny spells to consider.'

Cassy nodded. 'I get that, but she is your daughter, and you and Patrick getting married, well, it does change things.'

Fleur twisted her lips. 'Yeah. It does. But I don't want her to feel like I'm looking for approval. It's not that.'

'No, I know, but she might appreciate the heads-up before it happens. Or at least before she finds out second-hand.'

'I suppose. But what if she doesn't like the idea?'

Cassy raised an eyebrow. 'Then what? Are you not going to do it?'

'No, I am. I don't want her to feel weird about it. It's always been the two of us, more or less, and she's grown up now, I know, but I don't want her to think that things will change too much.'

'I think she'll be fine, Fleur. She likes Patrick. More than that, she trusts him. I don't think she'd be against it. If anything, she'd probably just want to make sure you're sure.'

'That sounds about right.'

Cassy took another sip of coffee. 'So? What's the plan? Talk to her first or tell her after?'

Fleur swirled the last bit of liquid in her cup and watched it settle. 'Maybe I'll just feel it out. If the right moment comes up before, I'll tell her. If not, I'll tell her after I've spoken to Patrick.'

'What's happened about the fainting episodes?'

'Nothing. She's been fine since.'

'Right.'

'It's all very strange. What more can we do when the tests are clear?'

Cassy glanced out at the containers again and shook her head. 'No, nothing, I suppose.'

'It's another reason I want to propose and do it.'

'I still can't believe you had this epiphany in a car on a motorway in England.'

Fleur laughed. 'Not quite; it was while I was in the study, but yeah. Romantic, isn't it?'

Cassy smirked. 'Deeply. Almost as romantic as this depressing coffee shop and our view of rusty metal boxes.'

'Well, it's a moment to remember, one way or another.'

Cassy shook her head. 'I can't argue with that.'

25

. . .

Fleur was lying in the bath. She turned the tap on, and held her fingers under the stream of water, watching as it gushed out in a frothy stream of warmth. She could think about one thing and one thing only: the crazy idea she'd got into her head to propose to the man she loved. She'd even gone and bought a ring, though she wasn't sure Patrick would wear it, but that was beside the point. As she adjusted the hot and cold taps, she wasn't really sure what to think about anything at all. She'd cooked up and schemed something completely out of her comfort zone and totally out of character, and now here she was about to make it happen. No turning back now.

After telling Cassy, she'd decided not to tell anybody else until after the deed was done. Despite a lot of to-ing and fro-ing, she'd decided not to run the fact that she was going to propose to Patrick past Lucy but instead present it to Lucy as a fait accompli. Letting her legs float up and become weightless, she stared at the little white IKEA lantern with perforated stars on the top sitting on the bath caddy and watched as a small battery-powered tealight candle flickered away to itself. As she studied the faux candle and marvelled at how good and realistic it was, she pondered not telling Lucy about the plan for Patrick.

Part of her thought it would be best to tell Lucy what she was thinking about doing; another part decided it wasn't any of Lucy's business. At the end of the day, she was the one who wanted to marry Patrick, and to be honest, not that she would ever voice her thoughts, she was a little bit over everything *always* being about Lucy. However, on the other hand, Fleur getting married, if indeed Patrick agreed, was significant. It would be something that majorly affected Lucy, so Fleur had tried to consider that too. The question that gnawed at her now was whether to confide in Lucy before taking the plunge. On one hand, Lucy was her daughter, who had often been her confidante, the person she'd been through a lot with. Sharing the monumental decision with her seemed only natural to some extent. On the other hand, Fleur felt deep down it was a decision she needed to make independently. Her relationship with Patrick was personal, and she didn't need anyone or anything to cloud her judgement. On top of that was the fact that if things didn't go as planned, she would prefer to handle the fallout privately.

While Cassy's support had been reassuring, it had also added a layer of pressure. Now, someone else knew about her intentions, and Fleur felt the weight of expectation. If she told Lucy, that pressure would intensify. What Fleur wanted to avoid was everybody knowing—like her sister, her daughter, and even her mum – and it becoming a massive thing. If she kept putting it off or indeed completely changed her mind altogether and everyone knew it would just turn into a big drama. Sighing, Fleur wiggled her legs under the water and imagined Lucy's reaction: surprise, excitement, and then, if she knew Lucy, there would be a barrage of questions and what-ifs.

Mulling the whole thing over, she decided that an upcoming speakeasy night at the deli she and Patrick were attending seemed like the perfect setting for the proposal. The intimate atmosphere, soft jazz, casual setting, candlelight, and the two of them in the roundabout place they'd met felt right. But with the evening fast approaching, Fleur knew she had to make a decision about whether to involve Lucy or not.

As the water began to cool, Fleur made up her mind. She would keep her plans to herself. Once she had Patrick's answer, she would share the news with Lucy. She let out a slow breath and dipped her fingers under the water, watching the ripples spread across the surface. She traced the patterns, feeling the weight of the day settle into her bones, the warmth easing the tension in her shoulders. As she reached for the soap on the wooden bath tray, she looked at the forever ring sitting right where her wedding ring had once been. The thought of her old wedding ring was suddenly in her face, a bit of a ghost of the past, a whisper of a different life. A memory drifted in, similar to the ones she'd had when she'd seen the picture of her with her dad.

How funny that back in the day she'd believed in the whole thing: the ceremony, the promises, the idea that she was in love and that it would be forever. And here she was doing it again with someone else. She could almost hear and see that day a blur of white and gold and the sense that she was doing the right thing and everything was exactly as it was meant to be, except, of course, it hadn't been. It really, really hadn't been.

Just as she was thinking about getting out of the bath, her arms draped over the edge, her phone buzzed on the stool next to her. The vibration rattled against the wooden surface and made her jolt slightly. Stretching an arm out, she lifted the phone and flipped it over to check the screen: Lucy. Fleur hesitated for a second. It was almost as if the universe had heard her thoughts and nudged Lucy to call her. She swiped to answer. 'Hey, Luce.'

'Hi, Mum.' Lucy sounded bright and casual. 'You okay? Are you in the bath? There's an echo.'

Fleur lifted a leg and let it float for a second, watching as the water lapped around her skin. 'I am.'

'Nice. A bit of self-care. Love that for you.'

Fleur smiled. 'Not sure it's self-care as such, but warm water helps for me, as you know.'

'What's it helping with? Problems at work?'

Fleur's heart gave a little kick. For a split second, she considered blurting out that she was planning to propose, that she had a ring, a plan, and a scheme, but she didn't.

Lucy continued. 'Anyway, I was just calling to say hi.'

'What's been going on at Dad's?'

'Not much. I've been at work mostly, so I haven't really seen them.'

'Right. How's the baby?'

'Fine, as far as I know. What's going on with you?'

Fleur pictured Lucy's face and how she might react if she told her what she was planning. She imagined that there would be surprise, then excitement, and then questions. 'You know me, Luce. I'm just plodding along as usual.'

'Alright then, I'll leave you to your bath. Don't make any major life decisions in there, okay?'

Fleur swallowed. *Just a small life decision incoming.* 'No promises.'

'I'll see you at the weekend.'

'Yep, looking forward to it. We'll go for a nice lunch. How are you feeling? Any of your funny spells?'

'Nothing. Not even a sniff of one.'

'Good.'

'Love you.'

'Love you lots.'

As soon as Fleur hung up, she popped the phone down and

stared at the ceiling. Lucy would find out soon enough. For now, the proposal was just for her.

26

Fleur stood in the kitchen with a cloth in one hand and a bottle of spray in the other, having just moved all the appliances and pots from the worktop onto the kitchen table. She'd sprayed and wiped the worktop until it shone. A fresh breeze came through the window, and she smirked to herself at the state of the situation around her. Here she was, going through the motions of a nice, normal life; a regular old cottage in a nice area, cleaning the kitchen, doing her chores, getting ready for the next work week. All of it normal and nice while on the inside, she was gearing up for a mammoth moment in her life. She, Fleur Champion, the woman who never did anything out of the ordinary, was going to pop the question to her unsuspecting partner.

As she took the little tray out of the bottom of the toaster, tipped its contents into the bin, cleaned it out, and slid it back into place, she wondered how the evening ahead of her was going to go. She and Patrick were off to a speakeasy, and she'd decided to take the bull by the horns and was planning to ask him over chowder. Not that she had any clue whether or not she was doing the right thing, but she'd decided that you only live once. Just as she was spraying the side of the kettle and wiping it until it gleamed, her phone buzzed with a call from Patrick.

'Hey, how are you?' Patrick asked.

Fleur felt ridiculously nervous about the evening ahead. 'Yeah, good. You?'

'You sure? You don't sound it.'

Fleur felt a quiver of butterflies go around her stomach. 'I'm fine. How are you?'

'Yeah, busy. I've got that meeting to go to, I'll leave as soon as it's over, so hopefully, I won't be late if the traffic's not too bad. But it is Friday afternoon.'

'Well, hopefully, you'll be home in time.'

Patrick exhaled on the other end of the line, the sound of rustling papers and a muffled voice in the background. 'I mean, I should be back in time, but you know how it is. One idiot on the M25 and suddenly my ETA goes from a civilised six-thirty to send out a search party a few days later.'

Fleur smiled, still wiping the kettle as if her life depended on it. 'Yeah, well, you would choose to try and run an empire for a living. Hardly surprising you end up spending half your time in tailbacks behind lorries with all the places you go.'

'Correction, badly driven lorries and honestly, some of these drivers make me worry for the future of humanity.'

'Good to know you've got your usual optimism about you today.' Fleur chuckled.

'It's part of my charm.'

'Lol.'

'Lol? You sound odd. Why do I get the sense you're up to something? Are you okay? You're not coming down with something, are you?'

Fleur gripped the cleaning spray. 'No, no. I'm not up to anything. Just head down cleaning and getting stuff ready for next week.'

'You definitely are. You're weird, and you keep doing that voice you do when you're pretending everything's fine but actually something's up.'

Fleur shuddered. 'There's nothing up. Can't a woman just want to go out for dinner without it being some big conspiracy?'

'A woman can, yes. You, on the other hand...'

'I'm just happy.'

'Hmm, it's not that; it's your voice. Suspicious.'

Fleur chirped. 'It's not suspicious, Patrick. I'm just full of the joys of spring.'

'Well, if I'm about to get lured into some elaborate scheme, can you at least promise me there'll be a good few beers this evening after the week I've had?'

Fleur rolled her eyes, popping the dishcloth onto the worktop. 'There will be beer and chowder. You should know; you have more experience of these speakeasies than me.'

'Good. That's all I ask. Alright, I'm about to go into the meeting, and then I'll set off. Hopefully, I won't get stuck behind some bloke who thinks 40 mph is an appropriate speed for a dual carriageway.'

'You definitely will. Just managing your expectations. I'm very experienced in traffic, unfortunately.'

'If I turn up late and hungry, just ply me with food and drink.'

'Duly noted.'

'See you later, when I will find out what you are up to.'

Patrick hung up, and Fleur stood for a moment, looking out the window. He'd got wind of her just by the sound of her voice. He was going to spend the entire meal trying to figure out what she was up to. Great. She glanced at the kitchen table, still covered in appliances and pots. Perhaps she'd change their plans, forget about the proposal altogether, stay in and, as Cassy had said, propose over beans on toast.

Funny, really, Patrick was already suspicious. She'd clearly not make a very good spy. He was going to turn up, sit opposite her in the deli, and spend the entire evening watching her like a hawk trying to figure out what she was up to. She picked up the cloth again and wiped the already spotless kettle. Maybe she should just cancel the whole thing. Stay in, open a bottle of wine, and forget she'd ever had the utterly ridiculous proposal idea in the first place. Pulling out a chair, she sat down, staring at the box holding the ring in front of her. She still hadn't worked out how she was going to do it, though she'd watched enough YouTube videos on proposing. She laughed to herself as she imagined just slipping it into the conversation between bites of chowder.

'Oh, by the way, Patrick, fancy getting married?' She said to herself. No. Way too blunt.

'You know, I love you more than anything, and I'd really like to spend the rest of my life with you, so what do you think? Marry me?' God, no. Too serious. He'd probably panic and run a country mile.

She leaned back in her chair, sighing. She needed something in between. Not too casual, not too dramatic. Something very "them". Deciding to just wing it, she tried not to think about it. After all, that was how she'd ended up in the situation in the first place. She hadn't planned to propose, and yet here she was, sitting in her kitchen, running through every possible way to pop the question like she was rehearsing lines for a play.

After checking the time, she left the kitchen, walked upstairs, and pulled open her wardrobe. What did one wear to propose? Something casual? Like it was just another dinner? Or something special? She pulled out a soft, floaty dress that made her feel nice but wasn't over the top. Slipping it on, she went to the mirror, smoothed it down, held her head to the side and made a few expressions. Ridiculous. Shaking her head, she decided she was making it so much harder than it needed to be and she'd just pop the question at some point in the meal and be done with it. Patrick loved her. She loved him. That was all that mattered. Easy. All she had to do was have a shower, get ready, make sure she looked like the bee's knees, and then actually do the deed. By the way her insides felt, easier said than done.

27

Fleur stirred her drink, watching as candlelight flickered against Patrick's face. He was mid-story, something about a driver he'd encountered earlier in the week, gesturing slightly with his free hand while the other rested against his glass. 'And then, get this, the bloke actually leans out his window and tells me I don't know how to drive. As if he wasn't the one doing twenty-five in a fifty while swerving across both lanes.'

Fleur laughed and tried to look interested, though her brain was only half-listening. Normally, she'd be fully engaged, teasing him about his dramatic retellings, and the banter would be bubbling back and forth, but all she could think about was the small box in her lap.

'So, yeah. That was Tuesday,' Patrick finished, shaking his head and taking a sip of his drink. 'How about you? How was your week?'

Fleur coughed, forcing her thoughts back to the conversation. 'Oh, you know. The usual stuff at work. A bit of a disaster with the training session, but Cassy and I managed.'

Patrick smirked. 'Let me guess. I'll go with the fact that the technology provided by the hotel let you down again or there was no parking, or both.'

'Obviously. The usual disaster with the hotel not having the facilities it claimed.'

Patrick chuckled, tipping his chair back slightly. 'That's what happens when you're a trainer for a living.'

'Or maybe I'm the problem,' Fleur said drily, taking a sip of her wine.

'Nah, never.' Patrick grinned.

Fleur rolled her eyes, but her heart was pounding. How was she supposed to just drop "will you marry me" into the conversation? *Oh, by the way, Patrick, fancy making things permanent?*

'Speaking of disasters,' Patrick continued, unaware of the emotional chaos going on in Fleur's head, 'I haven't even thought about what I need for LA and Maui. I keep thinking, "I'll do it at the weekend," and then the weekend comes, and I'm too busy doing anything but that. I have to get my presentation done and dusted and sent off to them soon, too.'

Fleur bristled at the mention of the holiday and her very new plans for it. 'I don't know why you're acting like you need to plan. You'll pack about four T-shirts and a pair of shorts and call it done.'

'You're not wrong. I'm just looking forward to it now. It's been a while since I've had a proper break.'

Fleur nodded and she gripped her glass. He had no idea. The idea of asking him to marry her suddenly felt more than gigantic or huge or anything. It felt monstrous and ridiculous, and she felt like an *idiot*. It had seemed so clear in her head, but now, sitting there, watching him, she wasn't sure she'd be able to get the words out or even if she wanted to. She was certain she was barking up the wrong tree. What in the name of goodness did she think she was playing at?

Patrick waved his hand in front of her face. 'Fleur?'

Fleur blinked, realising Patrick was watching the look on

her face intently and had clearly clocked that something was off. 'Sorry.'

'Are you okay? See, I knew it. You're acting all out of sorts.'

Fleur willed herself to be normal. 'Yeah. Just thinking about everything we need to sort before we go.'

'Like what?'

Like whether or not I'm about to completely change our entire relationship dynamic by asking you to marry me. She shrugged. 'Just the usual. Making sure we've got all the travel stuff sorted, double-checking we haven't forgotten anything, finishing and finalising things at work. We've still got a while to go but I like to be very organised.'

Patrick tilted his head slightly. 'Are you sure that's all that's on your mind?'

Fleur picked up her drink again, taking another sip to buy time. 'Of course. What else would there be?'

Patrick squinted as if he didn't quite believe her, but before he could say anything else, their food arrived. Alice beamed and placed two steaming bread bowls in front of them, the tops cut off and resting on the side of the plates. The thick, creamy chowder inside smelled incredible, rich with seafood and herbs, the steam curling into the dim light.

'Oh, this looks so good.'

Fleur was grateful for the distraction. 'I've been thinking about this chowder all day.'

'Same.'

Fleur dipped her spoon into the creamy broth; it was ridiculously good, perfectly seasoned, velvety, packed with fish and prawns, and just what she'd come to expect from a deli speakeasy. She closed her eyes for a second, letting the flavours settle.

'That good?' Patrick teased.

'Never gets old.'

Patrick laughed, and Fleur's mind drifted back to the question of the day. Maybe she could say something simple. Something easy, but then did she really want it to be casual? It wasn't just any old question. Nope, it was *the* question.

Patrick glanced up. 'You're definitely acting weird. You've hardly said a word now I come to think about it. I've been rambling on about my week and you've not said much.'

Fleur coughed. 'I am not acting weird.'

Patrick pointed his spoon at her. 'You are. You keep looking at me like you're about to tell me I've got two weeks to live. What is going on? Is there something wrong with Luce? Oh, for the love of God, not Ben again…'

'Nope.'

'Are you planning something?'

Fleur's heart just about stopped. 'Like what?'

Patrick narrowed his eyes. 'I don't know. That's why I'm asking. But you are up to something.'

Fleur shoved another piece of bread in her mouth. 'Honestly.'

Patrick wiped his mouth with a napkin. 'Don't tell me. I'll figure it out eventually.'

Fleur swallowed, nodding. 'I'm sure you will.'

As she sat there, Fleur's heart raced. The words were stuck to the roof of her mouth. She just couldn't get herself to actually say them. Best laid plans.

28

So much for Fleur making a big, grand gesture with her proposal. The whole meal had passed in a strange blur. A blur where Fleur's mind constantly circled around the idea of asking Patrick to marry her, only for her to lose her nerve each and every time. A little dissenting voice hissed at her that she was barking up the wrong tree entirely. She'd questioned what she was doing, so much so that the evening hadn't been all that enjoyable for either her or Patrick.

Leaving the deli, they walked in silence towards the River Lovely, the faint chatter and music from the High Street fading behind them. The night air was cool, the lighthouse towered in the distance, and as they approached the jetty, water lapped against the pilings, reflecting the glow of the streetlamps here and there in little pools of golden light. At the wharf, the riverboat chugged in, its hull knocking against the wooden jetty, and the strings of fairy lights hung around the vessel dropped shimmering patterns onto the dark water. Colin called out as he slung a rope over the bollard. 'Steady.'

Fleur watched the boat bump and judder as Colin cupped

his hands to his mouth. 'Getting a bit nippy down here on the river tonight!'

'Evening,' Patrick called back as he stepped aboard, Fleur following close behind. She was surprised to see that nobody else was getting on; there were only a couple of passengers seated at the back, wrapped up against the chill, and no one behind them. Patrick made his way to the top deck, settling into a seat while Fleur leaned against the railing. The lights of Lovely Bay twinkled on either side of the river, casting long, shifting reflections across the surface. Fleur exhaled slowly, watching the town drift past, and realised she'd missed her opportunity for popping the question and that she'd have to revert to Plan B. Not that she had a Plan B, but anyway.

At the next stop, the couple who had been sitting at the back of the boat got up and disembarked. Colin hung about for a bit, seeing if anyone was walking in the direction of the jetty before pulling away again, and the boat chugged down the river.

Patrick stood up and leaned over the railings, taking in the air. 'How nice is it this evening?' He looked up at the stars and shook his head.

Fleur hadn't really said a word since they'd left the deli, still wondering whether or not she was going to pop the question. It all looked so simple in the movies, even though normally it was the other way around—the old-school tradition already set in place. Here she was the nervous one and no longer a young girl dreaming of a white dress, but a bona fide grown-up with a lot of life experience on her hands wanting to make what they had permanent. All so very surreal.

She leaned over the railing, looking at the water glistening beneath the boat, then followed Patrick's gaze to the sky full of stars. It was a cool, crisp night without a cloud in sight, a deep, inky black as if the sky and stars would last forever. The sort of night Fleur loved, especially since moving to Lovely Bay. She looked up, didn't say anything, and stood lost in thought for a moment.

Patrick put his arm around her waist and squeezed. 'Are you sure you're okay? You're very quiet.'

'I'm fine. Just a lot on my mind.'

Patrick frowned. 'Is there something I don't know about? Is it the Lucy thing?'

'No, no, well, yes, of course, I'm worried about Lucy, but no, it's just, you know, stuff. I'm fine. It's nothing, just thinking about bits and bobs, you know.'

'As long as you're okay.' Patrick gave her another squeeze.

Fleur suddenly forgot all about the ring and all the ideas she'd had in her head and just blurted it out. 'Will you marry me, Patrick?'

Patrick froze and swore. 'What the heck? What?'

'Sorry...' Fleur winced. 'Bugger, it was meant to be, oh dear...'

Patrick stared at her, then started to laugh. 'What? Where has this come from?'

'I asked you if you'd marry me!'

'I gathered that! What like this all of a sudden? Right here leaning over the water, out of the blue?'

'I know, I know.' Fleur giggled. 'I meant to...'

Patrick was still laughing, shaking his head in disbelief. 'Fleur, are you actually asking me to marry you right now? Like standing here as if you're asking me if I want a cup of tea.'

'Yes! I mean, obviously, yes!' Fleur flapped her hands in front of her face as if she was trying to cool herself down. 'I had this whole plan; a big, grand gesture, and then the meal was weird, and I kept bottling it, and then I thought I was barking up the wrong tree, and then I got all in my head about the whole tradition thing and then, well and then here we are.'

'And then you just blurted it out?'

'Yes! And now I don't know what to do with myself because this was not how I pictured it at all!'

The boat swayed slightly as they drifted further down the river, the water glistening with reflections of the fairy lights. The whole town twinkled on either side of them and the lighthouse glinted in the distance. It should have been romantic, one of those magical, cinematic moments. But instead, Fleur was standing, hands on her hips, half-laughing, half-panicking, while Patrick stared at her like she'd just announced she was moving to Mars.

'So, what do you want me to say?' Patrick joked.

'Well, I mean, you could say yes. That would be a start.'

Patrick took a step closer. 'Of course, yes. I love you, Champo.'

Fleur's mouth opened, but no words came out. Then, instead of crying, as emotion overwhelmed her, she started to giggle. 'I feel like I'm supposed to cry or something, but I'm so happy and this hasn't gone as I thought it would at all.'

Patrick frowned. 'I don't know whether to be flattered or offended at this reaction.'

Fleur clutched the railing. 'This is a huge life moment and we're on the riverboat...'

Patrick chuckled and wrapped his arms around her. 'And I have a brand new fiancée.'

The word "fiancée" made Fleur go all mushy. 'Oh God, I'm someone's fiancée now. That's weird.'

'Yes, that is generally what happens when you propose to someone.'

'I didn't think that far.'

Patrick kissed Fleur. 'I love you, Champo.'

'I feel like I should redo it. Like, rewind and do the whole thing again properly.'

'Oh no, we're sticking with this. You asked, I said yes, and now you're stuck with me forever. No take-backs.'

Fleur looked at Patrick and then around her at Lovely as the weight of the moment settled. Stars shimmered above, the water glowed beneath them, and the boat chugged as Fleur let what had just happened sink in. She was going to marry Patrick.

She couldn't quite believe what had just happened. One minute, she'd been standing there, lost in thought, second-guessing herself for the hundredth time, and the next, she'd just blurted it out without an ounce of grace. Now here she was with her cards on the table. It felt huge, exciting, all-around nice and strange when she rolled the fact that she was going to get married around her head. It sounded like something out of someone else's life, something that belonged to the younger, more idealistic Fleur who'd once thought life followed neat, predictable paths. But nothing about her life in the previous few years had been neat, predictable, or smooth. In actual fact, it had been up, down, left, right, back and forth, and everywhere else in between. Here it was taking another turn altogether. 'This is not how I thought it would go.'

'How did you think it would go?'

'Well, for starters, it was meant to be over dinner by candlelight. I was supposed to be cool, elegant, maybe even romantic. There was a whole vision in my head; a beautifully put-together proposal, where I'd be collected and charming, and you'd be stunned into speechlessness by my impeccable timing and heartfelt delivery. Ha, joking, but yeah, not blurting it out like that.'

Patrick chuckled. 'Instead, you panicked, flapped your hands, and asked me as if you were offering me a biscuit.'

Fleur groaned. 'Exactly. I'm a disaster.'

'Works for me.'

Patrick nodded in Colin's direction. 'I think Colin's about to come over. He must have witnessed the whole thing.'

Fleur turned just as she heard slow, deliberate clapping. From the back of the boat, Colin leaned against the railing, beaming. 'Well, I guess I'll be the first to say congratulations. That was some show you put on there. I've seen a lot on this river, but this? This is a first. I don't think we've ever had a marriage proposal here, not that I know about, anyway.'

'Ahh.'

Colin shook his head. 'That was very nice. Congratulations, you two!'

Fleur chuckled. 'Thank you. Did you enjoy that?'

'Absolutely. What a way to end an evening shift. I was not disappointed.'

'Thanks, Colin.'

Patrick nodded. 'Appreciate it, mate.'

Colin patted Patrick's back. 'Well, I guess that gives us a very good reason to have a few drinks at the pub this weekend.'

'That, I can get behind.' Patrick chuckled.

Colin winked. 'Right, I'll leave you two to enjoy your romantic moment.'

Fleur rolled her eyes as Colin wandered back down the deck. 'The whole of Lovely is going to know about this before dawn.'

Patrick smiled. 'Let them be our guest.'

29

Fleur woke up, blinked a few times, and was rather disoriented about where she was. She'd been having a dream about her dad; she was young and had been upset at a party. Bill was in the dream telling her that, unfortunately, there were not very nice people in the world and that she was okay. For a second, Fleur forgot that Bill had passed away, and then it hit her like a sledgehammer as reality slammed into her brain. She looked over to the other side of the bed to see that Patrick was long gone. Because of years of having to get up in the dark for work, even on the weekend, he was not one to lie-in for long. Fleur suddenly sat bolt upright as another realisation struck her as she remembered what had happened the night before—the proposal. She wasn't quite sure what to think, but she did know that it hadn't gone to plan, that was for sure.

She smiled to herself as she recalled the boat, the startled proposal, and Colin. As the image of it went through her brain, she suddenly remembered that she hadn't even given Patrick the ring. Grabbing her dressing gown and heading down the stairs and into the kitchen, she decided she'd get the ring out later. Reaching for the kettle and after making herself a cup of tea, she went to find Patrick, who was sitting out in the garden.

'Morning.' Patrick looked up from his phone.

'Morning. How are you?'

'Yeah, I'm good. You? You were zonked out when I got up. I'm already on my second cup of tea.'

'Not too bad. I had a dream about my dad, so that was a bit strange.'

'Aww...'

'It was fine, weird though when you realise they're gone.'

'Yep.'

Fleur sat down on the chair opposite Patrick and curled her legs up beneath her. 'You okay?'

'I am. So, any regrets yet?'

Fleur narrowed her eyes and turned her head to the side. 'About what, exactly?'

'About proposing to me in what can only be described as a spur of the moment action.'

'Not quite. I've been planning it for a bit.'

Patrick raised an eyebrow. 'I'm still in shock.'

Fleur took another sip of tea. 'It was a perfectly unique proposal, that's for sure.'

'Unique is one word for it.'

'Charmingly unique.'

'And completely out of the blue,' Patrick countered.

'Spontaneous and memorable.'

Patrick laughed. 'Oh, I'll give you that. I don't think I'll ever forget the moment you just blurted it out and then started laughing.'

Fleur groaned, covering her face with her hands. 'I didn't mean to laugh.'

'It's not every day a man gets proposed to on a boat. It was sweet, I'll give you that. And definitely heartfelt. Romantic, though?' He shook his head. 'Not quite sure it ticks that box.'

Fleur giggled. 'Well, you know what? It doesn't matter. Because you said yes.'

'Yeah. I did.'

Fleur tilted her head. 'And you meant it, right?'

Patrick wrinkled his nose. 'Of course I meant it. I'd have said yes, no matter how you asked.'

Correct answer, Patrick. You can stay.

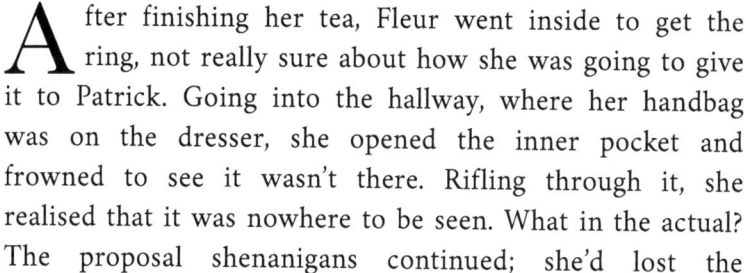

After finishing her tea, Fleur went inside to get the ring, not really sure about how she was going to give it to Patrick. Going into the hallway, where her handbag was on the dresser, she opened the inner pocket and frowned to see it wasn't there. Rifling through it, she realised that it was nowhere to be seen. What in the actual? The proposal shenanigans continued; she'd lost the blooming ring.

Her mind went over the night before; she'd taken the ring out in the deli and had it in her lap, but when she'd baulked on the question, she'd thought she'd tucked the ring back in the inner pocket of her bag, but it wasn't there. She couldn't believe it. After all the palaver and everything that had happened, she hadn't even given Patrick the ring—and not only that, she'd lost it.

Dumping the contents of her handbag onto the kitchen table, as if by some miracle the ring might magically appear amongst the receipts, lip balm, and rogue mints at the bottom, she tutted. As she rummaged, it wasn't there. Taking a deep breath and gripping the edge of the table, she spoke aloud. 'Okay. Think. Think. Think.'

The last time she'd had it was at the deli. She'd taken it out, meaning to give it to Patrick, and then it must have slipped off her lap, or she'd put it down and never picked it up again. No, she'd definitely put it back in her bag. 'Oh, for goodness' sake,' she groaned, rubbing her forehead.

All the build-up in her head, all the drama on the boat, and she hadn't even completed the proposal properly. She was officially the worst person in history at getting engaged. Realising that she must have left the ring in the deli, she went upstairs, quickly got dressed, grabbed her keys and her phone, called out to Patrick that she'd be back soon and headed straight back out of the cottage, practically jogging down the lane towards her car.

The deli was quiet when she arrived, the morning rush long gone. The scent of fresh bread and coffee filled the air as she pushed through the door. She scanned the floor and tables as if she might just spot the ring lying there.

Alice looked up from behind the counter. 'Morning. Coffee? Take-away? You look like you're a bit off-colour.'

'Morning, Alice. Worse. I think I left something here last night. Something important.'

'Oh?' Alice put down the tray she was holding. 'What was it?'

Fleur bit her lip, lowering her voice even though there was barely anyone else in the deli. 'An engagement ring.'

Alice's eyebrows shot up. 'An engagement ring?'

'Yes.' Fleur felt embarrassment creeping in. 'I had it in my lap, and I must have dropped it or left it somewhere and completely forgotten about it.'

Alice let out a slow whistle. 'Well, that's a new one. Most people lose sunglasses or a scarf—not engagement jewellery. Blimey! Did Patrick propose, and what you lost the ring? Ahh! I have Lovely gossip before Birdie. Well, that's a first. Wow! Congratulations!'

Fleur groaned. 'Thank you, but no, it's not mine! It's his.'

'What? I'm lost.'

'Long story. Look, sorry, is there any chance someone handed it in?'

Alice scratched her head. 'We had our usual tidy and set-up for the morning after everyone left, but I don't remember seeing anything. Give me a sec, I'll check out the back here, but I don't think so.'

Fleur's stomach twisted into knots as Alice disappeared into the back. She tapped her fingers against the counter, glancing around as if the ring might reveal itself to her in a moment of divine intervention.

Alice reappeared a minute later, shaking her head. 'Sorry, nope. Nothing back there.'

Fleur's stomach sank. 'You're sure?'

'I'll have another proper look in a bit before the lunch people start coming in, but if it's not behind the counter, then it's probably not here. Someone would have seen it.'

Fleur pressed her hands to her temples. This could not be happening.

'Hang on,' Alice said suddenly, clicking her fingers. 'Clive was in here after you left; he might have seen something.'

'Clive? Yes, he was next to me actually. We were tightly packed in that corner.'

'Yeah. You know what he's like, always lingering about, chatting away. He was helping me close up, actually—maybe he picked it up? He would have said though...'

'Okay. Okay. That's a lead, at least.'

'He's probably down at the jetty. He was in here very early this morning. He said he was on duty in the hut.' Alice said, nodding towards the door. 'If anyone's got it, it'll be him.'

Fleur nodded, already heading for the door. 'Thanks, Alice! I owe you.'

'You owe me a story!' Alice called after her with a grin.

'I do. Don't tell anyone if you don't mind. Nightmare!'

Fleur didn't even look back; she was already out the door, heading straight for her car and the jetty, praying that Clive had the ring and that she wasn't about to go down in history as the woman who lost an engagement ring before even giving it to her fiancé.

30

. . .

Fleur sank her teeth into her bottom lip as she drove along. It wasn't the end of the world if the ring was lost, not really. It was a standard, fairly small signet ring that hadn't actually cost a massive amount, but that wasn't the point. It wasn't because of the ring itself as such, but more the thought that had gone into it and the feeling behind it. She felt as if the ring signified a lot, even if Patrick just kept it on the side or in the glove compartment of his car and didn't actually wear it.

Fleur thought about lots of things as she indicated and turned in the direction of the river as little flashes of images went through her mind: when she was wearing the glittery pink dress at Lovely Manor, when she'd been caught in the rain, when Lucy had been ill, and at Cassy's fortieth birthday party. What had happened between her and Patrick had changed her even in the short time that she'd got together with him since the ball.

In the early days of them going out, she'd almost compartmentalised what they had. Thinking that what happened between them stayed in a nice little box that she could control and turn on and off precisely when she wanted to. At the time, she'd thought that she was correct in her assumption that she could turn that switch on and off. But now she knew that she'd been wrong. She no longer controlled the switch; she simply just always wanted it to be on. All in all, it was a funny place for Fleur to be. She'd never thought she would feel the way she did about anyone and certainly not that it would trigger feelings she hadn't expected and nudge her to want to marry someone. Yet here she was. Part of her still felt as if it was *preposterous*.

Reaching a side road not far from the main riverboat jetty, Fleur pulled into the side, turned off the engine, grabbed her cardigan, and hustled down in the direction of the jetty. Immediately scanning the area for Clive, she squinted as the river stretched out ahead calm and glassy, reflecting the grey of the sky. There was no sign of any of the riverboats; neither Colin nor Clive were anywhere to be seen. The little wooden hut where Clive usually sat was open, though, the door slightly ajar as if whoever was manning it had just stepped away for a moment.

Fleur looked around, glanced over at the railway station in the distance, hesitated for a bit, and then stepped forward, peering inside. A jumble of maritime bits and bobs and small business stuff looked back at her; maps pinned on one wall, a row of life jackets hanging in the corner, a small desk covered in paperwork, and a Thermos that had definitely seen better days. A distinct scent too: water, damp wood, coffee maybe, and a working life on the river hanging in the air. Seeing not a single soul, Fleur walked back out, peered down the river, and turned to the far side of the hut where a noticeboard sat lodged onto the timber boards of its walls. Filled with worn cork, it sported an assortment of pinned-up notes, ferry times, local event posters, and a few sun-bleached leaflets about boat safety. Right at the top, scrawled in large, loopy handwriting, was a sign: LOST PROPERTY? TEXT ME.

Underneath the sign, both Colin and Clive's numbers were

listed. Fleur exhaled, pulling her phone from her pocket and crossed her fingers. She tapped out a message quickly.

Fleur: *Hi Clive, it's Fleur. Bit of a strange one. I think I might have left something in the deli last night, and Alice said you were there after we left. Any chance you found an engagement ring? I popped down to the jetty because Alice said you were manning the hut this morning... Anyway, let me know. Thank you.*

She stared at the message for a second before sending. There was something ridiculous about the whole situation. How did people manage to get engaged without all this faff? Stuffing her phone back into her pocket, she leaned against the wooden railing of the jetty and let out a breath as the river lapped gently against the posts, salt and seaweed in the air. The river was very quiet with a few boats bobbing on their moorings, the distant sound of seagulls, and the occasional clatter of masts here and there. Tapping her foot, she wondered how long it would be until Clive got back to her. He probably didn't have the ring anyway. It was a bit of a long shot. Her phone buzzed.

Clive: *Bonjour. An engagement ring??? Who leaves engagement rings around?*

Fleur felt her nostrils go wide. *Just answer the question, for Fanny's sake.*

Fleur: *Yes, I know. I am officially the world's most incompetent proposer. Do you have it?*

A pause. Then another buzz.

Clive: *Relax. It's safe with me.*

Fleur sagged with relief and was so pleased that she felt as if little fizzes were coming out of her ears.

Fleur: *Thank God and thank you. Where are you?*

Clive: *Few minutes away. I'll meet you at the jetty.*

Fleur slipped her phone back into her pocket and let out a deep breath. *Crisis averted.*

She still had to actually give the ring to Patrick, but at least she wasn't about to go down in history as the woman who'd lost an engagement ring before even handing it over. A few minutes later, she heard the chug of the riverboat approaching. She turned, spotting Clive at the helm, looking pleased with himself as he pulled the boat alongside the jetty. He hopped off, tying up the rope, and turned to her with an exaggerated shake of his head.

'Fleur, Fleur, Fleur,' he tsked. 'What are we going to do with you?'

Fleur folded her arms. 'Oh, ha, ha. I know.'

Clive smirked, reaching into his pocket and pulling out a small velvet box. He held it up between two fingers. 'This what you're after?'

'Thank you. Where did you find it?'

'It was under my chair in the deli. Good thing I spotted it before it got kicked under the counter.'

'I can't believe I did that.'

'To be honest, I meant to give it to Alice this morning, obviously, but it completely slipped my mind. It was an early rise for me this morning and I may have had one glass of beer too many last night.'

Fleur chuckled. 'Right.'

'Colin told me what happened on the boat so I'd put two and two together, but then I had a call out this morning. I was going to get in touch when I got back. Anyway, here we are.'

'Thank goodness.'

'What I don't understand is how Patrick doesn't have this ring on his finger. Thought that was the whole point of a proposal?'

Fleur sighed, looking down at the box in her hand. 'I got a bit distracted by blurting it out and so I didn't even think about not having the ring. It's a long story...'

Clive raised an eyebrow. 'Distracted? You forgot to give him the ring.'

'I got sidetracked. I was having a moment.'

'Ahh, well, what goes on on these riverboats never fails to entertain.'

Fleur rolled her eyes. 'Right, well, now that I have it, I need to actually give it to him.'

Clive leaned against the wooden railing of the jetty, arms folded. 'It's funny. You've managed to propose but not actually hand over the ring? That's a new one…'

Fleur sighed, shaking her head. 'Yes, I know.'

'You'd better keep it safe now. So, what's the plan? Are you doing it here in Lovely, or is it some big grand affair? Up at the Manor maybe?'

'We're hoping for Maui.'

Clive let out a low whistle. 'Well, that's a step up from a registry office in town.'

Fleur chuckled. 'Yeah, it's a bit different, isn't it? But it just feels right. There's a lot to discuss, nothing concrete yet, but something about being by the ocean, somewhere beautiful, somewhere that's not tied up with I don't know, anything really. Just us, starting fresh.'

Clive nodded. 'I get that. Mmm, nice. Clean slate, clear waters, that tropical feel. Yes.'

'It won't be massive, just family.'

'So, when are you giving him that ring then?'

Fleur smiled. 'Soon.'

Clive straightened up, clapping his hands together. 'Right, no time like the present then. Now, go on, get out of here before you drop that thing again.'

'Okay. I'm going.'

As Fleur walked back in the direction of her car, the noise of a train approaching filtered through the air. She took in a deep breath and smiled. It was happening. The thing that had popped into her head was in progress. Good things were to come.

31

It was a few days later. Fleur had presented Patrick with the ring without any fanfare but with a whole lot of giggling and he was now wearing it on his left hand. Fleur had just had a shower, washed and dried her hair, and made a cup of tea. Patrick came in from work through the front, stuck his head around the kitchen door, and jerked his thumb upwards and joked. 'I'm just going to have a shower, and then we'll have the chat about the wedding and you tying me down for the rest of my life, correct?'

Fleur smiled. 'Yes.'

About fifteen minutes later, Patrick had showered and was sitting opposite Fleur, a bottle of beer in his hand, the top popped off. He laughed and looked a bit edgy. 'How funny that we're talking about where we're going to get married, even though up until you dropped the bombshell, I didn't know we *were* getting married.'

Fleur frowned. Patrick had an uncertainty about him she had never seen before. For as long as she'd known him, he'd always been calm, in control, and had a quiet, organised way about him. But now, he didn't look that way at all; his voice sounded a little bit laced with something on the edge of panic, was it? Whatever it was, it was unfamiliar. 'I know, it's, err, going quickly.'

Patrick took a gulp of beer. 'So, you mentioned doing it while we're away. Is that something you really want to do?'

'I think so. Why wouldn't we get married in Maui?'

'It just feels quite quick. You're sure you'd not want something more traditional?'

'Nope. What about you?'

Patrick shrugged. 'Details. Couldn't care less, just tell me where to turn up.'

'Ha.' Fleur rolled her eyes.

'There are a few other people to think about in this, though.'

Fleur thought about the fact that she was over worrying about everyone else all the time. 'Correct, yeah, however, really, I want to think about *us* and not about anybody else here.'

'Good for you to say that, actually. You're always considering other people.'

Fleur nodded. 'Maui it is then.'

'Great. We'll have to look into the legal side of it and see how that works. Even if we just do a ceremony out there and then have to do it again here later.'

'People do it all the time.'

Patrick made a wincing face. 'There is one fly in the ointment.'

'Your family?' Fleur pre-empted.

'No, no, they'll be fine. I can't see how it would be a problem. They'll love a little jaunt. Mum and Dad will probably combine it with a visit to my brother in Canada. Hopefully, they'll come too.'

'Yes, right, I thought that.' Fleur nodded. 'So what's the fly in the ointment?'

'Lucy.' Patrick stated.

Fleur inhaled slowly. 'Why is she a problem?'

'I know she'll be on board with it and happy about it, but what if there's something wrong with her?'

'I've already thought about that, obviously. But there's a hospital there if the worst comes to the worst. What do you do? Put your life on hold for the rest of forever because of a fainting episode, which we're not even really sure what it was. The tests said there's nothing wrong.'

Patrick nodded. 'I thought that too. But you just, I don't know. You never really know, do you? Alright, so let's actually think this through properly. If we do this in Maui, how's it going to work?'

Fleur leant back in her chair, pressing her lips together. 'Well, first, we need to see if the hotel can accommodate it. I mean, I assume they do weddings all the time, but they'd need some notice. We can't just turn up and hope for the best.'

'I'll email them in the morning. Worst case, they say no, and we have to find somewhere else, but I doubt that'll happen. There was a whole section on it on the website. Weddings in paradise or something.'

Fleur drummed her fingers against the table. 'And then there's getting everyone there.'

Patrick smiled. 'Bit of an important detail, that.'

'Captain Obvious.'

'So, who will come? We need to work out numbers first.'

Fleur counted on her fingers. 'Wendy, obviously. Cassy, if she can wangle it. Mum, Marvin. Lucy. Your parents. Your brothers and their lot.'

Patrick pulled a face. 'Mum and Dad will definitely come. Daniel and his lot I'm guessing they'd fly over from there. That actually makes it easier for them. Tom will probably be a yes, but Will—'

'Oh God, Will,' Fleur groaned.

Patrick chuckled. 'Exactly. He'll make a fuss about it being too far or too expensive, and he'll swear blind he wants to come, but somehow, he'll make it seem like we're the ones being unreasonable for doing it so far away.'

'Let's just assume for now that he'll find an excuse and won't come.'

Patrick tilted his head. 'Fair.'

Fleur took a sip of tea, still mentally calculating. 'That puts us at... what, fifteen to twenty?'

'Yeah, about that.'

'That's actually a nice number. Small, intimate, no fuss.'

Patrick smiled. 'Exactly how you wanted it.'

Fleur nodded. 'Yeah, but—' She hesitated. 'Do you think it's selfish? I mean, dragging everyone across the world for our wedding?'

Patrick leant forward, resting his forearms on the table. 'Let's be real, it's Maui. Nobody's going to be weeping into their passports about having to go on a luxury holiday for a wedding. I'm paying so that side of it is sorted.'

'True.' Fleur exhaled. 'So, we're really doing this?'

Patrick reached across the table. 'Yeah. We really are. Thanks to your proposal and mad cap idea.'

'Maui, then.'

Patrick squeezed her hand. 'Maui it is.'

32

Fleur Champion was panicking, big time. Patrick had gone off to sort out a problem at work, and once she was alone in her studio binding a book and reflecting on what she'd done, she'd realised that she hadn't really planned anything properly. She hadn't even told her own daughter that she'd asked Patrick to marry her. Ditto her mum and even her sister. She realised and panicked that she'd acted in haste, and now it was done and very much dusted.

Now she had to present it as a fait accompli rather than as something she was thinking about. This wasn't a problem, of course, she could do whatever she liked, and where her mum and Wendy were concerned, she didn't really care, but where Lucy was concerned, she now wished she'd run it past her first.

As she mulled it over, she walked down the stairs and decided to go for a walk on the beach to get a bit of fresh air and think it through. She wondered if sometimes she gave Lucy too much. Lucy was an adult; she was not a child. Fleur did not need to run things past her. On the other hand, Lucy had had an emotional year; her dad had just had a baby with somebody else, and now her mum was going to tell her that she was getting married. And not only that, but it was going to be soon and on the other side of the world. Ouch.

Fleur suddenly went cold, realising that she'd probably made a mistake in wanting to do everything quickly and that other people might not be quite as happy as her about, well, pretty much any of it. As she closed the front door behind her and walked down Lovely Pott Lane towards the beach, just as she was turning out of the end of the road, Birdie drove around the corner, pulled over, rolled down her window, and smiled. The Shipping Forecast played from inside the car, and Birdie raised her eyebrows. 'Hello! How are you? You're looking well, I have to say.'

'Thanks. Yes, I'm feeling well.'

'What's been going on with you, then?' Birdie asked as she reached over and turned down the Shipping Forecast.

Oh, you know, asked Patrick to marry me, Fleur thought in her head but didn't say. 'Not much, you know, same old, same old.'

'How's the notebook business going?'

Fleur smiled. 'Ticking along. I was just doing some orders then but thought I'd pop out for some fresh air.'

'Any more wholesale orders to keep you up at night?' Birdie chuckled.

'Well, actually, no. I have had a couple of enquiries, and another one from the people in Dublin, but to be honest, I pushed back on it. I've realised I'm no entrepreneur, it seems, and I feel as if I just need to play my own game with it. I'll stick to the markets and let it grow organically, you know? I'm not cut out to be the next dragon…'

'Well, there's a lot to be said for that, I think. Wholesale isn't great for everybody.'

'Yes, so true.' Fleur nodded in the direction of the cottage. 'I've actually spent most of the day in the studio, working on a new range of notebooks with a ruffle on them. It was my friend

Cassy who found the fabric, and I just love doing things like that. I think I'll stick with that for now.'

Birdie nodded. 'So, you've not been up to much then? No, err, things happening in your life? How's Patrick?'

Fleur laughed. Birdie clearly already knew about the proposal, but Fleur wasn't going to be broadcasting it before she'd told her own daughter. 'Oh, you know. Same old.'

Birdie shifted her car into neutral, and rested her arm on the open window as she smiled at Fleur. The sun had dipped low in the sky and pretty golden light shimmered over Lovely Pott Lane. 'So, what else have you been up to apart from getting lost in ruffles and vintage paper?'

Fleur hesitated for half a second, tempted to spill everything, but before she could say anything, a car approached from the other direction, creeping past at a near standstill. It was an old green Mini belonging to Margaret, one of the local B&B owners. She gave them both a wave as she inched by, her little dog perched on the passenger seat, staring solemnly out at the world.

'Busy, Margaret?' Birdie called cheerfully.

Margaret gave a dramatic sigh. 'Always. Got a full house this weekend—guests arriving in an hour. If you see me running up and down with a mop, no, you didn't.'

Fleur and Birdie laughed, waving her on as she carefully manoeuvred through the narrow lane.

'Honestly, I don't know how she does it. I struggle to keep my own house in order, never mind running a whole B&B.'

'Same,' Fleur admitted, glad that the subject had changed. 'Though I did have a big clear-out yesterday. The airing cupboard, Birdie. The airing cupboard.'

Birdie let out a low whistle. 'That's serious business. Did you find anything interesting in there?'

'A pile of towels I don't remember buying, a hot water bottle with a very questionable stain, and, oh, at least ten odd socks.'

Birdie snorted. 'I swear there's a parallel universe where all the missing socks are living in peace together.'

'Probably. Anyway, what about you? What's been keeping you busy?'

'Well, I've been thinking about opening another chemist.'

Fleur raised her eyebrows. 'Another one?'

'Mmm.' Birdie nodded. 'Over in Fairlight. There's nothing decent there, just that overpriced health store that sells dodgy supplements and charges over the top for a bottle of cough syrup.'

'Fairlight. That's not too far, is it?'

'No, only about twenty minutes away. I've been looking at a unit on the high street. Needs a bit of work, but it's got good foot traffic. And let's face it, everyone needs a chemist.'

'Exciting.'

'I keep going back and forth about it. Part of me thinks I should just be happy with what I've got, but then I wonder, why not? You need to keep pushing on in life, don't you? Change things up a bit...' Birdie looked pointedly at Fleur.

Fleur ignored the look. 'If it feels right, you should go for it.'

Birdie smiled. 'I like your attitude. Right. I'd better head off. I'll leave you to it. Don't do anything I wouldn't do. Let me know if you have any news.'

'That leaves me a lot of options,' Fleur teased.

Birdie winked. 'See you soon!' She pulled away, her car trundling down the lane, leaving Fleur standing there.

Fleur exhaled slowly, looking up at the sky, then back down towards the beach. She loved bumping into people now she'd been in Lovely a while. It was so nice to just chat and pass the time of day with someone. As she strolled down the lane, she thought about Lucy. She'd just have to get it out of the way and soon. The sooner it was done, the better.

With the sea breeze in her hair, Fleur glanced towards the beach and hoped that the sand between her toes would clear her head and work out how she was going to tell Lucy. It wasn't that she was worried about Lucy not being happy for her, more that Lucy had been through a lot. Her dad had just had a baby, a situation that was still new even if Lucy was over the moon about it. Now Fleur was about to tell her she was getting married. Grimacing, she again asked herself if she'd been a bit too impulsive.

Reaching the beach, she slipped off her shoes, the sand cool and soft beneath her feet. The tide was out and the water shimmered away as it stretched into the distance. A handful of people were dotted along the shore here and there; dog walkers, a couple of teenagers paddled in the shallows, an older man stood with his hands in his pockets, staring out at the horizon as if waiting for something. Fleur wandered slowly, letting the waves lull even though her thoughts were tangled.

Just as she got to the other end of the beach near the breakers, her phone buzzed in her pocket, dragging her back to reality. She pulled it out, frowning slightly when she saw Lucy's name on the screen as if Lucy had heard her thoughts.

'Hey, you.' Fleur pressed the phone to her ear.

'Hey, Mum.' Lucy's voice was light, but Fleur could tell she was preoccupied with something.

'Everything alright?'

'Yeah, yeah. Just thought I'd check-in. What are you up to?'

'Getting a spot of fresh air and wandering the beach. I needed to clear my mind.'

'What's on your mind?'

Fleur hesitated for a fraction of a second before deciding that there was no time like the present. 'Actually, there's something I need to talk to you about.'

'Okaaay.' Lucy dragged the word out. 'Should I be worried?'

'No, not at all. I'll just get straight to the point; I asked Patrick to marry me.'

Silence.

'Luce?' Fleur suddenly felt like she'd made a mistake by blurting it out.

'Sorry, I, what, wait. You proposed? What like to Patrick?'

'Err, yeah, who else would I propose to?'

'Mum!' Lucy's voice was animated, half laughing, half incredulous. 'What? How? When?'

'On the riverboat. It wasn't exactly planned, if I'm honest...'

'Clearly!'

'I know.'

'I mean, that's huge news. Congratulations!'

Fleur exhaled, relief washing over her. 'Yeah. It is.'

'And? What did he say? I presume yes or you wouldn't be telling me.'

'Yep, he said yes.'

'Ahhhh! So exciting!' Lucy squealed.

'I had a bit of a moment.'

'What kind of moment?'

Fleur sighed. 'The kind where I may have panicked and then laughed and, yeah, I forgot to actually give him the ring.'

'You forgot to give him the ring?'

'Yep.'

'I love this for you. This is the most *you* thing I've ever heard.'

'Thank you.'

'So, what happens now?'

Fleur hesitated. 'Well, it's going to be soon. Hopefully when we're away...'

Silence again. Fleur held her breath.

'Mum, what?'

'I know, I know, it's a lot...'

'Away? Hawaii? As in actual Hawaii?'

'Yes, well Maui.'

'As in, the other side of the planet?'

'That's the one.'

Lucy made a strangled noise. 'Wow. You really don't do things by halves, do you?'

'I suppose not.'

'Okay, let me get this straight. You propose to Patrick, forget to give him the ring, and now you're telling me that you're getting married in Maui? All this since the last time I spoke to you?'

'That's about the long and the short of it.'

'So, it looks like I'm coming to Maui.'

Fleur felt relieved. 'You are and hopefully Cassy and Aunty Wendy and Grandma too.'

'Gosh. Wow, you sound so happy, Mum. This is fabulous! What good news! First, I get a baby brother and now this.'

Fleur felt something in her chest shift. 'I really am happy.'

'That's all that matters.'

Fleur closed her eyes briefly and felt very grateful for Lucy's reaction. 'Thanks, Luce.'

'Look, I was only quickly calling you. I'm just getting to work. I'll speak to you later. This is so exciting! Love you, Mum. See you later.'

'Love you, Luce.'

Fleur stood and looked at the horizon for a bit. Lucy's attitude had done all sorts of things for her, including restoring her faith in the fact that she had done a good job bringing her up. One down, two to go. It was going to be interesting to see what Valerie was going to say. Valerie Champion, not that she knew it, was facing a test. She had better pass the test, that Fleur knew for free.

33

Fleur was sitting on a picnic bench down by the water, contemplating phoning her mum with her news. She'd taken a cup of milky coffee and a few squares of chocolate down to the beach and sat staring out at the water, wondering what drama her mum would come up with about the fact that Fleur was getting married. It was a blue-sky day in Lovely, with a real nip in the air and little white horses foaming on the waves all the way to the horizon. In the far distance, a thin horizontal line of clouds dusted across the sky, and a white speedboat in the distance had kept Fleur's focus occupied for a bit as she'd observed it bob up and down. She'd also watched a woman with a spaniel sitting on the bench not far from her, reading a book, enjoying the joys of Lovely life. Fleur sighed a little bit as she thought about the call and wondered how Valerie was going to react. With Valerie, one never could quite tell.

Back at the cottage, she turned the key in the lock, pushed the bottom of the door with her foot—the little trick she'd learnt to get the door to open—and made her way into the kitchen. Pouring herself a glass of water, she sat down at the kitchen table, propped her phone up, and dialled her mum. And breathe. After a few seconds, Valerie appeared on the screen, sitting on a camping chair with a denim jacket on, her hair tied up in a bright yellow headscarf, mountains behind her and the van to her left.

'Hi, Fleur. How are you?' Valerie chirped, appearing to be happy and full of the joys.

'Good, thanks. How are things with you?'

Valerie hesitated for a second. Fleur felt a drop in her stomach—what was Valerie going to say? But in an instant, the look was gone, and Valerie beamed and gestured behind her. 'Yes, good, thank you. We've had a lovely stay in these mountains. It's been absolutely gorgeous.'

'Oh, that's nice.'

'Yes, and I was just saying how much we love life. So good.'

Fleur swallowed. *Here we go again about how much she loves her van life and is enjoying it, blah, blah, blah...* Fleur braced herself to listen for a bit before she divulged her news. This was one of the occasions where she'd have to sit and take in everything about how amazing Valerie's new life was. Fleur pressed her glass of water to her forehead for a moment and tried to be calm and cordial. She could already feel her patience thinning, the way it always did when her mum went into full van life storytelling mode, especially when it involved Marvellous Marvin.

Valerie adjusted her headscarf and settled further into her camping chair. 'So, we decided to do this incredible hike. Absolutely stunning views, just breathtaking, and we were halfway down the trail when, oh, you won't believe it, I realised I'd forgotten my bag.'

Fleur forced a smile. 'Oh no.'

'Yes! Of course, Marvin being Marvin, well, he wasn't going to let that ruin our experience. Oh, Fleur, you'd have laughed. He only went and fashioned a makeshift bag for me out of my scarf! Can you believe it? Tied it up so perfectly, slung it over my shoulder—honestly, such a clever thing to do.'

Fleur clenched her jaw and nodded. 'Very, err, resourceful of him.'

Valerie beamed. 'Isn't it? He just thinks like that. Doesn't flap, doesn't stress, just solves problems, you know? It's one of the things I adore about him. He's got such an easy way about him, Fleur.'

Fleur exhaled through her nose, gripping the edge of the table with one hand. She could feel her window to tell her mum about the wedding slipping away, lost somewhere between Marvin the Mountain Man and his genius scarf-bag invention. Valerie was failing the test. 'Mum, I—'

'And the way he navigated the trail back down after that, well, it was honestly like watching someone completely at one with nature. You know, he's always been very intuitive about things like that. He said to me, "Val, you've got to feel the mountain, not just walk down it."' Valerie's eyes shone as she recounted the latest in Marvin's endless list of supposed brilliance. 'And honestly, Fleur, I did! I really felt it. You know, sometimes I think we rush through life without really being *in* it.'

Fleur pressed her lips together so tightly they almost disappeared. 'Hmm.'

'Anyway, it was just the most magical moment. The sun setting behind the peaks, the air crisp but not too cold, Marvin's hand warm on mine as we walked back down...'

'Mum!' Fleur snapped.

Valerie stopped mid-flow, blinking at her through the phone screen. 'What?'

Fleur forced her voice back to something resembling normal. 'Can we please talk about something other than Marvin for one second?'

Valerie frowned, sitting back in her camping chair. 'What's got into you?'

Fleur pressed her fingers to her temples. 'I've been trying to tell you something. Something important. But every time I open my mouth, you launch into another Marvin story like he's the Messiah.'

Valerie's expression flickered with something, not guilt, just irritation at being interrupted. 'Well, go on then. What's this very important thing?'

Fleur swallowed, her news was much more important than makeshift bags and hikes. 'Patrick and I are getting married.'

Silence. A long, stretched-out pause made Fleur's stomach lurch slightly.

Valerie's face was unreadable for a moment. Then, after what felt like an eternity, she let out a light, almost dismissive, laugh. 'Oh, Fleur, really?'

Fleur's heart sank. 'What do you mean, really?'

'I just mean, well, isn't it all a bit quick?'

Fleur felt a flash of anger rise up her spine. 'Mum!'

Valerie pulled a face. 'I just, I don't know, marriage? I didn't think you were that sort of person after, well, after the last one.'

Fleur blinked. 'What sort of person?'

'The sort that needs to get married. I thought you were, well, independent, now.'

Fleur clenched her fists under the table. So much for congratulations. 'I am independent, Mum. Loving someone and wanting to marry them doesn't mean I've lost myself.'

'I can't believe he asked you to get married. I didn't think I'd ever see the day after what happened the first time.'

Fleur shook her head. 'I actually asked him.'

Valerie looked both astonished, surprised, and as if she didn't believe her. '*You* asked him? Really? How does that happen?'

'I just decided, after Lucy and everything, that I want to make it forever with him. So, I thought about it the other day on the way to work, and then I thought, why not? I don't have to wait for him to turn around and be down on one knee and ask me. It's not as if it's 1930, is it? You know, we're modern women, after all.'

'Yes, yes,' Valerie nodded. 'That's exactly like me! I'm a modern woman.'

'Yes,' Fleur said, though she was not at all convinced by that.

'Although, I'm not sure I believe in marriage these days. I mean, why do you have to do that? I wish I hadn't bothered...'

Fleur shook her head, more than irritated that her mum was not gushing in congratulations, but instead turning it around again to her marriage with her dad. Talk about insensitive. Fleur swallowed down the lump of irritation rising in her throat. She should have known this would happen. Should have prepared for it, really. 'Well...'

Valerie let out a theatrical sigh and adjusted the scarf in her hair. 'I suppose some people still do it. But honestly, Fleur, I don't understand why you feel the need. It's just a piece of paper! Look at me—I've never been happier, and I don't need a certificate to tell me that I'm living my best life.'

Fleur clenched her jaw. 'Yes, Mum, I know you're living your best life. You remind me of it every time we speak.'

'Well, it's true!' Valerie trilled, oblivious to Fleur's rising frustration. 'I'm free! I can go where I want, do what I want, no one tying me down, no legal nonsense—just me and my van, seeing the world! It's liberating, Fleur, really. You should try it.'

Fleur inhaled slowly, pinching the bridge of her nose. 'Mum, I don't want to live in a van.'

'Well, not with that attitude,' Valerie laughed, completely missing the point. 'You know, you used to be more spontaneous, more adventurous. When you were younger, you had such a free spirit! Then you went and got married, settled down, and—'

'And had Lucy. And built a life,' Fleur finished sharply, unable to hold back the edge in her voice.

Valerie waved a dismissive hand. 'Well, yes, of course, and Lucy's wonderful. But you lost that spark! You started worrying about rules and plans and doing things the way everyone expects them to be done, and honestly, I just think it's a shame.'

Fleur felt her stomach tighten. It wasn't irritation anymore. It was hurt. Deep, dull, and entirely predictable. 'Mum. I am happy. I love my life. I love Patrick. This isn't about ticking a box, or following some old-fashioned idea of marriage. It's about us. It's about making a choice together and celebrating that.'

Valerie pursed her lips, unconvinced. 'I just don't see why it has to be official. It's so... traditional. I thought you were over it after—well, you know.'

Fleur exhaled through her nose, her grip tightening on her cup. 'Mum. You do realise this isn't about you, right?'

Valerie blinked, momentarily caught off guard. 'Well, of course, I know that, but—'

'Do you?' Fleur cut in, her voice quieter now but far more pointed. 'Because every time I tell you something about my life, you manage to twist it back to being about yours. I called to tell you I'm getting married, Mum. To share something happy. And instead of just saying, "That's wonderful, Fleur, I'm so happy for you," you've turned it into another conversation about how amazing your life is and how I should be living like you.'

Valerie opened her mouth, but for once, no words came out immediately. She sighed dramatically, reaching for her flask of tea and taking a slow sip. 'Alright. Well, congratulations, I suppose. When is it happening?'

Fleur hesitated. 'We're thinking of doing it in Maui.'

Valerie almost choked on her tea. 'Hawaii, Maui!'

'Yes, Maui. We want something small and intimate. Just close family and friends.'

Valerie raised an eyebrow. 'Sorry, do you expect everyone to just fly halfway across the world for this?'

'Nobody has to come, Mum. We're inviting the people who

matter, and if they can make it – amazing. If not, we understand. Patrick is happy to help out with flights and such.'

Valerie looked unimpressed. 'And you just assume I'll be able to drop everything and come along?'

Fleur gave a tight smile. 'Mum, you and Marvin have spent the last year swanning around Europe like a pair of nomads. I hardly think one flight to Maui is going to upend your life.'

Valerie pursed her lips but said nothing.

Fleur rested her elbows on the table. 'I want you there. That's why I'm telling you now. It's not happening tomorrow. We've got time to sort things out.'

Valerie sighed again, her fingers tracing the rim of her cup. 'Well, I suppose it does sound… lovely.'

'It's what we want.'

There was another silence, but this time, it wasn't quite as tense.

Valerie nodded. 'Alright. I'll talk to Marvin. See what we can do. I don't know if we can fly from Istanbul.'

'That would be great.'

'You're happy, Fleur? Really?'

Fleur met Valerie's gaze. 'Yeah, Mum. I really am.'

'Right. Well, darling, I'll see you later and talk to you soon. Congrats.'

'Thanks Mum. Speak to you later.'

Fleur looked away for a second and caught sight of a framed picture of her dad on the kitchen windowsill. It broke her heart that she was getting married and he wouldn't be there. But she was happier than she'd ever been, and at the end of the day, she was grateful for that. *Way to go, Champo. You'll be okay.*

34

Fleur skimmed the body of an email from work, which had pointed out to all staff who travelled for training purposes that there was a team-building exercise coming up in the calendar. She tutted to herself as she thought about the various team-building exercises she'd been part of over the years. The reality was that most of the people didn't last very long in the company anyway—although, to be fair, her friendship with Cassy had certainly blossomed through the job. However, there weren't that many people who had been doing it as long as they had. They certainly didn't need to team build with anyone especially if it involved dreary weather and outdoor activities that included mud and rain. Despite various attempts at team-building and staff retention, at the end of the day, the company had a fast turnover of staff, and just about everybody knew it.

Skimming back over the email, Fleur opened her calendar, noted the date, and then thought about the fact that she still hadn't told Wendy about the wedding. She'd told her mum not to say anything until she had spoken to Wendy and had asked herself a few times—or more like a hundred times—what on earth had possessed her to blurt out the proposal and act in haste in the first place. Spontaneity was nothing like Fleur, not at all. Most of her life was pretty straightforward and organised, and now she had thrown a random wedding proposal into the mix. All Fleur really knew was that her relationship, her move to Lovely Bay, her new life and just about everything was at a pivotal point. If someone had told her a year or so before that this would be happening, she wouldn't have believed them. But it was happening, right here in front of her eyes. Now she had to relay the latest development to her sister who could be stroppy at the best of times.

As she thought about Wendy and checked the time in Australia, she decided that she had to get the call over and done with before Valerie got in first. Flicking open WhatsApp, she looked at herself in the camera and smiled. Hopefully, Wendy wouldn't think she'd lost the plot and would be happy for her. A few minutes later, after messaging Wendy to see if she was free, Wendy came onto the screen and smiled.

Fleur decided to cut to the chase right away. 'Hey, how are you?'

'Hi! Good.'

'Look, I've got something to tell you.' Fleur took a breath and went in for the kill. 'I'm getting married.'

Wendy made a very exaggerated wide-eyed face. Her eyebrows flew up. 'What? You're getting married?' There was a pause. 'Sorry? To who?'

Fleur frowned. 'What do you mean to who? How many people do you think I'm getting married to in my life?'

Wendy burst out laughing. 'Patrick proposed? Aww!'

Fleur shook her head. 'No. Not that way at all.'

'Not that way at all? What do you mean?'

'I mean that *I* proposed to *him*.'

Wendy didn't say anything for a second, then squeezed her eyes shut and opened them again, as if she was trying to get her head around what her sister had just said. 'Sorry—*you* proposed to him?'

'Yes.'

'You mean that you, Fleur Champion, proposed to the man that you met in…' Wendy hesitated, narrowing her eyes. 'The same person who said they would never get serious with anyone again, let alone get married to someone? The same person who, when her divorce came through, said that she *hated* men? The same person who said that she was so glad she was independent?'

Fleur scoffed. 'The same person. That person is me.'

Wendy exhaled. 'It doesn't take a lot to shock me when I get calls from either you or Mum. I mean, last time, it was an infected finger and there was the Lucy drama, bless her, you moving to Lovely Bay, Dad, the cottage, Marvellous Marvin—everything. But this, this one is really up there. Not just a winner of the week but the winner of a lifetime. I did not see this coming.'

'I like to keep you on your toes.' Fleur joked.

'I don't know what to say!' Wendy let out a small gasp. 'Well, of course—congratulations! How amazing! Fantastic!'

'Thank you.'

'So when's the big day? I'll book my flights. It's been ages since I've been home.'

'You see, that's the thing. We're going to do it in Maui.'

There was silence for half a second. 'Wow. Now I *am* shocked.' Wendy started to laugh and wiped a tear from the corner of her eye. 'A Champo proposing, getting married, and doing it in Maui of all places! I mean, you do realise that if I had to list the top ten things I never thought I'd hear from you, this would be right at the top?'

'Yes, it appears I am full of surprises these days,' Fleur said sarcastically.

'Clearly! Oh, Mum must have loved this. What did she say?'

Fleur sighed, sinking into the chair at her kitchen table. 'Oh, you know, she made it about her, as usual.'

Wendy snorted. 'Of course she did. How did she manage it this time?'

'By going off on a tangent about how she doesn't believe in marriage, and how I should be out there living in a van and being free like she is.' Fleur shook her head. 'Honestly, I don't know why I expected anything different.'

Wendy smirked. 'Well, at least she didn't try to convince you to get married in the van. Count your blessings.'

'Don't give her any ideas.'

Wendy beamed. 'So, tell me more, then. Maui, eh? This was your idea?'

'Well, it started as just a thought, but the more I thought about it, the more I knew it was exactly what I wanted. I want to be on a tropical beach, watching the sunset...'

Wendy tilted her head. 'Exciting!'

Fleur smiled. 'The hotel is licensed to do weddings, so hopefully it will all come together.'

'Who's coming?'

'We don't want a big thing, but I'd love for you, obviously Lucy, of course, Cassy, if she can. Maybe her husband, if they can make it work and then Patrick's immediate family. No one else. It will be very small.'

'I wouldn't miss it for the world. Tell me more about this hotel.'

'Oh, it's gorgeous. Right on the beach, small but stunning, the kind of place that just feels right, it's not a budget hotel put it that way. They handle all the wedding stuff, which, frankly, is a godsend.'

Wendy laughed. 'Sounds great.'

'So, this way, it's simple. We get married on the beach, have a little dinner with our closest people, and then well, then we start the next part of life, I suppose.'

'I'll say it—I love this! I really do. I'm so happy for you, Fleur. After everything you've been through.'

Fleur swallowed. 'Thanks, Wens. I hope it goes well…'

'It will, we'll make sure it will. You're happy, Fleur. That's all that matters. It's been a long time. I can see it written all over your face.'

Fleur smiled back, realising for the first time in a very long time that she *was* happy, like forever happy. How nice did that feel? Nice.

35

Fleur sat at the kitchen table, her laptop open in front of her, a half-drunk cup of tea cooling by her side. The house was quiet except for an occasional hum of the fridge and the clock ticking on the wall. Clicking to open her inbox, she scrolled past the usual spam, work notifications, and emails she'd subscribed to but never actually read, before landing on the one she was looking for from the hotel in Maui. She clicked it open, her stomach flipping slightly at the sheer officialness of it all. Champo was getting married and it was looking back at her in black and white.

Dear Fleur,
Thank you for completing our wedding questionnaire! We are so excited to be working with you and Patrick to create your perfect Maui wedding. Seeing as you are already staying with us for over a week it's been easy to accommodate you.
Your responses have given us a great starting point, and based on what you've shared, we've put together a preliminary outline for your day.
Below is a breakdown of the key elements for your wedding:
Ceremony:

> Location: Beachfront (as requested)
> Time: 4 PM (golden hour—perfect for photos!)
> Chairs: White wooden with ivory cushions (unless you prefer something else?)
> Arch: Bamboo with soft draping and tropical flowers in your colour scheme
> Celebrant: Local officiant available
> Reception:
> Private oceanfront outdoor terrace at the resort
> Seating: Round tables, white linen, candlelit centrepieces
> Food: Customisable menu (attached for review)
> Drinks: Signature cocktail? Champagne on arrival?
> Cake: Two-tier (flavour of your choice—let us know)
> Other Details:
> Bridal bouquet: Tropical mix of soft greens and whites
> Buttonholes: Simple white orchids for Patrick and best man
> Hair & makeup: Available onsite
> Live music: Guitarist or ukulele player?
> Please review everything and let us know if you have any changes or specific preferences. We aim to make this process as smooth and stress-free as possible—our team will handle all logistics, so all you need to do is arrive, get dressed, and enjoy your special day!
> Looking forward to your thoughts.
> Best,
> Mia Parker
> Senior Wedding Coordinator

Fleur sat back in her chair, exhaling slowly. Well, that was easy. She scrolled back up, scanning through the list again and shook her head. It was all there. Everything she had imagined but hadn't really thought about in detail until the questionnaire had prompted her. The arch, the chairs, the flowers, the cake. It was all very professional if not a bit conveyor belt; by the sound of it, the hotel had done it so many times that all she and Patrick really had to do was say yes to things and sign the payment authorisation.

She clicked on the attached menu, her eyes flicking over the options.

Grilled mahi-mahi with pineapple salsa, macadamia-crusted chicken, fresh papaya, and prawn salad. Seared ahi tuna with coconut rice.

She didn't even need to think about it. It all sounded incredible.

Hi Mia,
Thank you so much for this—it all looks absolutely perfect. I can't believe how organised you are, this is already so much easier than I expected!
A few thoughts. 4 PM for the ceremony sounds great, the bamboo arch and white wooden chairs are exactly what we want—keep as is. The celebrant—I'd love to do a quick Zoom just to get a feel for him. No rush, just at some point before we arrive. The terrace for the reception sounds perfect. Definitely want candlelit centrepieces. Drinks—champagne on arrival and maybe a signature cocktail for guests? Something tropical but not too sweet.
Food—the menu looks amazing - happy to trust the chef's recommendations. Cake—two-tier is fine. I'll have a think about flavours! Hair & makeup—please book me in. Any idea on timings for that on the day?
Let me know what you need from me next.
Best, Fleur

Fleur sent her reply, sat back, and puffed out a huge blow of air. That was it and all she had to do. A few decisions here and there, make sure Patrick was looped in on the food, and then nothing much at all except get there and chill out. The hotel would take care of the rest. She stretched her arms above her head and yawned, not really able to let herself believe how easy it was turning out to be. All she really had to do was show up in Maui, put on a dress, shove a few flowers in her hair, and walk down the beach.

A few minutes later, her phone pinged with a reply and she read through another email from Mia detailing and answering all Fleur's points. She stared at the screen and shook her head as she computed that everything was taken care of: no stress, no faffing, no last-minute panic about logistics. She was getting married in Maui; it was going to be stress-free, easy, beautiful, and like some sort of dream. At least, she hoped it would be. She could but wait and see.

36

Fleur arrived at the door to a small conference room in a business centre, having stayed in a hotel room next door the night before, just in time to see Cassy step out with a face like thunder. She approached Fleur with a shake of her head and lowered her voice almost to a whisper. 'Head office does not have a clue. They really don't. That new guy from marketing has asked why we don't give our training courses with handouts as a rule. I mean, really? When was the last time you ever gave a handout unless there's a problem? We just have one old set to pass around if we need them. I thought we were meant to be doing stuff for the environment. That was company policy, wasn't it? A few years ago, they said that handouts were strictly forbidden. Something to do with paper and the planet, wasn't it?'

The look on Cassy's face was a picture, which made Fleur giggle. It was one of the moments between them she loved. They couldn't be manufactured, they just happened and always made Fleur laugh. Cassy did the funny high-pitched, squeaky voice she always did when she was highly irritated. Fleur had sometimes witnessed her use it on her boys as well—when they heard it, they knew they had better behave themselves and usually scarpered.

Cassy pointed to the coffee area on the other side of a small lobby section and made a coffee sign with her hand. 'I need a humongous dose of coffee. I'm leaving him to it.'

Fleur turned around and followed her. 'What did you say to him, then?'

'I told him to refer to the document, which is a PDF, and the section on the company's policy on the environment.'

'That's hilarious. These people—you can't make it up sometimes, can you?'

'Precisely.'

It had to be said, Cassy was looking on point. She had a beautifully cut pair of slim-leg Capri trousers in a gorgeous dusty pink, paired with a floaty silk blouse and a classic pair of loafers. The look on her face, though; not quite as pretty.

Cassy got them both a coffee. 'Honestly, Fleur, the absolute state of some of these people at head office. It's like they just pluck ideas out of thin air without thinking them through for more than three seconds. How about they get into the real world? I hate it when one of them turns up.'

Fleur nodded, stirring her coffee. 'What did he think was going to happen? That we'd all suddenly go back to printing out stacks of handouts like it's 1998? It was his department that made the whole "no paper, save the planet" policy in the first place!'

Cassy snorted. 'Exactly! And now they're acting like it's some shocking revelation that we don't have physical materials to hand out at a training session. He actually looked confused when I pointed it out. As if it had never once occurred to him that this was an intentional decision, not just some random oversight. I cannot stand it when one of them insinuates that we're incompetent. You and I run the tightest ship *ever*.'

Fleur shook her head. 'They must have meetings about

meetings, just to forget everything they decided in the last meeting.'

'I give it three months before they send out an urgent email reminding us that handouts are banned again and act like we're the ones being difficult for following their original policy.'

Fleur smirked. 'We should start keeping a bingo card for every time they contradict themselves.'

Cassy laughed. 'Anyway, enough about those absolute muppets. Let's talk about something actually exciting. My flights for the wedding are booked. I was up with the lark this morning. It's done. Show me the cocktails and tropical flowers.'

Fleur's eyes lit up. 'Really?'

'Yep! I found a great deal yesterday when you were delivering that session. A good flight time, decent layover on the way back, and—best part—the boys are sorted for the week, my holiday is approved, so I can actually relax and attend. Hooray.'

'Oh, that's amazing!'

'I wouldn't miss this for the world. I think it's going to be perfect. For the record, I love that you're doing it your way. No stress, no fuss, just you and Patrick on a beach, having the time of your lives. That's how it should be.'

Fleur nodded. 'That's what I keep telling myself. I just don't want to get caught up in the pressure of it all. I want it to be us, not some big production line for family we never even see and don't like that much.'

'You've done the hardest part—you've decided what you actually want. The rest is just logistics.'

Fleur agreed and smiled. She couldn't quite believe how easy everything had turned out. She crossed her fingers that nothing would change. Her best friend was coming to her wedding. All was right with the world.

37

Fleur tutted as she beeped the horn on her car and pulled into a spot just along from Ben's house. She'd gone there on her way home from a training course because Lucy had left her phone at Ben's and needed it that evening to go into London. Fleur could've swung for Lucy and her forgetfulness because there was *no way* she wanted to get caught up in going into Ben's house. Therefore, she'd WhatsApped Ben to say that she would beep when she was outside, hopefully meaning that she wouldn't have to suffer Sanctimonious Sarah and have to coo over the baby. That she could well do without.

On seeing Ben walk out of the house just after she'd beeped, waving Lucy's phone in his hand, she felt relieved not to see Sarah, wound down the window, and waved. Ben approached the car, didn't smile, and did not look happy, either.

'Everything okay with you?' Fleur asked, not really, truth be told, that bothered about his response. She was trying to be cordial.

'Yes, fine, thanks.'

Ben gave her the phone. She put it into the centre console

and rolled her eyes. 'She's a nightmare. She'd forget her head one day, wouldn't she?'

'Yep.' Ben was short, his tone clipped.

'Well, thanks for that then. Hopefully, she won't forget it again. Is everything alright with you?'

Ben had half turned to go. He turned back and his face looked like thunder. 'Actually, now you come to ask, no, everything is not okay with me. Not at all.'

Fleur frowned. 'Oh? What's happened?'

'Well, I would've thought that it would've been nice if you could have run it past me that you were getting married. Hearing about it from my daughter was, well, rude. Very rude.'

Fleur was so shocked and astonished by the cheek of Ben that she didn't know what to say, so she said nothing.

'It's a *huge* thing for Lucy after what she's been through, and I thought that you would've had the common decency to tell me yourself, considering our relationship and everything.'

Fleur stared at Ben's mouth, not quite computing quickly enough what he was saying. It flashed through her mind that he had a new partner and a baby and he had never even mentioned the fact to her. 'Right, umm okay. I'm not sure what you want me to say to that.' Fleur managed to blurt out.

Ben held his palms upwards. 'I mean, look at me, for example. When we were thinking about moving here, I phoned you and bothered to check with you. I ran it past you just as a common courtesy. Respect is what I think they call it out there in the world.'

Fleur shook her head in disbelief. Ben hadn't exactly asked her about moving, more told her and stated his intentions. He hadn't run it past her at all. She shook her head as irritation began to bubble. 'I really don't think it's any of your business, to be quite honest. I don't have to run anything past you regarding my relationship. Last time I checked we were divorced a long time ago.'

'I know you don't, but I just thought you'd have the common decency...'

Fleur held her hand up. 'The common decency? Really?'

'If it affects Lucy, it affects Sarah and me.'

Fleur was astonished. 'Right.'

'I just thought it would have been nice, considering that Lucy has had lots of problems. This is going to be *massive* for her to deal with. Marriage is a huge thing. I don't want her collapsing because of you...'

'What, like having a new sibling that's, you know, twenty-odd years younger than her? That's not a massive thing?' Fleur snapped back in irritation.

'That is completely different! We have involved Lucy right from the word go.'

Fleur took a deep breath and gripped the steering wheel. She hadn't anticipated the confrontation, especially not parked outside Ben's house. The irony of him lecturing her about communication and marriage wasn't lost on her, given his own life choices. 'Look, I understand you're concerned about Lucy, but our lives have moved in different directions. I didn't think my personal decisions required your approval.'

Ben's expression hardened. He narrowed his eyes and pointed his finger. 'It's not about approval, Fleur. It's about co-parenting. Major changes affect our daughter, and we should handle them together.'

Fleur nodded slowly, acknowledged his point, and decided to play the game just to keep him happy. *Idiot.* 'You're right. I should have informed you directly. But please remember, it works both ways.'

Ben looked momentarily taken aback, then sighed. He moved smoothly, without missing a beat, into lecture mode. 'Fair enough. We need to remember that we're a *blended* family and that this is not the fifties. Let's just ensure we're both more considerate moving forward, for Lucy's sake.'

Fleur managed a small smile, one she didn't mean but slapped on her face to keep the peace. 'Agreed.'

With that, Ben stepped back, and Fleur started the engine. Her mind raced with thoughts as she processed Ben's words. The term 'blended family' hung in the air between them, a phrase that absolutely carried the weight of Sarah's influence. 'Blended family?' Fleur's voice was tinged with incredulity. 'Is that what Sarah's calling it now?'

The little muscles at the side of Ben's jaw popped out. 'It's not just Sarah. It's a reality we need to face. Our lives aren't isolated; they're intertwined, and now there is a baby to consider, too. For Lucy's sake, we need to approach this as a unified front.'

Fleur heard her voice rising. 'Unified? That's rich coming from you. You made your choices back in the day without a second thought about how they'd affect Lucy or me.'

Ben was furious. 'I've always considered Lucy's well-being! Moving in with Sarah and having another child doesn't negate my responsibilities as her father.'

'Responsibilities?' Fleur shot back.

Ben's face flushed. 'Look, Fleur. This is about moving forward and ensuring our daughter feels secure amidst these changes. Sarah and I think you should have had the decency to tell us you were going off to wherever it is, Hawaii, to get married, yourself. I mean, even an email would have sufficed.'

'Pah! What, like you did about the baby? I've heard it all now. You are actually lecturing me about my personal life, now. Gold.'

'I just believe that major decisions, like getting married in Hawaii, should be discussed,' Ben insisted. 'Not just sprung upon us without warning. It's really not rocket science, Fleur. And let me tell you; I am not paying for anything!'

Fleur tried to calm herself down. There was little to no point in arguing with Ben. There never had been. 'I understand your point. Perhaps I should've communicated my plans more clearly. But you need to understand that my life doesn't revolve around seeking your approval.'

'I just want us to co-parent effectively. That means open communication, especially when our decisions impact Lucy.'

There were so many things Fleur could have said, but to be quite honest, she really could not be faffed. It was what it was, and some things, like Ben's arrogance, never changed. She felt the fight draining out of her. A battle with Ben was not one she had the energy for. 'Fine. Let's try to communicate better.'

Ben clearly felt as if he'd won. Let him think that. He really wasn't worth her time. As she drove away, Fleur had a little wry chuckle, more cackle, to herself. It had clearly got up Ben's nose that Fleur had very much moved on and was not only getting married but doing it *spectacularly*. Ben absolutely didn't like it when the boot was on the other foot. Shame. See how it feels, mate.

38

Fleur picked up the kettle from the fancy stove top on top of Cassy's range cooker in Cassy's beautiful kitchen and poured hot water into two mugs where she'd already put teaspoons of hot chocolate. The microwave pinged with a jug of hot milk, she whisked it and added it to the mugs, stirred them vigorously, picked the pair of them up and took them into Cassy's sitting room. Popping them down on the coffee table, she smiled at Cassy, who was sitting with her legs tucked up under her, a throw over her legs.

'I think I need you to live here with me. You can serve me cosy drinks every night of the week.' Cassy laughed. 'How much do you charge for your services?'

'I don't think I could cope with your household. It was bad enough having one girl—I don't know how you've coped with three boys. I really don't.'

'Yes, it's manic at times, but I do love them, not when I have to wash their stinky football kits, though.'

Fleur nodded. Cassy's boys were staying with their grandma, and her husband had a work event, so Fleur had gone over, and they'd had the house to themselves for the night. They'd had a takeaway salami pizza, shared a bottle of red wine, and chatted about everything under the sun. Fleur felt deliciously relaxed, wrapped in best-friend therapy, and a nice night off.

Cassy turned her phone screen around. 'I've just been looking at the pictures of the hotel. I can't believe we're going.'

Fleur nodded. 'I'm so pleased you're coming.'

Cassy put her hands together and tapped them a few times. 'I can't believe I've wangled it. The boys go to their grandma's and ten days off work. Bliss is what it feels like is incoming.'

'I know, it's going to be amazing.'

Cassy picked up her mug of hot chocolate and sipped. 'I really need it. I know I sound like a princess and I know it's *your* wedding, but I need a break. I feel like I haven't had any real time off for ages.'

'I'm hearing you,' Fleur replied with a nod and wide eyes.

'Remember when we were in that café and you said I needed a holiday? Now, not only am I getting that, but I'm going to my best friend's wedding on a tropical island. I mean, you can't really make it up. Who would've thought this would be happening a couple of years ago?'

'I know, right? You don't need to tell me. Remember when I moved to Lovely? Now look at me.' Fleur flicked her eyes upwards and chuckled.

Cassy smiled. 'Madness. Lovely, gorgeous, happy madness.'

'Something like that.'

Cassy leant back into the sofa. 'So, we're actually doing this. Heathrow to LA, then onto Hawaii, and then Maui. It sounds absolutely ridiculous when you say it out loud.'

Fleur grinned and curled her legs up beneath her. 'I know. We sound like celebrities. Or like we're off on some luxury honeymoon show swanning about first-class lounges with sunglasses on, pretending we're not completely shattered from the flight.'

Cassy laughed. 'Except, in reality, we'll be sleep-deprived, dehydrated, and waddling through LAX in compression socks, looking like we've been dragged through a hedge backwards.'

'Exactly. That's the part no one talks about when they go on about jet-setting. They don't mention the swollen ankles, the dodgy in-flight meals, or the sheer horror of having to navigate an airport after twelve hours of minimal sleep and maximum discomfort.'

Cassy shuddered. 'Oh gosh, the airport. I can already feel the stress. The security faff, the repacking of liquids, the existential crisis at duty-free where I start questioning if I need a £200 bottle of perfume because I've been in the air too long and have lost all sense of reality.'

'Ahh, it will be worth it when we get there.'

'Yup. I am kicking back for tropical time.' Cassy sighed happily. 'It's all going to look so beautiful, isn't it? The wedding bit, I mean...'

'I hope so. The ceremony on the beach, lanterns along the sand, the sun setting behind us, waves rolling in, blue skies, tropical flowers. What's not to love?'

'Oh, stop, you're going to make me cry.' Cassy fanned her face.

Fleur laughed. 'You'll be a wreck on the day.'

'I'm fully prepared to sob my way through the vows. I'll be one of those guests, clutching a tissue, weeping into my champagne.'

'Brilliant. That's exactly what I want from you.'

'Glad to be of service.'

Fleur took a sip of her drink and sighed. 'It's actually happening.'

Cassy nodded. 'It really is. I cannot wait now everything is booked.'

'Same.'

'The hotel is going to be amazing. It looks incredible in the photos. That open-air reception, the tropical flowers, the infinity pool that literally looks like it melts into the ocean. I may never come home. I might just conveniently miss my flight back and spend the rest of my life drinking Mai Tais by the pool.'

'Tempting. We'd never have to deliver a training course in a grotty business centre again.'

Cassy stretched her legs out. 'Champo, I'm really proud of you, you know. This is huge and you deserve every single second of it.'

Fleur felt a lump rise in her throat. 'Nah, don't be silly.'

Cassy clinked her mug against Fleur's. 'To Maui, to your wedding, and to my best friend doing all the fabulous things. Here for you, Champo.'

Fleur smiled. 'To all of it.'

Fleur felt a swirl of happiness in her stomach. For the first time in a long time, a long, long, long time, through ups, downs and roundabouts, everything felt exactly as it should be. She wasn't going to argue with that.

39

Fleur walked out of the cottage along the path at the rear of the house, opened the back gate and closed it behind her with a click. There was a lovely breeze in the air as she walked over crisp leaves lining the lane at the back of the house. The leaves gave a satisfying crunch underfoot and she nudged a pile of them with her foot making a few of them flutter up into the air. Margaret, one of the neighbours, chugged along in her little Mini and waved out of the window as she drove past. Fleur shrugged her jacket on because of the nip in the air. Although the sky was a pure, Lovely blue with not a cloud in sight, it was definitely getting chilly, and there was a crispness to the breeze coming in from the sea. Fleur nodded; before they knew it, the cold weather would be in, fires would be lit, smoke would rise in little plumes from chimneys all over Lovely Bay, the flannelette sheets would come out, Christmas would loom and the last of the nice days would be but a distant memory.

With that in mind, Fleur was trying to make the most of the weather before she went off to Maui. She and Patrick were going to an afternoon tea event at Lovely Manor or at least she hoped Patrick would be attending. He'd been delayed because he'd been called into work to sort out a problem where a flood had affected the electrics in a skyscraper his company managed. With his chief electrician away on holiday in Cyprus, he'd had little choice but to jump in his van and go and see what was what.

Fleur, in her wisdom, had decided to walk to Lovely Manor anyway, and if he didn't make it, she would enjoy the afternoon tea on her own. As she strolled with her basket over her shoulder, little cobbles on the narrow pavement nudged the bottoms of her shoes. A cool wind nipped at her neck as she walked past a beautiful house with a deep elevated deck where rosemary bushes spilled over onto the pathway. Looking ahead she could see one of Lovely Bay's prettiest churches in front of her, its steep spire with a cross on top poking up into the deep blue sky. Getting closer, she took in the arched windows underneath the top of the shell-tiled roof and looked at what appeared to her to be dragons on each of the four corners. As she got to the gate and peered in, it quickly flitted through her mind as she stared at the church's blue nave door that she could have had her wedding in Lovely. It would have been a nice enough occasion. Something, though, had told her that she didn't want a traditional English wedding in an old church on a summer's day, something of the like that she'd seen in Essex. She'd had enough of that the first time around.

Nope, she was going for all-singing, all-dancing tropical and was looking forward to the deep reds of hibiscus flowers, the tropical feel, lush mountains in the distance, thick, sticky air, and a wedding that was something else. For Fleur Champion's second stab at tying the knot she wasn't going with just run-of-the-mill, nope, she was casting her net much further afield. As she strolled and pondered, she also thought about the fact that if the wedding took place in England, it would've been a whole different ball game where the guestlist was concerned. There would have been extended family, this one, that one, and all sorts involved and our Fleur wasn't up for that. Going to Maui meant that it would be short, sweet, and the guest list was very contained. Just as she wanted.

As she walked past the main part of the church, she looked at a line of huge arched stained-glass windows with double doors underneath and six small windows going across the top, and wondered who had built the place and all the things it might have seen in its long life in the third smallest town in the country.

As the walk, the fresh air and, it had to be said, the stunning view of her surroundings, made Fleur decompress from this, that and the other, her mind wandered. It moved from thinking about the guest list and how short it was to her mum and Wendy. Wendy had been brilliant about the wedding news and not a problem at all—in fact, she'd been more than excited. She'd quickly booked a flight from Sydney to Hawaii and had not made much fuss about it whatsoever. She'd bought a beautiful floral dress and had been in touch with the hotel, booking herself and Lucy into a suite without any mention of money, budget, or anything like that at all. Wendy, it seemed, was very happy about the event and not only that was putting her money where her mouth was and was determined to have a good time.

Valerie, however, had been a different ball game altogether. As Fleur got to a pedestrian crossing and pushed the button, she sighed to herself as she thought about the various conversations with Valerie and how they had gone. Valerie had made the whole wedding in Maui all about herself at any given opportunity. She'd complained about the length of the flights, the size of the hotel rooms, the fact that the hotel wasn't near any major tourist attractions and the cost of just about everything.

After a bit of to-ing and fro-ing, Valerie and Marvin had come to the conclusion that the best thing for them would be to fly from Istanbul. Wendy had gone online and found a place where they would be able to leave the van for a few weeks and had even paid for it. Still, though, Valerie had complained whenever she'd been able to. So much for the globetrotting bohemian. Valerie had appeared to have forgotten about that.

In the conversations between Valerie and Fleur, there had been quite a few tangents that had been a bit of an eye-opener to Fleur; there were rumblings that Marvellous Marvin was perhaps not quite as marvellous at all. It had all started when Valerie and Fleur had been discussing the cost of flights to LA from Istanbul. Valerie had baulked at the cost because Marvin had insisted that they travel business class. Valerie had tutted and said that she would have been fine in premium economy. She'd been irritated and said that the trouble with Marvin was that he had champagne taste and beer money. In fact, Valerie had gone further and said that Marvin didn't have any money so who was he to talk about champagne in the first place?

To Fleur's complete and utter shock, Valerie had gone on to insinuate that the Marvin and Valerie love affair of the century had faded a tad. The reason being one very simple thing often referred to as "the root of all evil" by some; money. Valerie had relayed that after the discussion about the cost of business class flights that she and Marvin had had a conversation about money where Marvin hadn't ended up being happy. After a long heated discussion, it had turned out that Marvin had wanted to merge *all* their bank accounts. He wanted to be included in all of Valerie's financial decisions and to be able to get his hands on her money if and when he needed to. Marvellous Marvin wanted to be put as an "executor", as he had called it, on the money that Valerie had invested into ETF funds when she'd sold her house. According to Valerie, Marvin had insisted that the reason for this was in case something "happened to Valerie" and he needed to access the money to keep her safe. He'd mentioned medical bills, funds, not knowing what was around the corner, making sure that Valerie didn't get sick and all sorts.

Valerie, it appeared, had seen red flags and had not been that impressed.

All of it had left a very funny taste in our Fleur's mouth, but it seemed that Valerie was one step ahead of her. As Valerie had explained things to Fleur, it was clear that something had changed and Valerie had got wind of the fact that Marvin was perhaps digging for some gold. Marvellous Marvin's shovel, however, didn't seem to be getting very deep.

Fleur had felt really uncomfortable about what Valerie had told her for quite a few reasons. First of all, she'd always wondered if, underneath it all, Marvin was only after a meal ticket and Valerie's money. Secondly, right from the Big Announcement everything about it had made Fleur think that Marvin was weird, strange and not the sharpest tool in the box.

The other thing that had thrown Fleur was the fact that since the booking of the flights from Istanbul, Valerie's full-on gushing and hero worshipping of Marvellous Marvin had soured. Valerie had been almost dismissive of him when she spoke about money. Maybe the honeymoon phase with Marvin had finally come to an end. Perhaps the rose-tinted glasses were just that little less rosy now real life had started to take hold. Now van life wasn't quite as thrilling anymore and the bohemian experience wasn't quite as novel.

Fleur couldn't work it out. She *did* know that she didn't want it all coming to a head just as she was going to Maui so she'd tried to placate Valerie. As she walked along in the direction of Lovely Manor, she ummed and ahhed over the whole conundrum and wondered what was really going on in Valerie's head but tried to put it to the back of her mind. One thing she knew with her mother was that whatever happened, Valerie Champion would beat to the sound of her own drum and do whatever she wanted. There would be no one in the world who would be changing that.

∽

As Fleur got to the road that led up out of Lovely, where the manor sat on the hill in the distance, she stopped right where she was for a moment and looked up. Rolling hills, a beautiful old manor house, manicured gardens, and just pretty Lovely things as far as the eye could see. She'd got the tickets for the afternoon tea via Birdie and Cally at the chemist, and she wasn't really sure what it was going to be like. Right now, as she saw the manor glistening in the distance, she knew she'd made a good call—whether or not Patrick would make it, she could feel in her bones because of the view looking back at her, that she would have a nice time.

Adjusting the strap of her bag on her shoulder, she took a breath, letting her gaze rest on Lovely Manor. The building sat on the rise ahead, glowing under the early afternoon sun, framed by hills and perfectly maintained gardens. The slate roof gleamed, its steep gables and a row of tall, white-framed windows reflected the deep blue of the sky. Following the instructions that came with the tickets, Fleur walked past the huge main entrance gates and along a gravel path that curved towards a side entrance. Freshly cut grass lingered in the air, there was the faintest trace of woodsmoke from somewhere and she smiled as a couple in a car slowed and passed her.

Fleur reached the side gate, a tall, black wrought-iron structure flanked by thick yew hedges that had been clipped into perfect symmetry. She pulled her phone from her pocket and double-checked the message Birdie had sent with the entry details. A discreet keypad was set into the stone wall beside the gate. She keyed in the code, and after a brief pause, there was a soft click as the lock disengaged. Stepping through, she let the gate swing gently shut behind her. The gardens opened up in front of her, a perfectly maintained space of rolling lawns and carefully arranged flower beds. The main gravel path stretched ahead, but a smaller, winding path led towards the back of the manor, through a neatly trimmed rose garden. Fleur hesitated only a second before taking it, and trailed her fingers over the nearest rose bush as she walked. The petals were soft, the scent heady, a mixture of deep reds and pale pinks, the kind of English garden charm that was hard to replicate.

Despite herself, her thoughts drifted back to Valerie and the conundrum of Marvin. It wasn't just what her mum had *said* about Marvin; it was the *way* she'd said it. Valerie had always been someone who framed things in a way that suited her, who could make a decision sound like someone else's problem, but something about the whole situation didn't sit right with Fleur. The way Valerie had brushed off the issue when Fleur had asked a follow-up question. The way she had made it sound as if Marvin was now a bit of an inconvenience, rather than someone to be genuinely concerned about. The way Valerie had changed the subject so quickly after mentioning Marvin's complaints about money.

Fleur had picked up on it immediately—there had been something dismissive, almost casual, in the way Valerie had moved on, as if acknowledging it too much would make it more real. Fleur knew Valerie all too well and it was clear that Valerie had already realised she had made a mistake with Marvin but would never admit it, least of all to either of her daughters.

Fleur sighed, her steps slowing as she passed under an arched trellis covered in pale yellow roses. The scent followed her, soft and delicate, but didn't do a lot to settle the nagging unease about Valerie. Wendy had felt it too. That was the thing that stuck with her. Fleur had a tendency to second-guess herself, to overthink, but Wendy had been firm in her opinion that Valerie was pulling away from Marvin, not completely, but enough to make it obvious. Enough to suggest that something had shifted. The question was whether it was Marvin's behaviour that had changed, or if Valerie had simply grown tired of him.

Fleur reached the end of the rose garden, where the path widened and curved towards the back of the manor. In the distance, beyond the manicured lawns, she could see the marquee set up for the afternoon tea. The white canvas glowed softly in the sunlight, its open sides revealing glimpses of tables dressed with white linens, delicate china, and tiered cake stands.

Trying to flick the thoughts of Valerie away, Fleur tutted and shook her head. She didn't want to spend the afternoon stuck in her own head, going over the same thoughts about Valerie and Marvin again and again. There was nothing she could do about it. She was more interested in having a nice afternoon letting Lovely Manor work its magic. One thing she knew was that wherever Valerie went there would be drama. Not even a wedding in Maui was going to change that.

40

Time had flown by and there was no turning back. Fleur and Lucy were at the airport waiting at the desk at the entrance to a very fancy looking lounge. Fleur handed over their boarding passes to an immaculately dressed woman in a red suit with a gorgeous silk scarf and a neat bumped bun hairstyle. The woman beamed. 'Just checking your details here. Off anywhere nice?'

Fleur nodded. 'Yes, really nice, actually. We're going to Hawaii and Maui.'

'Ooh, lovely. For anything special? I've always wanted to go there. It's meant to be beautiful and very relaxing.'

'Actually, yes, I'm getting married,' Fleur said, not quite believing herself that she was, in fact, going to Maui to get married.

Lucy giggled. 'Yes, and I'm the bridesmaid. We're so excited!'

The woman handed the boarding cards back over. 'Oh, ladies, that is absolutely wonderful! Congratulations. Have a fabulous time. Okay, do go and make yourselves comfortable. Get yourselves a drink, you need to check the board because this is a quiet lounge, and we do not call passengers to flights, so keep an eye on the board.'

'Thank you so much.'

'If I were you, I'd head right past the buffet, go all the way along to your right and there's a really nice sectioned-off area that looks out over the planes. Most people don't get that far along so it's much less busy. You can make yourselves comfortable and have a few drinks and a bite to eat. You've got plenty of time before your flight.'

'We'll look out for it. Thanks for the tip.'

A few minutes later, Fleur and Lucy were walking through the lounge heading in the direction of the area the woman had told them about. Lucy giggled. 'Mum, this is so cool. I can't believe we are in a lounge at the airport on our way to Los Angeles. Like it's a dream!'

'I know.' Fleur nodded and laughed.

'Are you nervous?'

'Not really, just a little bit, sort of excited and a bit jittery. I'm not really happy about being on a plane for that long.' Fleur swallowed as she told the white lie. She was actually a tad scared about the plane but Lucy didn't need to know that. No need for the pair of them to be wondering if the plane would go down and they'd end up on the bottom of the sea.

Lucy agreed. 'I know, but it will be amazing when we get there, won't it? One of the girls at ballet school did a year in LA, she said it's fabulous, and the weather is amazing.'

Fleur pointed in the direction of the window, where the sky was a mixture of different competing greys and it had been drizzling since they'd left Lovely Bay. 'Well, it's got to be better than here at the moment. I think it's been raining for weeks, hasn't it?'

'Feels like it. Months more like.'

About ten minutes later, Fleur and Lucy were settled into a cosy spot near the windows overlooking the tarmac. They'd helped themselves to drinks and snacks from the buffet and were chatting away about what the hotel was going to be like once they'd got to Maui.

After lots of chatting, a quick call to Valerie and checking in on Wendy and Patrick, Fleur glanced at the departure board and noticed their flight had been delayed by two hours. Fleur groaned. 'Ahh! The last thing we need.'

'What do you think the reason is? It's worrying.'

Fleur attempted to keep her voice calm. 'I'm sure it will be fine.'

Lucy bit her lip. 'I hope so. I hope it's not an engine problem or anything like that.'

'I don't think we get to know that.'

'The idea of flying on a faulty plane is a bit scary.'

'I know, but they wouldn't let us fly if it wasn't safe. Let's try not to worry too much.' Fleur tutted to herself as she walked over to get another glass of champagne and wondered why it always felt in her life as things never went to plan.

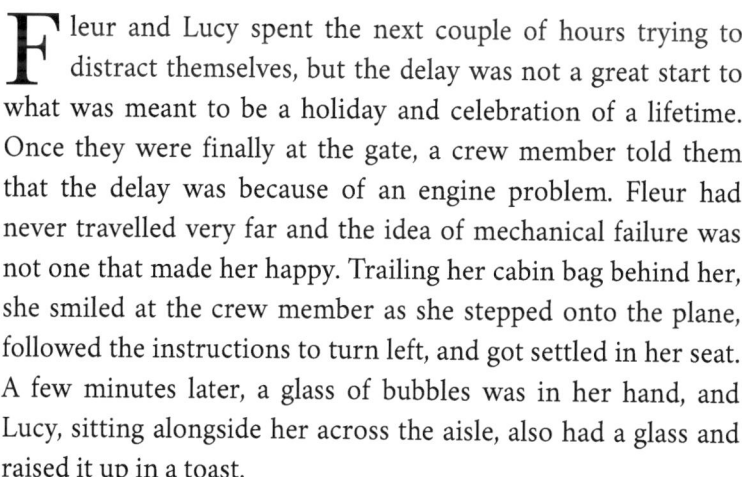

Fleur and Lucy spent the next couple of hours trying to distract themselves, but the delay was not a great start to what was meant to be a holiday and celebration of a lifetime. Once they were finally at the gate, a crew member told them that the delay was because of an engine problem. Fleur had never travelled very far and the idea of mechanical failure was not one that made her happy. Trailing her cabin bag behind her, she smiled at the crew member as she stepped onto the plane, followed the instructions to turn left, and got settled in her seat. A few minutes later, a glass of bubbles was in her hand, and Lucy, sitting alongside her across the aisle, also had a glass and raised it up in a toast.

'Wow, this is so nice. Thanks, Mum. Cheers.'

'You can thank Patrick. He's the one who booked these flights. Cheers.'

Lucy smiled. 'I can't believe we're on our way and you're getting married.'

'I know. You and me both.'

Lucy frowned. 'I've just had a thought. What about our bags? I hope they've not messed them up with the change of plane and everything.'

'I'm sure it will be fine. They do stuff like this all the time. We're in good hands.'

'Yes, true. They know what they're doing.' Lucy smiled as she took out the little utility bag in front of her and rifled through it. She held up a travel size lavender face spray and spritzed some on her cheeks.

Just as Fleur was putting her lap belt on, her phone pinged. She looked down and inhaled. *Here we go*, she thought. There was never a dull moment when Valerie was around.

'Who's that?' Lucy asked across the aisle.

'It's Grandma.'

Fleur read through the text and frowned.

'What?' Lucy questioned.

Fleur shook her head. 'That's weird. Grandma said that she's coming on her own now and that Marvin's not coming.'

'What? I thought they were leaving the van and having a holiday in America?'

'Yes, I know. That was the plan. They drove to Istanbul specifically for that reason, to that place where they could leave the van. Wendy sorted it out.'

Lucy shook her head. 'Marvin's not coming now? What? That's weird.'

'Grandma said she's had a bit of a change of plan. Marvin's coming later.'

'I hope she's okay.' Lucy whipped her phone out. 'I'll send her a message, too. So, Marvin's coming at a different time now?'

'Yes, it seems like it.'

Fleur's phone pinged again, and she read another message from Valerie. 'Alright, that makes more sense. Marvin is sorting out the van there and making sure it's fixed before he leaves, which is why Grandma's coming on her own.'

'Seems a bit last minute, doesn't it?' Lucy noted.

Little red flags waved in front of Fleur's face. Something wasn't right but she didn't know what. 'Well, I suppose that's what happens with vans. You can't choose when they go wrong.'

'Yes, true. Oh well, I'm sure she'll be fine. She's used to travelling now, isn't she? She's been telling me for ages how she spent years locked away just waiting to get out and travel. That it was always in her bones, so I'm sure she'll be fine on her own.'

Fleur smirked to herself. Never a truer word. Valerie was the one who was always pontificating about how much she loved travelling and how she was now able to do whatever she wanted and go wherever she pleased. How after Bill had died, she'd finally been allowed to let her inner bohemian come out to play. The thing was though that, actually, Valerie hadn't ever been on her own as far as Fleur could see. She grimaced to herself and crossed her fingers that Valerie was going to be okay. Let the Valerie drama begin.

~

Approximately twelve hours later, after quite a few glasses of bubbles, a nice long sleep and a few films, Fleur looked out of the window as the plane taxied and smiled over at Lucy.

Lucy craned her neck to see out the window. 'Oh wow, Mum, look at all the palm trees. It looks so warm and sunny, and we're not even there yet.'

'I know, wow, it's amazing. Bring on the sunshine.' Fleur checked her watch. 'According to this, because of the delay, we should be arriving at around the same time as Wendy. Actually, in fact, I think she's already here, so I'll message her.' Fleur looked at her phone as it beeped about six times, notifying her that she had arrived in America and that her home carrier would charge a daily rate for internet and text messages. Just as she was reading through the message, one came in from Wendy.

Wendy: *Hi, I'm already here! I worked out that you'll be coming in at the same place that I did, so I'll be waiting for you. So exciting!*

Fleur quickly messaged back.

Fleur: *We've just landed. We had a long delay. We're approaching the gate now, so we shouldn't be too long, depending on how immigration stuff goes. The weather looks great! See you soon!*

Lucy looked over from her phone. 'Yep, Auntie Wendy is already here. Seems she got here before us because of our delay.'

'Yep, I just got the same text. How funny; we've come from London, and she's come from Australia.'

'Yes, I know. Ooh, this is so fab! I can't wait to see her.'

Fleur nodded. So far, so good.

41

Fleur shifted in her seat, the leather on the taxi seat covering sticking slightly to the back of her thighs as warm, humid air seeped through the cracks in the air conditioning. It was hot, sticky, steamy and oh-so-very nice outside. The kind of sticky, tropical heat that clung like a second skin, thick with the scent of humidity, whatever that was, flowers, vegetation and something *very* foreign. Lucy wriggled beside her, pressing her face nearer to the window as the taxi wound its way down a long driveway lined with towering palms and thick bursts of frangipani trees heavy with yellow and pink blooms. A couple in shorts and t-shirts on white beach cruiser bikes waved at the driver as he went past and the driver gave a toot of his horn.

Lucy pointed to the trees. 'Wow, the colours. We're finally in Maui.'

Fleur gasped as the bay she'd seen in the hotel photos many times came into view. The most ridiculously perfect, postcard-worthy view, the blue so blue it didn't seem real, topped by deep tropical saturated greens. As the taxi got closer to the hotel, she could see shimmering waves curving into lush, green mountains beyond. The water so clear that even from the road it changed from pale turquoise near the shore to a deep, endless blue further out. Just a little bit stunning.

Patrick let out a low whistle from the front seat. 'Not bad, is it? It was worth the trek by the looks of it.'

Lucy shook her head. 'No. Not bad at all. I think I just fell in love.'

Fleur nodded. 'We chose well. This is amazing.'

Wendy gushed. 'Take me to the infinity pool and leave me there.'

The taxi slowed as they reached the entrance to the hotel, pulling up under a wide, thatched canopy framing an open-air reception area. A row of enormous clay pots filled with thick, glossy-leaved ferns lined a walkway to a concierge desk where staff in white shirts and beige shorts stood with beams on their faces. As soon as the driver opened the door, the scent of tropical flowers, vegetation and salty air filled Fleur's lungs. Stepping out in front of Lucy, she was instantly hit by the full force of the tropical heat; a heat that smelled of sunshine and greenery, frangipani and a full-on assault of humidity and warmth. The thick air wrapped around her and the long travel trousers she'd thought were a sensible idea felt as if they were thermals as they instantly clung to her legs.

Lucy climbed out behind her, stretching her arms and whisper-hissed. 'It's *so* hot! Oh my gosh, the reception is beautiful. I love it. I can't believe we're here.'

Patrick tapped his card on the driver's payment machine before swinging their suitcases onto the pavement. 'That's because we're in Maui, Luce. It's hot here.'

Lucy gushed. 'It feels like we're in an actual oven.'

Wendy nodded. 'It does!'

Fleur pushed her sunglasses up onto her head as she took in the hotel; it was exactly how it had looked in the photos except so very much better. As she stood for a bit as Lucy and Patrick fussed with the suitcases, she peered up at the high vaulted ceilings of the open-air reception. Thick wooden beams were dotted about, huge wicker fans turned lazily above, and a stone floor was covered here and there with sisal rugs placed just so. To the far right, a barman in a white shirt stood behind a wide timber curved bar lined with dark wooden stools pouring fresh pineapple juice into tall glasses. To the left, the space opened up onto a wide terrace, spilling out onto the most perfectly manicured stretch of green lawn Fleur had ever seen. Little paths lined with palms in pots led down in the direction of the bay and white wicker lanterns dangled from the trees. Sticky, balmy air, heavy with the scent of blooming flowers, rain-soaked earth and the smell of the bay was so thick that Fleur felt as if she could almost touch it.

A smiling woman in a floaty coral dress approached, a clipboard in one hand and four fresh flower leis draped over the other. 'Aloha! Welcome to Lana Lai Resort,' she said warmly, placing a lei over Fleur, Wendy and Lucy's heads.

Lucy beamed, touching the soft petals around her neck. 'Thank you.'

'I'm Keira, one of the front desk team. You must be Fleur, Patrick, Lucy and Wendy, is it?'

'Yes, that's us.'

'Fantastic. We've been expecting you and the rest of your party. Your suites are ready, and the wedding team has everything scheduled for your arrival. Would you like a welcome drink?'

Fleur hesitated, glancing towards the bar. 'That would be lovely. We've been travelling for what feels like an eternity. It's so hot.'

Keira gestured towards the seating area just beyond a table groaning in vases of tropical flowers. 'Take a seat, relax for a moment, and we'll bring them over. We do things a bit differently here; no check-in desks, lines of queues or roped-off bollard areas where you stand in line and people bark orders at you. I'll be personally checking you in and then I'll take you to your room if you want me to or you can have a wander and chill and go as you please. We take relaxing and vacationing very seriously here. You booked a six-star boutique experience for a reason; we aim to fulfil that for you right from the word go. You won't be disappointed.'

Fleur nodded, swallowed at the mention of the six-stars and how much the boutique experience was costing them and followed Patrick and Lucy over to a wide, white-cushioned sofa nestled beneath a massive wicker light fitting. She sank down, feeling the journey start to ebb away as she looked around; piles of neutral-coloured cushions were expertly placed on long, low sofas, gigantic green palms sat in oversized wicker plant pots, rattan side tables held giant softly lit lamps, quiet footsteps, freshly cut flowers stuffed into white clay vases, hushed voices, and clusters of oversized coffee table books sat here and there ready to be opened with a long drink. Six stars looked back at her.

A couple of minutes later, tall chilled glasses full of something pale and citrusy, with fresh mint leaves floating on top and condensation running down the sides, arrived on the table. Fleur took a glass, sipped and sighed. 'Oh, that is good. Just what I needed.'

'So good,' Wendy agreed.

Patrick tasted his and nodded approvingly. 'I could get used to this.'

'It sure beats sitting on the M25 on a Monday morning wondering if you're ever going to make it to work.'

Keira returned a few minutes later with a folder and an iPad tucked under her arm. After they'd handed over their identification documents and checked in, Keira smiled. 'Okay, so just to go through a few details for you. Your suites are ready now and your luggage will be taken up shortly. Fresh fruit and drinks will be delivered daily and you just need to let us know what housekeeping requirements you prefer. The wedding team has arranged a meeting for tomorrow morning to go through the final touches and your pre-wedding spa treatments have been confirmed for the afternoon. Let me know if there's anything else you need in the meantime.'

Fleur blinked. 'Oh, yes, the spa treatments.'

Keira smiled and tapped the iPad. 'Yes, part of the wedding package. A full body massage, facial, and a relaxing soak in the ocean-view bathhouse.'

Patrick grinned. 'Well, that's you sorted then.'

Fleur shook her head in amazement. 'This place is ridiculous in the best possible way.'

Keira laughed. 'We like to think so.' She handed over a key card. 'Your suite has an ocean view. Let me know if there's anything you need.'

Fleur took the card. 'Thank you so much.'

'My pleasure! And again, welcome to Maui.'

Fleur turned to Lucy, Wendy and Patrick, feeling an almost surreal wave of happiness flood through her. So far, so good. 'Right. Let's go check out our new home for the next week.'

Patrick grabbed the last of their hand luggage, Wendy rolled her suitcase behind her, and Lucy practically skipped ahead towards the pathway to the rooms. As they walked along, Fleur exhaled slowly. She was in Maui, she was getting married. It really was happening. It was bliss.

After seeing Lucy and Wendy to their room, Fleur pushed open a heavy wicker-covered door and was immediately hit by a myriad of lovely scents from a diffuser on a rattan side table; lemongrass, lavender and eucalyptus filled her nose as she slipped off her shoes and sighed. Popping her bag down, she walked in taking in a huge bed draped in white linens, dress cushions in every possible permutation of white and cream, a tasselled runner on the bed and a cluster of potted palms nestled into the corner. Oversized dark rattan fans rustled above, white gauze curtains moved at the doors and Patrick was standing on the balcony looking out in the direction of the bay. Strolling past floor-to-ceiling wicker shutters, Fleur stepped out onto the balcony and was hit by humidity, a lush scent from blooming frangipani, bees buzzing and the sounds of the sea. For a moment she was overcome, not quite believing it, not quite all there. She smiled at Patrick, put her hands over the balcony and held her face up to the sky. 'Holy moly this is nice.'

'What a dump, eh?' Patrick joked.

'Totally awful. Dreadful.'

Patrick laughed. 'I have to admit I was slightly concerned about what it was going to be like when we got here.'

'I know. You never really know even when you've paid the best part of a mortgage for it.'

'So true, but so far it's exceeded expectations from my end.'

'Mine too.'

'Happy?'

'Very.' Fleur closed her eyes for a second. 'Long days of doing nothing. No training materials, no emails from work, no Etsy orders, no housework, no anything.'

Patrick put his arm around her waist and kissed her. 'Just getting married to me.'

Fleur nodded. Worked for her.

42

Fleur opened the door to the balcony and felt the gorgeous tropical air hit her. Picking up a jug of iced tea that had just been delivered, she placed it on the table, and sat down. Tapping on her phone, she connected with her mum, who was sitting at the airport in LA. Valerie did not look her best; she appeared tired, stressed, grumpy, overwhelmed and was nervously twirling her hair. The look on her face would have made anyone wary. Fleur knew it only too well.

Fleur gulped and plastered a smile on her face. 'Hey, Mum, how are you?'

Valerie sighed. 'I'm fine, actually, I'm not fine. I'm quite stressed, to be honest, Fleur. I could have done without this.'

Fleur ignored the last bit of the comment and smiled. 'So, what's happened with Marvin?'

Valerie ran a hand over her face. 'He just gets very stressed about the van.'

'I don't understand, Mum. How is he upset about the van when, really, it's not even his? You were the one who bought it and you have the money to fix it when stuff goes wrong. I can't see what the problem is. Am I missing something?'

'Yes, but it's *ours* now.' Valerie stressed the word "ours" heavily and sighed. 'He's very invested in that van. He wanted to stay there to make sure it's fixed.'

'I don't get why he'd be happy to let you travel on your own. He said he wanted to stay with the van, did he?'

Valerie flapped her hand and twirled her hair. 'Yes, yes, that's what he said. He was very stressed. I don't care what he does.'

'So he's going to come in a couple of days?' Fleur clarified.

'Yep.'

'What about the wedding?'

Valerie sighed. 'I don't know, darling. It was important for *me* to be there for the wedding. Obviously, not so much for him.'

'It's not too much to ask though, really, is it?'

'Well, I suppose not.'

Fleur smelt a rat; Valerie was being elusive. 'What have you done about his flight?'

Valerie flapped her hands again. 'Well, he looked at the cancellation terms and it was easy. The code we booked meant we had to pay a small fee to cancel it and that's it. So he's going to rebook.'

'What he's just going to book one at the last minute once the van is fixed? Really?'

'Yes, from Istanbul to LA. The same as me. It's quite simple.' Valerie twirled her hair with her right forefinger.

'Right. Well, I hope you're okay and Marvin gets the van sorted.' It killed Fleur to say that but she was trying to be nice to her mum.

Valerie made a funny dismissive wiggling movement with her hand and pursed her lips. 'Darling, thank you, it's just such a long way and you sprung it on us so quickly. Really, Fleur. I'm not being funny but some consideration would have been good. I'm not as young as I used to be. I can't go gallivanting all over the show hither and yon.'

Fleur was dumbstruck. This coming from a woman who'd

sold her home and taken off to Europe in a van. The same woman who'd told Fleur to lighten up and be more impulsive. Fleur ignored her mum's words. 'So, Wendy and I will be at the airport to meet you and take it from there. All you have to do is get on the plane there. Don't worry about anything and we'll see you soon.'

'Yes, okay, darling, thanks. I'll message you when I'm on the plane and just before take-off. You will make sure you're there, please. Don't be late.'

'No, we won't. See you soon.'

Fleur put the phone down and sighed. Something about the issue with Marvin and the van didn't quite sit right as far as she was concerned, but she couldn't work out what. Why was Marvin being so dramatic about the van? At the end of the day, it was just a van, and he hadn't even been the one to pay for it. It had been Valerie who had bought the van. For somebody who was apparently such a globetrotter and loved to wanderlust, it seemed strange that a trip to America and Hawaii wasn't as important as getting a starter motor on a ten-year-old van fixed. The more and more Fleur thought about it, the less and less it didn't add up. Valerie too; weird, elusive and just odd. As if she was trying to make out the trip was too much for her to avoid speaking about the real reason Marvin was delaying.

She was pouring another glass of iced tea when the doorbell went. Getting up to answer, Wendy was standing in the corridor in swimmers with an oversized white shirt over the top, white-framed sunglasses on her head, white flip-flops, and a very large wicker beach bag, Wendy smiled and took in the fact that Fleur was still in her robe, and stepped inside.

'Morning, how are you?'

'I'm just having iced tea on the balcony. Patrick's gone for a swim with Lucy. Would you like one?'

'That sounds nice. Ours went straight into the fridge.'

'It's delicious.' Fleur followed Wendy through to the balcony. 'I've just come off WhatsApp with Mum.'

'Yes, she messaged me.' Wendy shook her head. 'There's something weird there. Like, I don't know, but don't you think it's strange that all of a sudden, Marvin isn't coming yet? I thought they were thick as thieves. She told me in Greece that she would never travel without him again. She kept avoiding my questions...'

'I thought the same.'

'He's saying that he's staying there just because of a starter motor. I don't know, it just seems really odd to me.' Wendy wrinkled her nose.

'I just assumed it's because he was attached to the van.'

Wendy shrugged. 'Well, some people are like that but, nah, it's not right. She's not telling us something. Elusive is the word.'

'Yes! It's not his van at the end of the day, either.'

'Well, he thinks it is.'

'You're right. There's something else. I can just *feel* it. You don't not go to what's pretty much the other side of the world when you're not paying, with the person that you've just spent every day of your life with. It just doesn't make sense.'

'When you say it like that it's even more dodgy. Yeah, she's up to something,' Wendy agreed. 'There's something going on here that we don't know about.'

Fleur sighed and rolled her eyes. 'The next drama with Mum. Spare us.'

Wendy tutted. 'I thought we'd seen enough with the infected finger.'

'Tell me about it. There was the Big Announcement, too. Really, why are we surprised? She was always going to make this all about her.' Fleur swirled the ice in her glass. 'Honestly, I don't know what to make of it. It just doesn't sit right. If Marvin is such a globetrotter, he'd be on the next flight, wouldn't he? Stuff the starter motor.'

Wendy crossed her legs and tucked her sunglasses into her beach bag. 'Exactly. But instead, he's staying behind for what? A starter motor? I mean, Fleur, come on. That's ridiculous. He's acting like the van is some sort of lifeline.'

'Right? He is supposedly this free spirit, world-traveller type. A man of adventure, all about the experience. So why is he clinging to that van like it's the only thing keeping him grounded?'

'Maybe because it is?'

Fleur frowned. 'What do you mean?'

Wendy leaned forward. 'I've been thinking about it and I don't think their relationship is as picture-perfect as mum makes out.'

Fleur snorted. 'I could've told you that.'

'Think about it. She's spent the last couple of years acting like she's found this amazing new lease on life like they're this bohemian, carefree couple roaming around Europe without a care in the world. But I think it's more complicated than that.'

Fleur narrowed her eyes. 'You think it's all an act?'

'Not completely. I'm sure she's happy in some ways, but maybe it's not all it's cracked up to be this van life malarkey. Her life before was very *stable* with Dad. Maybe Marvin's not as keen on this whole travelling, loved-up-in-a-van lifestyle as she wants us to believe, either. Maybe he's clinging to that van because it's his safety net. Maybe, deep down, he knows that if they weren't doing this whole travelling thing, they wouldn't have much holding them together. Which is why he's started to try to get his hands on her money. Plus, she's not getting any younger...'

Fleur blinked, letting Wendy's words settle. 'You think the van is their relationship?'

'Yes, and if that's the case, why would he want to leave it behind?'

Fleur leant back in her chair. 'God, that actually makes sense.

Like, if he really wanted to come here, he'd have figured it out, wouldn't he?'

'Exactly. Mum's not telling the truth. I know that look she does and when she keeps touching her hair, I bet she was doing that when you spoke to her. She's trying to keep up appearances, pretending it's all fine when deep down, she must be fuming or they've had a fight and she doesn't want to admit it.'

Fleur thought back to the video call. Valerie had looked tired, not just from travelling, but from something else. Defeated, almost. Wendy was right, she *had* been doing the twirling her hair thing. 'You might be onto something. I don't know. I hate the thought of her being taken for a ride.'

'Me too, but let's be real, Mum's not an idiot. If she's ignoring the signs, it's because she doesn't want to face them.'

Fleur sighed, rubbing her temples. 'So, what do we do?'

Wendy shrugged. 'Nothing. Yet. We just watch and wait. If Marvin shows up in a few days, fine. But if he doesn't? Then maybe it's time to ask some questions or just drink cocktails and let her get on with it.'

Fleur exhaled slowly. 'I just don't want to see her hurt.'

'I know. But sometimes, people have to realise things on their own.'

Fleur nodded, though the uneasy feeling in her stomach didn't disappear. Whatever was going on, she had a feeling they hadn't heard the last of it. Typical that it was happening when she was getting married and it was meant to be all about her. In the Champion family, some things never changed.

43

Fleur stepped onto soft, warm sand, and slipped her sandals off as the last of the day's heat settled around her. The sun dipped low on the horizon and cast long, golden streaks across the sky, and turned the ocean into a shifting sheet of amber. Talk about glorious. A breeze drifted through palms, wide, glossy leaves rustled and lanterns strung up between wooden posts and low-hanging branches flickered along the beach. Everything felt as if someone somewhere had specifically designed things with one aim and one aim only; to relax. Fleur, it had to be said, was making the most of it.

'This place is so gorgeous.' Cassy turned in a circle to take it all in. 'Absolutely gorgeous. I mean, look at it. The lanterns, the little tables on the sand, the paths through the trees, the sunbeds. The fact that I can literally hear the waves as I order a cocktail? What's not to like?'

Fleur smiled. 'I know. I keep thinking I'm going to wake up and find out we're actually sitting in some dodgy hotel restaurant back home, drinking overpriced cocktails with a sticky menu talking about how bad the attendees at the event were that day.'

Cassy shuddered. 'Please, don't even joke about that. I don't want to be reminded about going back to work. It feels as if we are a million miles away. I do miss the boys, though.'

Patrick, who was walking slightly ahead with Cassy's husband and his brother, turned back. 'Are you two planning to stand there admiring the place all evening, or do you actually want to sit down and get a drink?'

'We're taking it in.'

He led the way towards a row of tables beneath a wooden pergola, draped in white fabric that fluttered in the evening breeze. A few other guests were sitting along the edge of a rattan beach bar, chatting, candlelight flickered and the air was full with a sticky tropical humidity. The faint strum of a guitar weaved into the sound of the waves rolling onto the shore. As they settled at a table, a waiter appeared, beaming at them as he put down a small lantern in the centre of their table. 'Welcome! Would you like to start with something to drink?'

Cassy nodded. 'Yes, please. A cold, tropical cocktail that will make me fuzzy around the edges.'

Fleur giggled. 'Make that two.'

Patrick eye rolled. 'You two are on a roll by the looks of it.'

Cassy waved one of her hands dismissively. 'We are on an island for a wedding. If we can't have ridiculous cocktails now, when can we?'

Fleur sighed and let her eyes flick between the sky and the candles on the surrounding tables. 'It is pretty perfect here, isn't it? Every part of the hotel is just so nice and well-designed. When they claim it's six-stars, it really is.'

Patrick reached for her hand under the table and gave it a squeeze. 'I'm so pleased it's worked out well.'

Ten or so minutes later, the waiter put down a tray with an assortment of fancy boutique cocktails. There was not a cocktail umbrella or dodgy plastic stirring stick with a fake pineapple in sight.

Cassy sighed. 'Oh my gosh, look at these beauties. Fleur, we've made it in life. This is so me. I don't want to go home. If it wasn't for the boys, I wouldn't...'

Fleur picked up a tall glass with passion fruit floating on top and took a sip. She raised her glass. 'A toast.'

'To what, exactly?'

Fleur gestured around her. 'To being here, in this beautiful place, to the fact that we've actually pulled this off, and to I don't know, just all the good stuff.'

Cassy clinked her glass against Fleur's. 'To all of that.'

Cassy's husband laughed. 'To swimming in the bay...'

'Yes, and to that.'

Cassy put her drink down. 'So, do you feel ready? Girlfriend's getting married!'

Fleur hesitated. 'You know what? I actually do.'

Cassy raised her glass again. 'One more toast, then.' Cassy smiled. 'To your last few days as an unmarried woman. To the next few days being absolutely perfect and to the fact that you, my dear friend, my gorgeous Champo, are finally getting your happily ever after.'

Fleur's heart felt as if it was going to explode. 'I'll raise my glass to that.'

~

A few hours later, Patrick had gone for a stroll with his parents, Lucy, Cassy and her husband had gone back to their rooms and Fleur sat at the beach bar on a stool next to Wendy in balmy evening air she couldn't quite get enough of. Wendy looked relaxed, happy and pretty in a floral maxi dress and frangipani in her hair.

Fleur sipped her cocktail. 'So, what do you think about Mum?'

Wendy shook her head. 'Can't work it out. How do you

think she looks?'

'I don't know. When we picked her up at the airport, she seemed happy enough, didn't she?'

'I know. Almost as if she's *too* happy. Something's up with her, no doubt about it.'

'Oh well, we'll soon find out. She'd totally changed her tune from when I spoke to her. Maybe she's actually just trying to think that this is about me...' Fleur rolled her eyes.

Wendy smirked and took a sip of her cocktail. 'You know what it's like when Mum's around—there'll be drama, for sure. I reckon she thrives on it these days. I never really saw it before but I suppose that was because we were young and I guess Dad protected us from it.'

Fleur shook her head. 'I'm not going to worry about it.'

'No, don't,' Wendy agreed and turned her wrist over to look at her watch. 'She should be here any minute. She said she was going to have a shower and freshen up before joining us.'

'I'm sure we'll find out what she's up to. It won't take long. She won't be able to contain herself. You know what she's like.'

Right on cue, Valerie came strolling across the bar in a royal blue dress, one-shoulder bare, very high-strappy sandals with ankle ties, a deep tan, and looking exponentially pleased with herself. She was full of the joys of spring, with large, dangling earrings swaying as she walked, a stack of bangles jingling on her arm and a huge faux tropical flower in her hair. All of the tiredness and irritability that she'd shown at the airport was long gone. She clapped her hands together as she reached the bar and swished around. 'Hi, darlings! Oh, this is fabulous! I'm having a wonderful time already. You see, I've always wanted to go to Hawaii! But Maui, yes wow! I could live here!'

Fleur had to stop herself from rolling her eyes. Wasn't this the same woman who had declared that Hawaii was too much for her? That she could have done without it? Now, here she was, back in full wanderlust bohemian mode, as if she had been desperate to arrive all along. 'Yes, it's really nice here. Glad you like the hotel.'

Wendy took a cocktail menu from the bar, turned it around to Valerie, and then grabbed another one of the wicker stools, pulling it so that there was a triangle of seating. She pointed to the one next to the bar she'd been sitting on and indicated for Valerie to take a pew. 'Here, Mum, you sit there, and I'll sit on this one. You can lean on the bar then.'

Valerie smiled, adjusted the stool a little, scooped up her blue dress, pulled it up to show off a tanned knee and sat down. She tugged at the fabric of her dress, letting it slide down a little over her shoulder and smoothed the skirt over on her lap. 'Well, girls, isn't this lovely? We're finally here. I have been so looking forward to this and now here I am!'

'Yes, it's such a gorgeous place.'

Valerie picked up the cocktail menu, glanced down at it, then back up again with a slight frown. 'I think I'll have this one with pineapple, tequila, lime juice. Sounds good to me. I wonder if they do doubles.'

'I don't think you want a double cocktail, Mum. They're pretty strong anyway.' Wendy frowned and held up her glass. 'Mine is quite potent.'

'Oh well, you only live once is what I say,' Valerie replied with a funny hooting laugh.

Wendy gave Fleur a look. 'So, what's happened with Marvin?'

Valerie made a strange, dismissive gesture with her hands and automatically reached to twirl her hair. Another exchanged look passed between Fleur and Wendy. 'Oh, to be frank with you two, I don't know what's happening with Marvin, darlings. He, well, oh you know how it is. I've left him to it. I can't be doing with it all.'

'You can't be doing with it all?' Wendy repeated. 'What does that mean?'

Fleur's thoughts raced. After all the times she'd had to listen to Valerie going on and on about how perfect Marvin was, how he had opened up her world, now here she was suddenly saying she couldn't be doing with him. Valerie had changed her tune completely. Even her body language was different. Fleur was having difficulty getting her head around it and wondered if the cocktails were a lot stronger than she'd first thought.

'What I mean, girls, is that sometimes in life you have to do what *you* want to do, and that's why I'm here,' Valerie said breezily. 'Marvin was fussing about the van and all sorts, so I left him to it. I can't wait around for him to lose his, well, his you know what, about vans and suchlike. As you girls know, I don't need that sort of thing in my life. Lived with it for too long you see.'

Fleur ignored the dig about Bill and frowned. 'So, hang on, he's not coming at all?'

Valerie wiggled her hands. 'I don't know, you know. Don't fuss and complicate things. You always were such a fusser Fleur. Fuss, fuss, fuss. Honestly, you didn't get that from me.'

'I'm not fussing and complicating things, Mum. He's your partner, and he's currently in Istanbul, and you're over here, and you're meant to be going on holiday with him after this. Are you saying he's not coming? Have you, well, sort of, broken up with him? Is that it?'

Valerie batted her hand in the air, her bracelets jangled like crazy, and she waved her fingers near her face as if she was swatting away a fly. 'No, no, no. It's fine. It's fine. Don't worry about it. No need for anyone else to get involved. If he makes it, he makes it; if he doesn't so be it. Girls, if I've told you once; in our family we don't wait around for people, am I right?'

Wendy looked startled. 'What? I thought you paid for his ticket! When's he going to come?'

'No idea,' Valerie replied as if it was completely normal that the person she'd spent the best part of the last few years with, in a van, travelling across Europe, wasn't coming to Maui with her.

'What about your holiday in California?' Fleur wrinkled her nose.

Valerie twirled her hair. 'No idea. Details, Fleur, darling. I'll just maybe change my flights and come back home for a bit. It's just a quick ride in a plane after all.'

Fleur stilled at that thought. Valerie being closer wasn't really something she'd factored in or particularly wanted back at home. She felt awful for even thinking it. She actually preferred Valerie in a van in Europe now she'd got used to it. 'Oh. Okay.'

Wendy raised her eyebrows and tapped the side of Valerie's arm. 'Is he not coming at all? I can't believe it! Mum!'

Valerie held her hand up and shook it so that the bangles clattered together at her elbow. 'Everything runs its course, girls. I did try to bring you up like that. Never rely on anyone.'

'So, what about the van and everything?'

There was another dismissive flick of Wendy's hand and absent twirl of her hair. 'Oh, he can have it for all I care. I mean, what's it to me? A stupid piece of metal with a bed inside. To be frank, it wasn't even that comfy…'

'Mum, what the hell? What do you mean what's it to you? I can't believe this!' Wendy exclaimed. 'You've just left him there? You're not going back to the van? Are you saying that? I'm confused. What *are* you saying?'

Valerie wiggled her phone in the air, her rings catching the light. 'It's the digital age, girls. I don't need anything. I don't need a van. I have my money invested, and I can do everything from my phone right here, right now.'

Fleur pressed her lips together, biting back a comment. She vividly remembered when Valerie had had an infected finger, how she'd acted as if it was the end of the world, unable to do *anything* for herself. Valerie wasn't anywhere near as independent as she liked to think she was.

Valerie tutted. 'Marvin is more worried about whether or not he's connected to the internet, always looking at his phone, always on that thing Chirp or whatever it's called now and to be honest with you, girls, I'm just *over* it all. You know, I'm a wanderlust, a bohemian traveller, a globetrotter. I don't need to be stuck in a van with, you know, someone who looks at his phone all the time.'

Fleur didn't know what to say. She shook her head and kept quiet. Valerie had flipped from one thing to the next. When she'd been at the airport, she'd told Fleur she wasn't getting any younger, now she was back to the bohemian traveller spiel.

Wendy's chin dropped. 'Mum! Are you telling us you've just walked away from this relationship and you're not going back?'

Valerie dipped into her handbag, waved her passport above her head and beamed. 'I have my passport and my phone, and that's all that's needed.' She jerked her thumb in the direction of the rest of the hotel. 'I packed everything I might need with me. I have anything of value in my possession. As I said, I am a wanderlust at heart. Wherever I lay my hat, that's my home.'

'Blimey. I'm actually gobsmacked.' Wendy stated solemnly, tipped her glass back and drained her cocktail.

Valerie wriggled on her stool to get comfortable, reached for her cocktail and took a slow sip, her bracelets jingling as she placed it back on the bar. 'Look, girls, I know I've talked and talked about van life, but let me tell you—it is not all it's cracked up to be.'

Fleur shook her head, not sure what to say but it didn't matter because Valerie was on a roll.

'I mean, people romanticise it, don't they? Oh, the freedom! The open road! Waking up to a new view every day! But what they don't tell you is the reality of it. Cold nights, dodgy Wi-Fi, breaking down in the middle of nowhere, and don't even get me started on the sheer amount of damp you have to deal with.'

'Damp?' Wendy raised an eyebrow.

'You wouldn't believe it and the constant need to be connected to some sort of power source. I mean, Marvin was obsessed with it. He'd park up and spend the first hour working out where to plug in or how to get the best internet connection. And it's a story for another day, the queues for the showers at some of those campsites. Grim. When I say grim, I mean gutter-level.' Valerie held her right hand out in front of her and indicated in the direction of the floor. 'Absolute gutter. The debacle of trying to dye your hair in a van, too. That is something else. You wouldn't believe some of the things I've seen, girls.'

Fleur pressed her lips together, trying not to laugh at the idea of her mother who as far as she knew had always liked fluffy bathrobes, proper towels, bathrooms with mood lighting and marble countertops, roughing it in a queue for a communal shower block. 'It's never been my cup of tea.'

'Honestly, I know I made it sound like the best thing ever, but I think I was just trying to convince myself. At first, it was exciting, but after a while... I just felt a bit—' Valerie twirled her wrist in the air, searching for the right word— 'untethered.'

Fleur frowned. 'Untethered?'

'Yes. Rootless. You know I've always been a bit of a free spirit, but even I started feeling like I needed something more solid. A proper base. A home. So, I've been thinking...'

'Here we go,' Wendy muttered, lifting her drink to her lips, realising she'd drained it and placing it back on the bar.

Valerie straightened, a glint in her eye. 'I need to start making smart decisions with my money. The money from the sale of the house has mostly just been sitting there, and I think it's time I did something with it. More investments, girls. That's what I need to focus on now.'

Fleur placed her cocktail carefully back onto the bar. 'Investments.'

'Yes! You know, I've always been interested in property. Maybe a little place in Italy, or something by the coast in Spain, Sicily is meant to be a great place for expat retirees. Or something closer to home.'

Fleur's stomach tightened. *Closer to home.* She flicked a quick glance at Wendy, who raised an eyebrow but said nothing. 'Right,' Fleur said slowly. 'And by closer to home, where do you mean?'

'I'm not sure yet.'

'So, you're seriously thinking about moving back?' Fleur asked.

Valerie lifted a manicured hand, wiggling it slightly. 'Not necessarily *moving* back permanently, but you know having something there. A base, as it were. A place to go when I want to. Just so I don't feel like I'm floating around all the time.'

'I thought that was what you were after. Well, this is all very, umm, interesting.'

Valerie smiled, clearly pleased with herself, and picked up her cocktail. 'Isn't it just?'

'Hmm.'

'So, you two girls have the pleasure of me *all* to yourselves.'

Fleur swallowed and closed her eyes for a second. She wasn't quite sure what to think about that.

44

Fleur walked along a path with Cassy, not far from the hotel, on their way back from the hairdresser's. She'd been in to talk to the stylist about what they were having done to their hair the next day, and to make sure everything was set. As they strolled and chatted, she looked up at a long beautiful line of green and yellow frangipani trees, the lush tropical vegetation thick around them. Everything seemed saturated in deep green, and the air was heavy with a scent so flowery and sweet, it was almost sickly. Sunshine streamed down onto the road, little rays slipping through the trees making dapples of light on the path. Fleur looked up at the deep green of the trees, smiling as a few pink frangipani flowers punctuated yellow ones here and there. Picking up one of the flowers from the path, she tucked it into her hair. Cassy followed suit, bending down picking up a yellow frangipani and popping it behind her ear.

'Well, this is the life. I could get used to this every year.'

'It really is. I wonder what the weather's like at home.' Cassy queried.

Fleur turned her mouth upside down. 'Who knows? I don't care.'

'We know it won't be like this for sure.'

'Nope, not in a million years.'

'How was your mum last night?'

Fleur sighed and shook her head. Valerie was up to something. Fleur knew it. She just wasn't quite sure what yet. 'She was fine. But there was something up with her.'

'Like what?'

'Like she was acting strangely. And then the whole thing where she said she was going back to her room for an early night—it doesn't add up.'

Cassy wrinkled her nose. 'What do you mean? Doesn't add up? Why not?'

'I mean that I think she was up to something.'

'Like what?'

Fleur shook her head; she had an inkling that Valerie was interested in a man. 'I don't know. She was chatting to that man at the bar, remember? And then when I said to her about going back to her room, she told me it was because she had a headache. But then, later I went to get some ice because Patrick and I were having a nightcap on the balcony and she was coming out of the toilet by the reception. I asked her what she was doing, and she said she'd changed her mind and was going to have a little stroll on the beach. When I said I'd go with her and that she couldn't go walking on the beach in the dark on her own, she was adamant that I didn't. Like *really* adamant. She wasn't having any of it.'

Cassy raised her eyebrows. 'What do you think she was up to, then? Meeting him on the beach or something? Would she feel safe doing that?'

'I don't know, but she looked all dreamy and weird. She had a funny look on her face.'

'What kind of look?' Cassy frowned.

'The one she had when she first told Wendy and me about

Marvin. Sort of like the cat who got the cream.' Fleur shook her head.

Cassy stared at her. 'Wow, you don't think—'

'I think she might have done, yes. Don't say anything to Wendy or anyone, but I know that look on my mum's face and I think she was probably going to the bar to meet up with him.'

'Really? Would she actually do that? With someone she's just met?'

'She's already been for a walk with him. Then she went for a drink with him.'

'Wow. She doesn't waste much time, does she?' Cassy laughed.

'I know, right?'

'How does that make you feel?'

Fleur shook her head. 'Pretty rubbish I suppose. I wonder who she is, you know? Sometimes, it makes me think that my whole life and childhood was a lie. I don't know. I don't really have much choice here, do I?'

'I suppose you don't, really.'

'It is what it is. She was with Dad for all those years, then Marvin, and now it's been like five minutes since that came to an end, if it has, and she's jumping in at the deep end with someone else if I'm right. I guess she deserves a holiday romance...'

Cassy tutted. 'Does she? Last time I checked I thought this holiday and occasion was meant to be all about you. She should keep that in mind.'

'You don't need to tell me. I'm well aware of it.'

'It's quite unbelievable. You know I've heard everything about her since she went off to do van life but, gosh, the last few days have been an eye-opener. She's well, I don't want to step out of line, but Fleur, she's *very* self-centred.'

'Oh, I know. You're telling me nothing I don't already know.'

'It's like she's literally making up for what she believes to be lost time.'

Fleur shook her head. 'I can't be bothered with it anymore. It is what it is, and my mum will do whatever suits her because, let me tell you, she's going to do it anyway. So there's no point in me wasting any time or energy on it. Let her have her holiday romance, if that's what's happening.'

'I do see what you mean about ignoring it but I'm saying for the record that she's unbelievable in my opinion. This was meant to be about you...'

'You live and learn, don't you?'

'You certainly do.'

Fleur picked up another frangipani flower and twirled it between her fingers before bringing it to her nose and inhaling deeply. 'Wow, these smell lovely. We're going to have them in our hair tomorrow. Do you think they will last? I don't want mine to wilt.'

'She said there's a treatment they do to keep them nice for the whole day.' Cassy sighed, stretching her arms up. 'It's just so nice that we're here.'

'Doesn't feel like we're in the USA at all. More like a little slice of paradise.'

'Who would've thought that my best friend would be getting married in paradise?' Cassy smiled and nudged Fleur on the arm.

'Absolutely mad, isn't it?'

'It all started when you moved to Lovely Bay and things have gone like lightning since.'

'It did. Now, look where we are.'

Cassy smiled. 'You know what? All this and what has happened to you has really made me realise that I need to try and *do more* with my life.'

Fleur made a funny face and then wrinkled her nose. 'More with your life? Like what?'

'Ahh, I don't know. There's always budget to take into account, but sometimes I think, wow, months have gone by and all I've done is work, make dinner, clean the house and look after the boys. Rinse, repeat and then do it all again the next week.'

'Yeah, I know, I feel the same sometimes. So, what grand plans have you got to change that?'

Cassy laughed. 'No idea but I'm going to try and make more things happen. Actually, I was going to ask if you could make me a notebook that I could use for it. The Get-Cassy-a-Life notebook.'

Fleur chuckled. 'Of course. I like the sound of that. What sort do you want?'

'I just want one for bits and bobs, you know? Like the one you showed me before, where you note down stuff about things you're interested in, places you want to go, bucket lists, that sort of thing.'

'Too easy. If there's one thing I know how to do...'

'So, what do you do? Every time you see something you like or are interested in you note it down and refer to it when you need to?' Cassy questioned.

Fleur nodded. 'Exactly. It's good to do because you forget stuff. You can just refer to it when you want and, yeah, remember things etcetera.'

'It'll help me keep track of all the amazing things I want to do with my life.' Cassy giggled.

'Go on then, like what?'

'I don't know... I think I might do something like a tap dancing class. Something to expand my brain and my fitness, that sort of thing. I know I'm getting older, and I want to stay active.'

Fleur chuckled. 'So, we're doing a tap dancing class in the new year, then, are we?'

'We are.'

Fleur burst out laughing. 'Can you imagine? We'd be like a couple of fairy elephants.'

'We should make it ballet, then we could wear a tutu.'

Fleur giggled as they carried on down the path, the frangipani-scented air thick and warm around them, the sun dipping lower in the sky, golden light in the leaves. As she laughed, she had a life moment. A good one. Here she was in Maui, strolling under the trees, laughing with her best friend and not a care in the world. Oh how life had changed for the better. Oh how pleased she was with that.

45

Fleur stood in front of the full-length mirror in the suite, staring at her reflection, heart thudding and pulse racing. She might be saying it herself but the dress was perfect.

She'd been fairly sure about it, of course, but now, standing in the suite with sunlight filtering through the shutters, the ocean breeze lifting the edges of the white fabric ever-so-slightly, it felt just right.

Wendy, standing a few feet behind her, whistled. 'Oh my goodness. You are stunning. You look like one of those impossibly effortless, cool-girl brides you see in those fancy Instagram reels. The ones who pretend they just threw something on but actually spent six months curating their entire aesthetic. I can't believe how lovely the dress is. It fits you like a dream!'

Fleur chuckled. 'I can assure you there was no six-month curating. More of a panic-search followed by a blind hope for the best.' She turned and looked over her shoulder. 'Gosh, it looks so much better with the hair and flowers and everything.'

Cassy, perched on the edge of an armchair, tilted her head. 'It really is gorgeous.'

Fleur ran her hands over the silky fabric. It was exactly what she'd wanted—floaty, light, effortless and not too over the top. A soft, draped silk that skimmed rather than clung, a gentle dip at the neckline, delicate lace tracing along the edges of the straps. Nothing fussy or heavy. Just simple, timeless, and exactly her. 'I love it.'

Wendy grinned, hands on hips. 'Right, do a twirl so we get the full picture.'

Fleur rolled her eyes but turned slowly and made a funny face.

Cassy clutched her heart dramatically. 'Oh, stop. You're going to make me cry and I've only just got my mascara on.'

'You are going to be a mess, aren't you?'

'A total mess. We're talking full tears, blotchy face, embarrassing sniffing and I am not sorry about it. I'm *so* happy for you. This is emotional already and we've not even started yet.'

Wendy padded over in bare feet. 'Patrick is going to absolutely lose his mind when he sees you.' Her voice caught. 'Dad would be so proud.'

Fleur's stomach flipped. The thought of Patrick, standing on that beach, waiting for her, made her heart squeeze. She touched Wendy's arm at the mention of Bill, their dad. 'He would be over the moon if he could see the pair of us. You reckon?'

'Yup, he so would' Wendy peered in the mirror and frowned. 'We're glowing. How did that make-up girl do that? I need to put her in my suitcase and take her to Sydney.'

Fleur squinted at her make-up and turned to the side to examine her updo. It was a perfect soft tumble of curls at the nape of her neck with a few loose strands and fresh frangipani flowers pinned in at the side. She'd instructed that she wanted minimal make-up that was fresh, dewy, nothing too heavy and just glowy. Whatever had been put on her face had followed the brief and exceeded it.

Cassy sighed dreamily. 'Ugh. This is like a dream. You are going to glide down that beach like a boho goddess and Patrick is going to have to steady himself to avoid passing out on the spot.'

Fleur laughed. 'You're getting carried away with yourself. No more bubbles for you.' She felt a bit the same though; sort of hyper about the fact that she was getting married on a beach to Patrick where she would walk barefoot down a candlelit aisle with the bluest ocean stretching out beyond, with Patrick standing there, looking at her like she was the only person in the world. At least she hoped that was how it was going to go. A knock at the door made them all turn.

'Who's that?' Fleur frowned, glancing at the clock.

Wendy padded over and opened the door 'Ahh. It's your daughter, bearing what appears to be a very important delivery.'

Lucy stepped in, a smile on her face, holding a small, white box tied with a ribbon. 'I have a gift.'

Fleur frowned. 'What's that?'

Lucy crossed the room and gave the box to Fleur. 'It's from Patrick.'

Cassy let out a full squeal. 'Oh my. A pre-ceremony gift. The romance.'

Wendy swatted her. 'You're hyper.'

Fleur untied the ribbon to reveal a delicate gold bracelet, simple and elegant, with a tiny charm in the shape of a frangipani flower. She swallowed. 'Ooh.'

Cassy clapped a hand over her mouth. 'Oh. That's it, I'm gone. I need tissues. Immediately.'

Fleur turned the bracelet over in her fingers. It was engraved on the back. 'Forever. P.'

'Wendy shook her head. 'I'm not one for being soppy but this is next level. First the ring and now this. Thank goodness you're marrying him because he's a keeper, for sure.'

Cassy sniffed dramatically. 'This is going to be the best day.'

Fleur touched the bracelet and smiled. The day was going to get better.

46

Fleur stood at the edge of the timber decked area jutting off the side of the cocktail bar area of the hotel, looking out over the beach, a bundle of nerves and thrumming with anticipation. Everything was all set and ready to go. No backing out now. Peering in the direction of the lawn where the wedding was taking place, she felt a little flicker of nerves in her chest. All of it looked just as she'd hoped and dreamed; pale linen-draped chairs on either side of a central aisle, an arch drowning in tropical flowers and frangipani, rows of flickering candles in beautiful white lanterns leading down to where Patrick would be standing in just under half an hour. The sky the kind of perfect holiday blue that she'd never really seen before and a heavy, tropical, full feel to the air.

Sighing in pleasure and a deep satisfaction of a job well done she let it all settle inside and around her. Here she was ready to go. From the proposal to the dress to the planning and emails with the hotel to the flights, the nerves, and the unbelievability of it all. It was all about to come together and she couldn't wait to see it through. Our Champo was getting wed.

Somewhere behind her, Cassy was saying for the tenth time

how amazing everything was and Wendy was adjusting her dress in front of a large, gilded mirror. Lucy was standing next to the photographer's assistant deep in conversation and her mum was sitting on a chair looking down at her phone. Everything had been planned to within an inch of its life and was exactly as it should be. It couldn't really be any more perfect. There was only one thing that could have made it better; her dad.

Just as Fleur was looking in the direction of the bay admiring the deep blue of the ocean, she suddenly frowned and looked down at her arm. A single fat raindrop right in the middle of her forearm. Surely not. Frowning, she glanced up. Strange; the sky was still so blue and so untouched that it made no sense that rain might be involved. Another drop and then another. Fleur turned around and peered backwards and felt her eyes go wide. Coming in at the double were rain clouds and before she could even get the words out, the heavens opened.

'Oh my goodness!' Cassy shrieked, leaping back from the table, clutching a glass of bubbles to her chest as though it needed saving before anything else.

Wendy swore under her breath, reaching for a napkin from nearby tables as if that would somehow help.

Lucy's mouth dropped open. 'Oh. My. Actual. What in the world do we do now?'

Fleur just stood there for a second, as a beat of pure stunned silence stopped her from doing anything, then gathered up her dress and made her way undercover. One of the wedding planners and a couple of hotel staff came rushing out from nowhere, waving clipboards and shouting instructions. The little delicate flower arrangements—meticulously placed on every single chair—were being swept off into the wind and a few of the lanterns had fallen over.

'Someone get the covers! Move the chairs! Archway plan going into action!'

Cassy let out a wild laugh, grabbing Fleur's wrist. 'Classic. This cannot be happening. We couldn't just have a normal, breezy, perfect tropical wedding, could we?'

Fleur blinked at her. 'Five minutes ago, there wasn't a cloud in sight. How can this be happening?'

Cassy shook her head. 'Now what do we do?'

Lucy stared at the sky in pure disbelief. 'I specifically checked the forecast. It literally said no rain. What is this? It has come from nowhere.' She pointed to the right. 'That way is still blue...'

The wind picked up, a small white linen-draped table wobbled and a stack of candles toppled into the sand. Valerie, who had been comfortably sipping a mimosa under the canopy, let out a deep sigh, crossed her legs, and shook her head. 'Typical. You spend all that money on a tropical paradise and still end up with British weather. It's followed you. You see, that's precisely why I left. That and the whole Brexit debacle.'

'Not helping, Mum,' Fleur bit out, blinking as rain landed on her face.

Valerie tutted. 'Well, at least you'll remember it.'

The wedding coordinator skidded up to them, clipboard held over her head although she was slightly breathless, she still appeared to be very in control. 'Okay, okay, minor setback, but don't panic, we've got an indoor contingency plan. We can move the ceremony inside the main terrace. This sometimes happens so we're well set up for it.'

Fleur's stomach sank at the thought of the wedding moving inside. She'd wanted the beach, sand beneath her bare feet, soft lanterns lining the shoreline, and the bay as a backdrop to their vows. 'Nope,' she said automatically. 'No, we're not moving inside.'

Cassy turned to her, hair already frizzing. 'Erm, babe, but what exactly do you plan to do instead? Manifest the rain away?'

Fleur pressed her lips together. This was not what she had

planned. She'd imagined walking down an aisle lined with frangipani and soft candlelight, her skin warm from the sun, her dress billowing slightly in a sea breeze. Not rain and in an indoor wedding in a function room; she'd had a gutful of function rooms in her day job. She wasn't moving inside. She wasn't giving up on the dream of the wedding. There had to be another way. She looked back towards the beach, where the staff were calmly securing whatever they could and moving things undercover.

Mia nodded. 'You can wait if you like. It comes and goes very quickly here. It wasn't forecast as you know.' She looked up at the sky. 'I think if we give it an hour you'll be fine. I'll talk to the celebrant, he'll be fine with that. Up to you. You never know we might get a rainbow; those are the really special ceremonies. I'll get a tray of food delivered and some drinks and you can sit it out. If not, we can go inside. Everything in there is set up. It's not a problem.'

Fleur nodded. 'Yes, I'd like to wait please.'

An hour later, just as quickly as it had arrived the rain had eased, more drinks had been consumed, Valerie was quietly getting sozzled, and the outdoor ceremony area had again been set up. The air was different, stilled, heavy with warmth, and a thin veil of mist fluffed upwards from the sand, curling over the wooden chairs, wrapping itself through the lanterns, making everything sort of hazy. The sun was again back, the clouds burnt away here and there leaving a soft, fluffy light that made the entire area appear to glow.

Lucy whispered from beside her as she gripped the handle of a white umbrella. 'Mum, look at it! It's made everything misty. It's so pretty.'

Fleur nodded. The entire wedding set-up was transformed,

the rain appearing to have softened everything. Just as she was standing looking out in the direction of the bay a rainbow formed going from left to right, the bay underneath it. Fleur felt her chin drop. Utterly, completely, totally magical.

Cassy chortled. 'You're kidding me. A rainbow! I take back everything I said. Look at it! Fleur, it looks like some sort of enchanted island. The downpour has turned it into something out of a dream. Ahh, look at the sunshine peeking through. This is next level.'

Fleur exhaled again, letting herself really take it all in. The beach glowed under the bursts of sunlight, the sky shimmered as if it had been painted in glittery blues and golds and the rainbow stretched behind the floral arch as if someone somewhere had quietly placed it there just so. She giggled it couldn't have been better. The rainbow sealed every single deal she'd ever had in her head.

The wedding coordinator signalled for people to take their seats until it was just Fleur and Lucy left on the decking area looking out in the direction of the archway.

Lucy whispered and pointed to the rainbow. 'Mum, you look like an actual princess in a dream.'

'Do I? So do you. Right, well let's get to it then. It's now or never.'

As Fleur walked along beside Lucy, she could feel warm, rain-dampened sand shift beneath her feet, the rainbow framed the bay and mist curled gently at her ankles. She breathed it in as she slowly stepped along the lantern-lined aisle in the direction of Patrick. Inhaling the scent of tropical flowers, sea air, and the last traces of warm rain, she tried to bottle the smell so she'd remember it forever. With the guitar music strumming, Patrick stood waiting, his linen shirt slightly damp, a look in his eyes she'd never seen on top of a beaming smile.

As she reached the arch, Lucy stepped to the side, Patrick reached out and took both her hands. 'Hey.'

Fleur tilted her head, smiled and whispered. 'Bit of a dramatic twist, wasn't it?'

Patrick chuckled, his grip tightening slightly. 'Champo, I'd expect nothing less. You look stunning. Just *so* beautiful. I love you.'

Fleur smiled. 'Right back at you.'

The wedding celebrant, an older Hawaiian man with kind eyes and a gentle smile, stepped forward, nodding towards them. 'I think we can all agree—this is already a wedding none of us will forget.' He turned around, peered up at the rainbow and smiled. 'We haven't had one with one of our rainbows for a while. That always means it's *very* special.'

A little ripple of laughter passed through the handful of guests and Fleur relaxed, her shoulders dropping slightly as she chuckled. It didn't matter that it had rained because standing with Patrick's hands around hers, with the sun glowing over the bay, her daughter beside her, and her best friend watching, she smiled as she felt as if something tapped the side of her head, telling her she was more than okay. All of it, from the moment she'd met Patrick had been wonderful and messy, unexpected and crazy, up, down, busy, and most of all just *right*. She looked up into Patrick's eyes and felt hers fill with a few tears. *Way to go Champo, you'll be okay.*

She lost herself for a bit as the celebrant proceeded, not really hearing him until she again found herself standing on the beach. She smiled as she heard the celebrant. 'And now, your words.'

Fleur swallowed, feeling a tiny flutter of nerves. Not because she wasn't sure, she'd never been more sure of anything in her life but because suddenly, the moment felt so big, so much bigger than she'd expected. Emotion rolled over her like a wave.

Patrick went first. He sounded happy, sure, confident, full of life. 'I wasn't expecting you to arrive in my life and definitely not when you did. You turned my world inside out, Champo, and I wouldn't change a second of it. I can't imagine a life that doesn't have you in it, and I wouldn't want to. So today, standing here in the place you've always dreamed of, in front of the people we love, I promise you this: I will stand by your side, always. I will love you, even on the days when life feels messy and hard. I will never, ever take you for granted. And most of all, Fleur Champion, I will love you *forever*.'

Fleur felt as if she was the only person in the world. She took a breath. 'I don't think I really believed in the idea of forever before you. Then I met you and it turns out, with you, forever is easy. It's the easiest thing in the world. Who even knew? You have made me laugh when I wanted to cry, held me together when I felt like falling apart, and shown me what it means to be loved in a way that I didn't even know was a thing. Like actual love and you love me for *me* and just me. I love you, too.'

As the rainbow stretched across the sky, the last traces of mist curled around their feet and Fleur felt tears plop out of the corners of her eyes and slide in a warm trail down the side of her cheeks. As she looked up at the rainbow, she pursed her lips together and closed her eyes for a second. She felt as if something tapped the side of her head. This was her moment. Her forever had finally begun.

Buy my next book The Bookshop Pretty Beach

THE BOOKSHOP PRETTY BEACH

The Bookshop Pretty Beach

When a bookshop enters the Pollyverse you know it's going to be a *small-town,* **meet cute,** *bookworm's* dream... think *book ladders,* crammed shelves, piles of books forever, reading lamps and overstuffed curl-up-and-dream chairs. Say hello to The Bookshop in Pretty Beach.

Starting over was never part of Daisy's plan... but neither was working in her eccentric uncle's dusty old maritime chandler building in the heart of Pretty Beach—let alone turning it into the *cosy bookshop* she's always dreamed about. With a tight budget, a cast iron work ethic and a past chock full of setbacks, she's more than determined to make it happen.

What she doesn't need? An infuriatingly smug, exceptionally handsome man to get in her way. Daisy knows his type—men like him don't just spend time in small seaside towns without a motive. Anyway, she doesn't give a stuff because she is NOT looking for love, at least that's what she thinks... little does she know a feel-good meet cute hero is about to sweep her off her feet.

'When Polly does bookshops it doesn't get better. ... so good you'll want to turn over the closed sign, hide in a bookshelf, and stay the night snuggled up with a quilt.'

>>>The Bookshop Pretty Beach

READ MORE BY POLLY

(Reading Order available at authorpollybabbington.com)

The Bookshop Pretty Beach

A Cottage in Lovely Bay
    Sunshine in Lovely Bay
    Forever in Lovely Bay

One Nice Day in Lovely Bay
    One Sweet Day in Lovely Bay
    One Perfect Day in Lovely Bay

The Summer Hotel Lovely Bay
    Wildflowers at The Summer Hotel Lovely Bay
    Seashells at The Summer Hotel Lovely Bay

The Old Ticket Office Darling Island
    Secrets at The Old Ticket Office Darling Island
    Surprises at The Old Ticket Office Darling Island

READ MORE BY POLLY

Spring in the Pretty Beach Hills
    Summer in the Pretty Beach Hills

The Pretty Beach Thing
    The Pretty Beach Way
    The Pretty Beach Life

Something About Darling Island
    Just About Darling Island
    All About Christmas on Darling Island

The Coastguard's House Darling Island
    Summer on Darling Island
    Bliss on Darling Island

The Boat House Pretty Beach
    Summer Weddings at Pretty Beach
    Winter at Pretty Beach

A Pretty Beach Christmas
    A Pretty Beach Dream
    A Pretty Beach Wish

Secret Evenings in Pretty Beach
    Secret Places in Pretty Beach
    Secret Days in Pretty Beach

Lovely Little Things in Pretty Beach
    Beautiful Little Things in Pretty Beach
    Darling Little Things

The Old Sugar Wharf Pretty Beach
    Love at the Old Sugar Wharf Pretty Beach

READ MORE BY POLLY

Snow Days at the Old Sugar Wharf Pretty Beach

Pretty Beach Posies
  Pretty Beach Blooms
  Pretty Beach Petals

* * *

Printed in Dunstable, United Kingdom